2.B

# HIGH DESERT

Center Point
Large Print

Also by Wayne D. Overholser and available from Center Point Large Print:

*The Durango Stage*
*Proud Journey*
*Pass Creek Valley*
*Summer Warpath*
*Fighting Man*
*Ten Mile Valley*

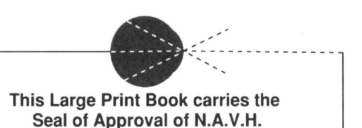

**This Large Print Book carries the
Seal of Approval of N.A.V.H.**

# HIGH DESERT

## A WESTERN DUO

# Wayne D. Overholser

CENTER POINT LARGE PRINT
THORNDIKE, MAINE

First Edition
January 2018

Printed in the United States of America
on permanent paper.
Set in 16-point Times New Roman type.

ISBN: 978-1-68324-657-2

Library of Congress Cataloging-in-Publication Data

Names: Overholser, Wayne D., 1906-1996, author.
Title: High desert : a western duo / Wayne D. Overholser.
Description: First edition. | Thorndike, Maine :
    Center Point Large Print, 2018. | Series: A Circle V western
Identifiers: LCCN 2017043579 | ISBN 9781683246572
    (hardcover : alk. paper)
Subjects: LCSH: Large type books. | Western stories. gsafd
Classification: LCC PS3529.V33 H54 2018 | DDC 813/.54—dc23
LC record available at https://lccn.loc.gov/2017043579

# HIGH DESERT

.

# TABLE OF CONTENTS

# HIGH DESERT

# I

Traveling eastward, Murdo Morgan left the pines in midmorning and came into the high Oregon desert. He made a dry noon camp under a wind-turned juniper, drank sparingly from his canteen, and rode on. The sky was without clouds; the sun laid a hot pressure upon him. Sage grew in rounded clumps as far as he could see, the smell of it a desert incense in his nostrils.

He forked his black easily in the way of a man who rides much, the dust of uncounted miles upon him. His face was high-boned, his nose thin; features that had marked all the Morgans he had ever known. They had marked his father who had left Paradise Valley sixteen years before, a broken and defeated man. They had marked his three brothers who lay buried below the valley's east rim.

Today Morgan rode across country he did not remember. Tomorrow he would be in Paradise Valley. He pictured it now with the nostalgic eagerness of a grown man returning to his boyhood home. He had long dreamed of this return, of how he would stamp Broad Clancy under his boot heels, of how he would smash Turkey Track's hold on the valley.

They had been childish dreams inspired by

a boy's lust for revenge, a lust that had been blunted by the years. A different purpose had brought him back, although Broad Clancy would not believe it. There was another dream, a greater one than the boy dreams, that Morgan wanted to turn into reality.

The town of Irish Bend lay ahead, but Morgan could not guess the distance in miles. The country seemed entirely strange. It was late spring, and the desert, never really green, was feeling the surge of its scant life.

He remembered that it had been fall when he had ridden out of the country with his father, but it was not the difference in seasons that made the desert seem unfamiliar. The years had dimmed his memory of these empty miles. At twenty-seven he retained few of the thoughts and images that had been bright in the mind of an eleven-year-old boy. Even the dream had changed, and grown with time. Now it was a lodestar calling him back to risk his life and every cent of money he had.

Morgan followed an east-west valley, rimrock forming an unbroken line to his left. A jack rabbit broke into the open and kicked high into the air. A band of antelope raced away from Morgan to fade into the sage. In late afternoon, he came to a herd of cattle carrying the Turkey Track brand, evidence that Broad Clancy's domain spread far beyond Paradise Valley.

Dusk caught him with Irish Bend still not in sight. He made camp beside a tar-paper shack, built a small fire, and cooked supper. When he was done with the fire, he kicked it out, for his was a dangerous business, and he had learned long ago that a man silhouetted against a night blaze made a good target.

Darkness folded about him, the last golden glow of sunset dying along the snowy crest of the Cascades. Morgan lay on his back, head on his saddle, eyes on the stars set in a tall sky. There was this moment when he could thrust worry away and let the dreams build, but another night would bring its sultry threat of violence. He wasn't fooling himself. He knew Broad Clancy too well.

But this night was to be enjoyed—the desert smells, the desert wildness, the great emptiness of this land with its rimrock and buttes, its juniper and sage. It shouldn't be an empty land. The valley bottom could be irrigated, the lower slopes of the surrounding buttes dry-farmed. Given normal luck and a boost from Providence, a thousand families could make a living on land that now supported only Broad Clancy's Turkey Track and a handful of settlers. That was Murdo Morgan's dream—to place a thousand families on land that would be theirs.

He gave himself to speculation about the tar-paper shack. Four walls with a broken window and no door, a roof partly stripped by the wind, a splintered floor. A few newspapers in the corner. Portland *Oregonian*s, Morgan noted, not yet yellowed by age. And outside, almost covered by wind-blown sand, was a weather-grayed cradle. Homemade and crude, but hinting at a poignant story.

Knowing Broad Clancy, Morgan could guess the story. Clancy would tolerate only a limited number of nesters on his range and only at places he designated. His men had come here, probably late at night, routed the nesters from their beds, and started them on their way. And a baby had learned to sleep without its cradle.

The run of a horse brought Morgan upright. He listened a moment, placing the horse to the east and gauging its speed. It was coming directly toward him. Pulling saddle and blanket away from the shack, he hunkered there to listen.

Another horse was coming from the south. Morgan waited, tense, not hearing the first horse for a time. Then they were both in front of the shack, and a man called: "Peg!"

Morgan heard the girl's laugh, gay and soft.

"You'd ride through the whole Clancy outfit to get here, wouldn't you, Buck?" she said.

"It was a fool risk," the man said irritably.

The girl laughed again, tauntingly this time. "Afraid, Buck?"

"You know I ain't. I just ain't goin' to stand for

you playin' around with Rip and eggin' me on at the same time. You're making up your mind tonight."

"What makes you think I see Rip?"

"There's talk enough. Is it me or Rip?"

"You men are all fools." There was the creak of saddle leather as she stepped down. "You're wasting time, Buck."

"I want to know."

"Of course, it's you."

"Then I'm tellin' you, Peg. If I ever catch . . ."

"Buck, are you going to kiss me?"

He swung out of the saddle then. Morgan saw them come together, the two shapes mold into one, heard whispers of talk that reached him as blurred sounds. From what he had heard about the valley, Morgan guessed this would be Buck Carrick, a nester's son.

Buck flamed a match and held it to his cigarette, the glow of it making a brief brightness. He had a handsome square face, his eyes dark and widely spaced, his chin a fighter's chin. About twenty-five, Morgan guessed. Old enough to be in love and foolish enough to meet this girl at risk of his life.

Peg, for some reason Morgan hadn't heard, was suddenly angry. "I won't ride off with you, Buck," she was saying, "and I didn't have you come here for Rip to shoot! If that's the way you trust me, get on your horse and keep riding."

"I told you this was the night you were makin' up your mind," Buck said. "You've kept me danglin' for two years. I can't stand it no longer."

"Let me go!" the girl screamed.

"We'll get married in Prineville and . . . well, take the stage to The Dalles."

"Your dad will . . ."

"We'll be out of the country before he knows anything about it."

"You're crazy, Buck!"

"That's right. Crazy with lovin' you. Crazy with wantin' you. Crazy with worryin' what Rip Clancy is doin' to you. I love you, Peg. Ain't that enough?"

"No. Not nearly enough. I'll never marry you."

"You said I was the one. That's all I need to know."

Morgan had crawled through the sage to the shack. He came to his feet, gun fisted.

"Let her go, Buck. It's too dark to see what you're up to, so don't make any fast moves."

The girl jerked out of Buck's hands and ran to her horse. Buck stood still, a square black shape in the starlight. "Who are you?" he asked.

"Makes no never mind to you. Mount up and get."

"I ain't leavin' her with you," Buck said

doggedly. "How do I know what you're figgerin' on?"

"I ain't keeping the girl," Morgan said. "But if she rides, you'll sit pat for a spell."

"Maybe I'm not in a hurry, mister," the girl said.

"Then you ain't smart."

"You're wrong on that."

"Go on, then."

"I hope I'll see you again."

"Don't ever see her," Buck groaned. "She'll drag you through perdition. She's poison."

Peg was in the saddle now, her laugh gay and without the shadow of fear.

"Why, Buck, I thought you liked my poison."

Turning her mount, she rode eastward. Morgan held Buck there until the sound of her horse was lost in the desert stillness.

"All right, son," he said then. "Remember what I said about fast moves."

"I ain't forgettin'," Buck said bitterly, "and I ain't forgettin' what you done tonight."

"I hope you won't, because you'll thank me someday. Go on now. *Vamoose*."

But Buck stood motionless as if listening. Morgan heard it then. More horses. Coming toward them.

"I didn't see anybody all day," Morgan said. "Now the desert's alive."

"It's Peg's work," Buck said with deep sourness. "She does that to a man. She's a fever in your blood if you look at her twice. I'm warnin' you, mister. Stay away from her."

The sound of horses came through the night.

"Got a guess on who's coming?"

"Rip Clancy and some Turkey Track hands. Chances are Peg met 'em and headed 'em this way."

"Then you'd better be making dust. I'll hold 'em off."

Buck stepped up. "You don't owe me nothin', friend. This roan I'm ridin' can outrun any nag they've got."

"I've got my own reasons for not wanting a ruckus to bust out. Get moving. Run your horse for a few minutes. Then pull up and take it easy."

"I know a few things," Buck said resentfully. Cracking steel to his horse, he disappeared.

Morgan remained at the shack, his back to the wall. There was no moon, and the starlight made a thin glow on the desert.

His lot had been a lonely one. No mother that he could remember. His father dead when he was twelve, nerves shattered and health broken by Broad Clancy's lead, the dream a prodding ambition until the moment of his death. That dream had been Murdo Morgan's inheritance.

The lonely years then. A chore boy on one ranch after another. A cowhand in Montana. A lawman in tough Arizona border towns. Finally, the Colorado mining camps. Then his luck had turned. He had grub-staked a prospector and the man had struck it. That had given Morgan his stake, enough to buy the wagon road grant that made up half of Paradise Valley.

Morgan smiled now as he thought of the Cascade and Paradise Land Company. He was that land company, but it was just as well Broad Clancy didn't know it for a time. Clancy hated the company enough. He would hate it twice as much if he knew the company and Murdo Morgan were one and the same.

Clancy had used this range for years, government and company land alike, ignoring the fact that the odd sections of a strip six miles wide on both sides of the old wagon road belonged to the company. The company had made no effort to collect rent, and Clancy had neither offered to pay nor lease the land.

With high disdain for the right of private property, he had considered all the valley open range and had acted accordingly.

# II

Because Morgan's life had been a lonely and womanless one, his thoughts turned to the girl, Peg. He wondered what she looked like. He heard again the light tone of her laughter. It had been a fine sound to hear. It would stay with him like a sweet haunting tune he had heard whistled. Then a sour note turned his thoughts bitter. There had been no trouble in the valley since Morgan and his father had left. Now this Peg had Buck Carrick and Rip Clancy in love with her. It would take a woman, he thought, to stir up a feud at a moment when he, Morgan, was bringing trouble enough of his own.

He caught the blur of running horses. Four of them pointed directly toward the shack. Morgan wondered what kind of girl this Peg was who would allow her flurry of anger to turn her from Buck to the Clancys.

They were there then, reining up in a whirling cloud of dust that drifted toward the shack.

"Come out of there, Carrick!" a man in front called.

"He's gone," Morgan said. "If you boys'll keep riding, I'll go back to sleep."

"Who the devil are you?"

"Makes you no never mind, does it, friend?"

"You're on Turkey Track range. Get off."

"Reckon I'm hurting the bunchgrass? Or are you looking out for the sagebrush?"

"Actin' smart won't buy you nothin'. I said to drift. This is Rip Clancy talkin'."

"A Clancy don't cut no bigger swath than the next man." Anger honed a fine edge to Morgan's voice. "I aim to finish my sleep."

"You'll sure finish it if . . ."

"We're getting sidetracked," a gravelly voiced rider beside Rip said. "This is just a drifter. We're after Carrick."

The man loomed a head taller than Rip, and was wider of shoulder. Morgan could tell nothing about him beyond that, but his was a voice a man would never forget.

"Why don't you light out after Carrick?" Morgan asked. "He allowed you didn't have an animal that could run with his roan."

Rip cursed shrilly. "He's just a braggin' fool! Where'd he go?"

"South."

He told them the truth and knew they wouldn't believe it. He smiled, thinking they would look for Buck in any direction but south.

"I've got a hunch he's in the shack," Rip said uncertainly. "I'm goin' to take a look."

"I wouldn't, sonny," Morgan breathed. "It's too dark to watch you right close, so I'm thinking you'd better stay where you are."

"You ain't tough enough to stop us!" blustered Rip.

"Maybe not," Morgan drawled, "but I've got an iron in my hand and five slugs that says I'll make a nice mess out of your bunch while I'm trying."

There was silence then except for the heavy breathing of the Turkey Track men. The one behind Rip sounded as if he had asthma.

21

This was an old and familiar business for Murdo Morgan, but he didn't like it. Somewhere along his back trail he had lost his appetite for powder smoke. He had come here to build, not to destroy. But this was a matter of living or dying.

"What you doin' on this range?" Rip Clancy demanded.

"My business, sonny."

"You're a stranger," Rip said arrogantly. "I'll tell you somethin' you need to know. Around here folks do what Broad Clancy says. If they don't, they have trouble. Buck Carrick knew he was off the reservation when he came here. I think he's inside now and you're coverin' up for him. If we find him, we'll make wolf meat out of him."

"What's between you and Buck Carrick is nothing to me. Right now, my business is to keep you on your horse."

"If Buck's inside," the big man said, "it makes two guns, and he ain't worth gettin' killed over. We'll wait till the sign's right to get him, Rip."

But Rip Clancy was too young and too much in love to consider the risk.

"There's four of us," he said darkly. "This hair-pin can't be as tough as he acts."

A smart man wouldn't walk into it. Not with the darkness as thick as it was and with Morgan standing with his back to the shack wall. What light there was worked to his advantage.

The gravelly voiced man knew it. Another time

Rip would have known it. But Buck Carrick had met Peg here.

The bitterness that thought roused in Rip was a potion deadening his instinct of self-preservation.

"Too bad you're bent on committing suicide tonight," Morgan murmured. "You ought to give yourself time to play your string out with Peg."

It was a long shot that might work either way. Morgan heard Rip's indrawn breath, heard him ask—"What do you know about Peg?"—in a high nerve-tightened voice. Then a faint challenging cry came from the south, and a gun sounded, muffled by distance.

"Reckon that'd be Buck," the gravelly voiced man said. "Let's get him!"

Wheeling their horses, they pounded south toward the gun blast. Morgan felt admiration for Buck Carrick. He had waited out there in the sage to pull the Turkey Track riders off because it was his fight and none of Murdo Morgan's. With a fast horse under him and a black night to hide in, he could play fox and hounds with a better than even chance to get clear.

Murdo built a cigarette and smoked it before he went back to his blanket. Horse sounds faded and desert emptiness was all around him again.

He vaguely remembered the Clancy kids. There was Short John, older than Morgan, about fourteen when Morgan had left the valley and a runt for his age. Morgan remembered a girl named Jewell. She would be in her early twenties now. This Rip was the youngest. He had been little more than a baby when Morgan and his father had ridden out of the country.

Then the memory of Peg's rich laugh crowded the Clancys out of Morgan's mind. He wouldn't like her. He wouldn't like any girl who played two men against each other to satisfy her own sense of importance, but he would never forget her. . . .

It was early morning when Morgan swung to the south, put his black across the shoulder of a juniper-covered butte, and looked down into Paradise Valley, with the huddle of buildings that was Irish Bend centering the flat. Beyond the town lay the dirty pool of water that was dignified by the name Paradise Lake. South of it a patch of hay land was a bright emerald in a gray setting. Again, nostalgia struck at Murdo Morgan. He and his father had paused here to blow their horses. Morgan had had his last look at the valley then. Sixteen years ago, but the memory was a bright picture perfectly fitting reality. Rimrock lined the northern part of the valley. Farther east it rose into several jagged ridges known as the Hagerman Hills. They broke off into a series of round buttes forming part of the eastern and all of the southern rim of the valley.

Clancy's Turkey Track buildings were directly

below Morgan. Far across the valley was the site of the old Morgan place. The sharpest picture of all the memories that had clung in his mind from that day sixteen years ago was the sight of smoke rising from the cabin. Clancy had not waited until they were out of the valley to burn it.

Morgan turned his eyes to the north. Along that edge of the lake alkali glittered in the morning sunlight like a patch of white frost. Farther north, just under the rimrock, was another white area Broad Clancy had named Alkali Flats.

Morgan sat his saddle for a long time, bringing every detail back to his mind. Then his thoughts turned to Ed Cole. Cole was a San Francisco man Morgan had met in Colorado years before as a field representative of a land company. After he had secured his option on the wagon road grant, he had looked Cole up and told him he was $100,000 short.

"I'm working for the Citizens' Bank now," Cole said, "and I believe I can wangle the loan for you. As a matter of fact, we had been dickering for the valley ourselves, but we felt the price was a little steep."

"I'd be beholden to you," Morgan said.

"Not at all, son. A straight business proposition."

"Ought to be a good deal for the bank. The valley's worth five times what I'm asking to borrow."

Cole laughed. "You're an optimist, Murdo. Not many bankers would agree with you."

"Why, Ed, that . . ."

"I know." Cole held up a carefully manicured hand. "I've been there. It's good land if it had water on it, and there's a lot of it, but don't forget you've got Broad Clancy to buck and you've got a handful of squatters like Pete Royce there at the lake, and the Carricks below the east rim, who won't want to move. What's more, you're a long way from a railroad. That valley isn't worth a nickel if you don't get settlers on it. How are you going to do that?"

Morgan had an idea, but it was his notion and not Ed Cole's. Shrugging, he said: "I'll figure on it." And he had left Cole's office.

# III

For a time, Morgan had waited. Then, when the loan had been approved, he had gone immediately to the office of the Gardner Land Development Company. He had never met Grant Gardner, but he had heard of him, a capitalist who was more interested in using his wealth to develop farm colonies than to make money.

But Grant Gardner was harder-headed than Morgan had heard he was.

"I admire your courage, Morgan," he said

26

frankly, "but I don't admire your business sense. You've put a fortune into that road grant and borrowed a hundred thousand to boot. I know the Citizens' Bank and how they do business. If you slip when the time comes to pay, you'll lose your shirt."

"I've got till October," Morgan said. "By that time, I'll have the land sold."

Gardner threw up his hands. "Morgan, you're a lamb among wolves. How are you going to get a thousand families into your Paradise Valley by October?"

"I figured on your help. I had a wild notion you were the same kind of dreamer my father was. From the time I remember anything, I remember him talking about how land wears out and folks will have to keep moving west. He said we had to plow up new land to support a population that's growing all the time. He wanted to help the settlers when they came to Paradise Valley, but they didn't come in time. If I'm wrong about you, Gardner, I'll have to get a job punching cows 'cause I sure will lose my shirt."

For a long time, Gardner sat studying Morgan, pulling steadily on his cigar, fingertips tapping his desk.

"You're not wrong about me, Morgan," he had said then. "I'm a dreamer and a gambler to boot. I've taken some long chances on land development, and folks have called me crazy the

27

same as I'm calling you, but I have a conviction that the future of the West lies in agriculture, not the cattle business. We've all got some kind of a job to do or we wouldn't be here. My job is to bring about the settlement of land that can be profitably farmed."

"You're talking my language now," Morgan had told him.

Gardner had shaken his head. "Afraid not, Morgan. I can't see that you've got much chance with your wagon road grant. I've been successful because I've picked my land developments carefully. It strikes me you've been carried away by the memory of an idealist father who left you with some fantastic childhood notions."

"Maybe that's right," Morgan had agreed doggedly, "but I've seen men who had enough nerve to take long chances pull off some crazy-looking propositions. I'll pull this one off if I get the help I need. I've got to have a national organization to sell the land. You've got it. Would you put Paradise Valley over for ten percent of the sales?"

Gardner thought about it. Then he nodded. "Yes. I don't have anything to push at the moment. I'll give you that much of a boost."

"There's another thing. I'll sell the bottom land in small tracts, but a farmer needs water to make a living on that kind of acreage. There are some creeks flowing into the lake that run enough water for a thousand families if we had the reservoirs in the hills."

"A million dollars?"

Morgan had shaken his head. "I'm no engineer, but I'd say half of that."

"Figure me out of it," Gardner said flatly. "I'm not that big a gambler."

"My idea is to use a lottery to sell the valley," Morgan went on.

Gardner laughed shortly. "It can't be done, Morgan. The laws of the United States forbid it."

"I'll get around that by letting 'em bid on every piece of land after it's drawn. We'll have a government man there to see it's done the way it's supposed to be."

Gardner scratched the end of his nose. "You've got more head than I gave you credit for, Morgan. Tell you what I'll do. I'll sell the land for you and push the lottery idea. I'll send a crew to handle the land sale and I'll be there myself. If you've got settlers who'll buy, and if they're the kind who'll work and don't expect something for nothing, I'll put in your irrigation project."

"That's all I'm asking," Morgan said.

Morgan rose and reached the door before Gardner warned: "Don't expect any mercy from the Citizens' Bank or Ed Cole."

"I won't need it. I'll have the money."

"When do you plan the sale?"

"September First."

Gardner nodded approval. "Good. That's time enough. Keep me informed. I'll be in Irish Bend before the First of September."

So Morgan had taken his black gelding from the livery and ridden north. He thought of the warning Gardner had given him about Cole and the Citizens' Bank, but it did not worry him. He had known Cole personally for six years, and regarded him as a friend. In any case, the money had been loaned and Murdo Morgan owned the wagon road grant. If Gardner did his selling job, the money would be on hand before October.

Now, with his eyes on the valley, a faint premonition of disaster slid along Morgan's spine like the passage of a cold snake. He would have to dispossess the nester families or talk them into buying the land they squatted on.

Broad Clancy was a tougher problem. Yet Morgan held no sympathy for either the nesters or Clancy. They had stubbornly settled on land they had selected regardless whether it was government land open to entry or company property.

A gray dirt streak of a road cut through the sage from the north rim to Irish Bend and wound on to the south buttes, twisting a little to the west so that it ran directly to a sharp peak rising boldly above the lesser hills. It was Clancy Mountain, and behind it in the high country was Clancy marsh, Turkey Track's summer range.

It was poor graze along the north edge of the valley with rock ridges extending like giant fingers southward from the rim. Except for Pete Royce at the lake and the Carricks farther east, the squatters had all located along the north edge of the valley. The bulk of the bottom land was rich with bunchgrass growing among the sage clumps—good graze, an empire worth fighting for.

Morgan put his black down the steep slope to the valley floor and, keeping north of the Turkey Track buildings, lined directly across the valley to Irish Bend. The sun climbed until it was noon high, rolling back purple shadows that clung tenaciously to the Hagerman Hills to the east. It was a still day, utterly without wind, stiflingly hot for so early in the season.

Reaching Irish Bend shortly before noon, Morgan stabled his horse. "Treat him right," he told the hostler. "He's come a ways."

The hostler nodded, tight-lipped, and said nothing, but suspicion was plain to read on his long face. Morgan stepped through the archway. He stood for a moment in the sun's glare, gray eyes raking the street, a lock of black hair sweat-pasted to his forehead.

He made his appraisal of the town without hurry, taking his time building his cigarette. He

31

had the pinched-in-the-middle look and the wide shoulders of a man who had spent most of his life in the saddle. His face and hands were tanned a dark mahogany, his clothes and holster and gun butt were black. In many ways, he looked like any of the Turkey Track riders who idled along the street, yet he was a stranger, and therefore set apart.

Morgan left the stable and moved toward the hotel, passing the Elite Saloon and going on across the intersection made by the town's single side street. He walked with studied indifference, feeling many eyes watching from the hidden places of the town. Suspicion was here. When his purpose became known, that suspicion would turn to open hostility.

A tight smile cut at the corners of his lips. He understood this and expected it. A man who has lived with danger as a constant traveling mate develops a feeling that is close to instinct. He was like a dog setting his face toward a wolf pack, bristles up, muscles tensed.

Irish Bend had been no more than a single store sixteen years ago. Now it was a cow town supported and permitted to exist by the grace of Broad Clancy. When the time came, every hand would be against Murdo Morgan because Clancy willed it so.

This was the way it had been with Morgan. He had been looked upon with distrust before.

It was never pleasant, and it left its mark upon him. There had been the fights, and they, too, had left their marks—the white scar on his left cheek almost hidden under the dust clinging in his black stubble, the welt of a bullet on his left hand.

This was Paradise Valley, this was the town of Irish Bend, remembered in the well of Morgan's memory, and yet entirely strange. Here was harbored a wickedness spawned by suspicion, a shadow across the sun. It struck at Morgan from the false-fronted buildings, from the alleys, from the wide, rough street. There was a sort of grim humor about it. Broad Clancy was a small man, but he threw a long, wide shadow.

The tantalizing smell of cooked food rushed along the street to Morgan. He had not eaten since dawn and he had been conscious of a rumbling emptiness in his stomach for hours.

He turned into the hotel and immediately stopped. A girl stood behind the desk and Morgan's first thought was: *This is Peg.*

Immediately he knew he was wrong. She was small, perhaps twenty-two or three, with eager blue eyes so dark they were nearly purple. Her hair was as golden as ripe wheat fit for the binder. Her lips were full and red and quick-smiling. No, she wasn't Peg. That gay, reckless laugh had given him a picture of her, and this girl didn't fit the picture.

She motioned to an archway on his left.

"There's the dining room if that's what you're looking for."

"Thanks. Just couldn't seem to get my eyes on it."

"I noticed that."

As he turned through the archway, he heard her laugh follow him, low and throaty. She wasn't, he thought, displeased.

There were a few townspeople in the dining room—two settlers with mud caked on their gumboots, and one table of cowmen. They left as Morgan took a seat, and he had only a passing glance at them. One was young and small, one a thick-bodied wedge of a man, the other middle-aged and smaller than the first with a head overly large for his body and the conscious strut of a man who is certain of his position and power.

Morgan watched him until he disappeared into the lobby. He was Broad Clancy and he fitted Morgan's memory of him as perfectly as Paradise Valley had.

Morgan stepped back into the lobby when he finished dinner. He saw with keen pleasure that the girl was still at the desk.

"I want a room," he said.

Nodding, she turned the register for him to sign. A pen and bottle of ink were on the desk, but he didn't write his name for a moment. To look at her was like taking a deep breath of fresh air after coming out of a tightly closed room.

He saw things about her he had not seen before—the smooth texture of her skin, the dark tan that could have come only from the long hours under the sun, the freckles on her pert nose, the perfection of her white teeth when she smiled.

She dipped the pen and handed it to him. "You have to sign your name."

"I'm sorry." He dropped his gaze, not realizing until then how directly he had been staring at her. He scratched his name, gave San Francisco as his home, and laid the pen down. "When you've been thirsty for a long time, you just can't stop drinking when you come to water."

Capping the ink bottle, she swung the register back, but she didn't look at his name for a moment. Her eyes were lifted to his and he saw no suspicion in them. Again, he thought she was not displeased. She did not belong here. She seemed to stand in the sunlight away from Broad Clancy's shadow.

Then she looked down at the register as she reached for a key. She froze that way, one hand outstretched, lips parted, and warmth fled from her face.

"Morgan. Murdo Morgan." She straightened and gave him a direct look. "I suppose you think you're a brave man to come back."

"I never laid any claim to being a brave man," he said laconically.

"Would you admit you're a fool?"

"That might come nearer being right."

She clutched the edge of the desk, knuckles white. "I don't think you're either one. Only the devil would return for revenge."

"If you'll give me my key, I'll find my room, ma'am. Then maybe you can tell me where Broad Clancy would be."

"Do you think I want my father's blood on my hands?" she asked hotly. "Or do you deny you returned to kill him?"

"Yes, I'll deny that. If I kill him, it will be because he forces me."

"You're a liar as well as a devil." She pointed at the black-butted gun that snugged his hip. "Your brand is easy to read."

He placed his big hands, palm down, on the desk and leaned toward her. "Look, Miss . . ."

"You were eleven when you left!" she cried. "You're old enough to remember that my name is Jewell."

"Jewell Clancy." He said the words as if he could not believe they were her name. "I have seen desert flowers, but I didn't expect to find one here."

She blushed, but her smile did not return. "You can't stay here in the valley. Don't start the fight again."

"I don't intend to start it. I want a room and I want to see your dad."

"I remember the day you left. I was in the store when you and your father rode by. I'll never forget. I've thought about it so many times. We'd killed your brothers and you'd lost your home, but you weren't crying. You were grown up, even then. Let it go at that, Murdo. All the killing you can do will not set right the wrongs we did."

"I know that," he said roughly, "and I'm tired of being called a liar. I didn't come back to kill your dad."

He saw the pulse beat in her throat, the tremor of her lips. He sensed the struggle that was in her, the desire to believe him battling what her reason told her to believe.

"Even if you were telling the truth," she whispered, "Dad won't believe you. You'll find him with Short John and Jaggers Flint in the Silver Spur. Flint's a gunman, Murdo. He'll kill you. I think Dad hired him as insurance against your return."

"Then a lot of things will be settled," he said lightly, and turned to the door.

"Don't go, Murdo!" she called.

He swung back and had a long look at her. He saw her lips stir and become still. He sensed the rush of emotions that the ghost of a past not dead brought to her.

"Looks like I'll have to do without that room," he said, and left the hotel.

# IV

Murdo Morgan was a direct man without an ounce of sly cunning in him. It was a mark of Morgan character, the same as the thin nose and high cheek bones had marked Morgan faces. He knew that this meeting with Broad Clancy might decide his future and the future of the valley, and he hurried his steps as if to hasten destiny's decision.

There were a dozen riders strung along the bar, and another group at a poker table. Turkey Track men, Morgan knew, for they were not squatters, and there was no other spread within fifty miles or more of Irish Bend. If there was a fight they would back their boss, and that made odds that gave Morgan no chance at all.

The Clancys and Jaggers Flint were standing at the street end of the bar. Morgan paced slowly to them, feeling again the covert scrutiny of every man in the room, exactly as he had felt it when he had first ridden into town.

Broad Clancy was not over five and a half feet tall and spindly bodied. His face was as wrinkled as the last overripe apple in the barrel. He had placed his expensive wide-brimmed Stetson on the bar and his head, Murdo saw, was entirely without hair. He turned, green eyes staring briefly at Morgan from under hooding gold-brown brows, then coldly gave Morgan his back.

Short John, Clancy's oldest son, now about thirty, was the way Morgan remembered him. He was smaller than his father, but he was much like the older man, with the same green eyes and the bushy gold-brown brows. There were differences that Morgan noted—wavy brown hair worn long, mutton-chop whiskers that seemed out of place on so young a man, and an intangible something that gave Morgan the impression that Short John had never lived his own life, but that he was forever under the shadow thrown by his father.

Short John turned his back to Morgan with the same contemptuous indifference Broad had shown. The slow smile that spread Morgan's mouth did not lighten the gravity of his face. He recognized this for what it was. The Clancys didn't know him and they pretended not to care. They were the king and the crown prince; he was a stranger approaching the court. Let him bow and scrape the way other strangers did.

Anger stirred Morgan, but he kept it masked with an urbane expression. The great pride he always associated with small men was here in Broad Clancy, and to a lesser degree in Short John.

Uncertainty had always been Morgan's lot; trouble as natural to expect as the sunset. He had been taught by the very circumstances of his life to learn to read men. He came to the bar now and stood beside Broad Clancy, knowing that any way he played this would be a gamble, but that if he pegged Clancy right, there was one way that offered a fair chance of winning.

"You're Clancy, ain't you?" Morgan said, his tone a cold slap at the man's dignity.

Broad Clancy stiffened. Short John turned, an audible breath sawing into the sudden quiet. Jaggers Flint, standing beyond Short John, exploded with an oath.

"That's him, boss. That's the huckleberry who held the gun on us last night at the Smith shack."

It was the gravelly voiced man who had been with Rip Clancy the night before. He stepped away from the bar, cocked and primed for sudden and violent trouble. Trouble was his business; he made his living that way. He was waiting to kill now, waiting only for the signal from the man who had bought his gun.

According to Jewell, this was the man Broad Clancy had hired as insurance against Morgan's return. Morgan knew the breed. Flint had a streak that was mean and cruel, but if he was like a hundred others Morgan had known, he had another element, a weakness that would break under the pressure of hard courage. Now Morgan searched for that weakness.

"That's right, Clancy," Morgan said. "I met up with this man last night. I think you cheated yourself when you agreed to pay him fighting wages."

Quick interest brought a bright glint in Clancy's green eyes.

"Why?"

Morgan waited, letting the tension build, watching Flint's muddy brown eyes grow wide and hard and wicked, watched desire grow until it had brought him close to making a draw.

"When you pay a good price, Clancy," Morgan said with biting contempt, "you deserve a good product. All you got is a phony. Just big brass buttons and an empty holler."

Desire faded in Flint's eyes. He swallowed and choked.

"Nobody talks that way . . . not to Jaggers Flint," he finally said, in a vain attempt to sound tough.

Morgan waited for the signal of his intent, the down drop of a shoulder, the tightening of his lips, the fire glow in his eyes. But Flint stood motionless, glowering, and Morgan prodded him with a laugh.

"It's been a long trail, Clancy," Morgan said. "Things ain't the way they used to be. You didn't hire men like this when you cleared the valley of the Morgans."

Clancy's eyes narrowed. "What do you know about the Morgans?"

"I know quite a bit about the Morgans, but that

ain't the reason I'm here. I want to talk to you. I don't take to being jumped by a gun dog. Tell him to draw or drag."

Clancy was frankly puzzled. He nodded at Flint without taking his eyes from Morgan. The gunman muttered an oath as if reluctant to drop the matter, but he moved back to his place at the bar with greater speed than the occasion required.

He had cracked. Morgan doubted that the man would ever have the courage to make a face-to-face draw against him, but he would be a constant threat as long as he and Morgan were both in the valley. Morgan had aroused the hate that Flint and men of his kind hold for another who has broken them. There would come a day when that hate would find expression.

"Your business?" Clancy asked in a dry dead tone.

"I'm Murdo Morgan . . . representing the . . ."

"Morgan!"

The word was jolted out of Clancy. He stood stockstill, eyes twin emeralds sparking under the bushy brows, stiff-shouldered as if the temerity of Murdo Morgan in coming here had stunned him momentarily.

"I don't think you've forgotten the Morgans, Clancy."

"Murdo Morgan." Clancy seemed suddenly to come awake. "You came back to kill me, didn't you? Go ahead . . . but if you down me, you'll have a rope around your neck inside of five minutes."

"I didn't come to kill you, Clancy," Morgan said patiently. "What's been done has been done. I'm representing the . . ."

"I don't give a cuss what you represent!" Broad Clancy bellowed. He jerked a thumb toward the street. "Get out! I'll give you two minutes to dust out of town."

The men at the poker tables had risen and moved to the bar. More than a dozen guns. Morgan knew he could take Broad Clancy and perhaps Short John. He couldn't take them all. But Clancy made no motion for his gun. There had been a time when he would have, but the years had slowed his draw and he had no desire to die.

"All right," Morgan said with biting scorn. "You're not as bright as I remember you. I came here to talk over a proposition that's got to be settled before the summer's finished. There'll be lives . . ."

"Turkey Track stomps its own snakes!" Clancy bawled. "We make our own laws and we enforce 'em. I've got nothing to talk over with any blasted stranger, and least of all a Morgan."

Short John and Jaggers Flint had moved up to stand close behind Clancy, the others forming a packed triangle farther along the bar. Morgan was entirely alone. A strong current ran against him, a current that would have washed a lesser man through the door and into the street.

"Forget I'm a Morgan," he said. "Put Smith or Jones or Brown or any handle onto me you want to. If you'll listen you might be able to save the Turkey Track. If you don't . . ."

"You've used up most of your time," Clancy said coldly. "Ride out of the valley."

For a moment Morgan had forgotten the barkeep. If he was shot in the back, there would be no avenging justice. Only a quick burial. They would plant him below the east rim beside the three Morgans who had lain there for sixteen years. He backed along the bar until he could see the apron. The man straightened and laid a shotgun on the mahogany.

Morgan's smile was a cold straight line that toughened his bronze face.

"You used to be a fighting man, Clancy," he said coldly, "but you're old and you're afraid, so you hire lobos like Flint and wink at a barman to shoot a man in the back. I'm not here to argue. I came here to find a way to stop a fight, but if it's fight you want, it's what you'll get."

Morgan backed out of the Silver Spur and slanted across the intersection formed by Main and the side street. He paced along the front of the Elite Saloon and past two empty buildings, moving with challenging slowness.

Stepping into the livery stable, Morgan paid

the hostler and got his black, ignoring the open malice on the man's face. Mounting, he rode across the street, stepped down in front of the post office, and tied his mount. A hasty departure from town would mean that he had been stampeded by Broad Clancy, an advantage he could not afford to give the cowman.

Morgan paused in front of the post office, shaping a smoke and lighting it, eyes on the pine-fringed slopes of the Sunset Mountains. A white cloud bank lay above the pines, slowly building into grotesque shapes.

When he had shown his defiance, Morgan tossed his cigarette into the street and turned into the post office. He bought a card from the white-haired postmistress, scratched a line to Grant Gardner in San Francisco, and mailed it.

"Murdo."

It was Jewell Clancy's voice. He wheeled back to the wicket. The girl was standing where the old lady had been a moment before, her gaze speculative and interested.

"Do the Clancys run the post office along with everything else in the valley?" he asked.

"No. It's the only place where I could talk to you without Dad seeing me. When I saw you come in, I ran around the back."

"I had a notion you didn't want to talk to me," he said.

Still, her gaze was held on him as if trying to

cut away the tough exterior he showed the world, as if pondering the real motives that had driven him back after all the years. He saw no fear of him in her eyes, no bitterness, no hatred.

She was grave, not even a hint of a smile lingering at the corners of her full red lips.

"I was outside the Silver Spur," she told him, "and heard what you said. I . . . I was wrong about you. You didn't come back to kill Dad."

"Thanks for the confidence. I didn't expect to hear it from a Clancy."

"Why did you come, Murdo?"

He took off his hat in a quick gesture as if suddenly remembering it was on his head, a gesture of gallantry that plainly surprised her. He held his silence for a time, pondering her reason for asking him. Perhaps Broad Clancy, regretting he had not listened, had sent Jewell to find out his mission.

"I'll tell your dad when he's of a mind to listen," he finally said.

"They say all Clancys are stubborn," she said, "but Dad is the stubbornest of all of us. If he wasn't, he'd have seen what I did. When you backed Flint down, you could have forced a fight on Dad and killed him. That's how I knew I was wrong."

"If I'd come here to do a killing job," Morgan murmured, "I wouldn't have used the Morgan name."

"I thought of that, too." Her smile brought back a little of the warmth he had first seen on her face. "You see, I'm almost as lost as you are. Dad can't understand how a Clancy can see two sides to the trouble."

"Can you?"

"Yes, but it wasn't all Dad's fault. Or did you know that?"

"No."

"Someday I'll tell you about it. That isn't important now. If you aren't here to kill Dad, you're here for another reason. If I knew what it was, I could help you."

"No, you can't help."

"Dad will keep on thinking you're here to kill him," she urged, "so he'll kill you first."

"I reckon he'll try."

"Auntie Jones is the postmistress. If you want me, get word to her."

"Thanks."

Morgan left the post office. Again he paused outside to build a smoke. He was still there when Jewell came through the doorway behind him and walked gracefully across the street, a hand lifting her skirt from trim ankles as she waded through the dust.

# V

The afternoon sun pressed against Morgan's back as he took the east road out of town. The miles fell behind, miles that were monotonously alike; flat sandy earth, sage, and rabbitbrush, an occasional juniper that seemed to huddle within itself to hold the small moisture that its roots drew from the arid land.

Then Morgan topped a ridge and came down to Paradise Lake. It was no thing of beauty. Tules grew profusely in the muck along the west end of the lake. A long-snouted hog, suddenly aware of human presence, snorted defiance and crashed into the swamp growth.

On the north shore of the lake the alkali flat, entirely without life, shimmered in the sharp brightness of the sunshine. It was worthless, but the south side of the lake was the most valuable part of the valley. Here were thousands of acres that could be farmed without water, for it would always be moist from the lake. Pete Royce's place, the only farm in this part of the valley, took up but a small fraction of the rich black soil that stretched south from the lake.

The road skirted the front of Royce's farm. A brown haystack from the previous year bulked wide in the field between the road and the lake.

Around it, grass, belly-high on a horse, bowed in long rhythmical waves before the hot wind. Southward, gray desert stretched in sage-studded ridges toward the buttes.

Presently Morgan came to Royce's cabin. It was made, he guessed, of lodgepole pine brought from Clancy Mountain. There was a scattering of sheds and corrals and, what was most surprising, a well-kept yard between the cabin and the road. Even without the obvious evidence of the washing on the line, Morgan would have guessed a woman lived here.

Dismounting, Morgan watered his horse at the trough. A saddled bay gelding was racked at the hitch pole in front of the cabin. The door was open and, as Morgan turned to step back into the saddle, he heard a laugh, gay and feminine. With a sudden sharpening of interest, Morgan realized that the girl, Peg, was inside.

Morgan would have ridden on if he hadn't heard the girl ask: "What are you going to do about the company man when he shows up, Rip?"

"I'll fill him so full of lead he wouldn't float in the lake," Rip Clancy's voice said. "It'll take more'n a company gunslinger to run us Clancys off our range."

Stepping around the trough, Morgan walked up the path that cut across the lawn. Something was wrong. Only Ed Cole and Gardner and his organization knew that Morgan was coming to Paradise Valley.

Morgan paused in the doorway, an angular shape nearly filling it, right hand idle at his side. "I'm the company man you're expecting, Clancy," he said coldly. "Now what was it you were going to do?"

Young Clancy and the girl were sitting on a leather sofa pushed against the north wall. Grabbing his gun, Clancy came up from his seat as if a giant spring had shot him upright. Then he froze, color washing out of his scrawny-thin face. He was considering the black bore of Morgan's gun.

"You're plumb fast with the talk," Morgan said contemptuously, "but a mite slow on the draw."

Morgan would have recognized Rip as a Clancy. He had the same arrogance and exaggerated pride, the green eyes and bushy brows, but they were red, not gold-brown, and his hair was red. He straightened, slender hands moving nervously as he sought a way out of this.

"I know your voice!" he cried. "You're the *hombre* who covered up for Buck last night, ain't you?"

"That's right."

"I should've plugged you," Rip said regretfully. "Flint talked me out of it. I didn't think he was that short of nerve."

"A Clancy wouldn't be short of nerve, would

he? Want me to put my iron back and give you another chance to draw?"

Rip ran the tip of his tongue over thin lips. He shot a glance at the girl, his sharp features growing sharper as hate pressed him, as the humiliation of this moment cut deeper into his pride.

Morgan let the tension build until Rip flung out: "You've got the edge now, mister! Go ahead and walk big. There'll be another day."

"I'll wait for it, sonny."

Morgan remained in the doorway, gun hip-high, watching young Clancy narrowly. He sensed a cold courage in the boy that had been lacking in Broad and Short John. As he watched, a wicked grin broke across Rip's narrow face.

Without turning, Morgan saw he had made a mistake. He had seen only the one horse, and it had not occurred to him that Rip would have another man with him. Now, from the mocking triumph in the boy's eyes, he knew someone was behind him.

There was no time to think about it, to let it play out. He whirled with the unexpectedness and speed of a striking cougar, his gun lashing out with a ribbon of flame. A bullet burned along Morgan's ribs, but the man in the yard didn't fire again. Morgan had moved with perfect co-ordination of instinct and muscular speed. His bullet had knocked the man off his feet as if he had been sledged by an axe handle.

Time had compressed and run out for Murdo Morgan. Rip Clancy was behind him with a gun on his hip and all the opportunity he needed. Morgan spun back. Then he held his fire. The girl had gripped Clancy's wrist.

"No, Rip!" she was screaming. "No!"

Morgan reached Clancy in two long strides. "I'll take that cutter. I didn't think the Clancys would whipsaw a man like that."

"The man you shot wasn't a Clancy," Peg said without feeling. "He's Pete Royce."

Clancy stood still as Morgan took his gun. He stood with shoulder blades against the wall, face bone-hard, eyes frosty emerald slits.

"What kind of a woman are you, Peg?" he asked hoarsely. "I'd have killed him if you . . ."

"I know," the girl breathed. "And I've got an idea about any crawling thing that would shoot a man in the back."

Red crept into Clancy's cheeks as he felt the girl's scorn. He held his position, saying nothing. Morgan holstered his gun and knelt beside the man in the yard. The bullet had creased Royce's skull. It was a shallow wound, enough to knock the man cold, but unlikely to be dangerous. Morgan lifted him and carried him into the cabin.

"Is there a sawbones in town?" Morgan asked.

"Doc Velie. Go fetch him, Rip."

Young Clancy didn't move for a moment,

52

sullen green eyes whipping from Peg to Morgan and back to Peg. He had been beaten; he had taken the girl's contempt, and pride had been torn from him and trampled underfoot.

"All right," Clancy breathed. "Don't figger I'm done with you, mister, and I've got an idea that when Pete gets up and finds out what you've done, Peg, he'll take a blacksnake to you."

"I'll kill him if he does," the girl said flatly. "He'll never beat me again."

"Big wind blowin' off the lake," Clancy jeered. "He'll curry you down like he's done before. Or maybe I'll do it myself. You've had your fun playin' with me and Buck Carrick. One of these days I'll have some fun of my own."

Clancy stalked out, hit saddle, and went down the road at a hard run, cracking steel to his horse every jump.

Morgan watched while Peg washed the crimson trickle from her father's face and stopped the flow of blood with a bandage.

"Sorry I had to shoot him," Morgan murmured.

"You've got no call to be sorry." She rose and faced him. "I wouldn't have been sorry if you'd shot him between the eyes."

"He's your father?"

"So he says. I'm not proud of my blood."

Morgan built a smoke, standing lax, back against the wall. This was the first opportunity he'd had to appraise the girl, and he took his time with his cigarette, head bent a little, eyes fixed on her.

Peg Royce was tall, with dark eyes and cricket-black hair combed sleekly back from her forehead and tied with a bright red ribbon. She was eighteen or twenty, Morgan guessed, with a woman's full-bodied roundness. She stood beside the couch, ramrod-straight, making her study him as coolly as he studied her. She came toward him then, moving in a graceful leggy stride.

"You're a fighting man," she breathed. "I felt it last night, and I had proof just now. You're worth any three men in the valley, but that isn't enough. The company should have sent an army."

She stood close to him, head tilted, the fragrance of her hair a stirring sweetness in his nostrils, red lips invitingly close. He saw the pulse beat in her white throat. She set up a turbulence in him, speeded his heart until it was pounding with hammer-like beats in his chest.

"I've done all right," he said. "With your help."

"I won't always be around," she said with a shrug. "You'll be fighting the whole Clancy outfit. Dad and the rest of the nesters will be taking pot shots at you. You won't live the week out."

"I never gamble with anybody's life but my own." Morgan slid past her into the yard. "Keep your dad quiet till the doc gets here. Head wounds are pretty tricky."

"Nobody keeps Pete Royce quiet," she said with sharp bitterness.

"Why do you hate him?" asked Morgan.

"Because of what he's done, and what he will do. You'll hate him before you're done. You're here to get him off company land, aren't you?" She shook her head. "He won't go, and he won't pay for the land. Go in there and put a bullet through his head. You'll never get him off any other way."

She stayed in the doorway, scowling against the sun. Looking at her, Morgan saw the lines of discontent that cut her forehead. Suddenly she put it away. She laughed, as gay and free a laugh as she had given Buck Carrick the night before.

"You wouldn't kill him when he couldn't fight back, would you? You're that kind of a fool. The trouble is Pete Royce and Arch Blazer and the Clancys don't play by rules."

"You're pretty as an angel," he said in a puzzled voice, "and as tough as a boot heel."

"That's me," she said gaily, and came across the yard. "Nobody knows what I am. Maybe I don't myself, but I know a little about the game that every woman has played since Eve had her fun. I'll use a man to get what I want, and I'll have a winner when the last hand's dealt. A lot of the pious people like the Clancys say I'm bad, but I'm honest, and that's more than you can say for them."

"Is it honest to play one man against another until one of them is dead because of you?"

"Who's dead?"

"Buck Carrick might have been after you put Rip onto his trail last night."

"I didn't do anything of the kind, Murdo Morgan. Don't make me worse than I am."

"Then why did Rip come to the shack after Buck?"

"I'd met Buck there before. Old man Carrick hates me. That's why we meet at the shack. Rip probably saw me ride across the valley."

"How did you know my name, and that I'm a company man?"

"The wind talks," she said lightly, "and I understand it. I saw you watering your horse. That's why I started talking to Rip about the company man. We don't have many strangers here, so I made a good guess who you were."

"You wanted me to come in?"

"Sure. I wanted to see a fight. You know. Get a man killed over me."

He had called it right. She was as tough as a boot heel. There was little shame or modesty about her. She would use a man to get what she wanted, exactly as she had said. Suddenly he was angry. There was no good reason for it except that he resented her coolly confident smile, her frank assurance that she could have him and use him exactly as she had used Rip Clancy and Buck Carrick.

"Thanks for keeping Clancy off my back," Morgan drawled.

"Don't thank me. I wanted you alive. Don't forget I'm going to hold that winning hand on the last deal."

He stepped into saddle. He sat looking down at her, knowing he had no reason to stay, but not wanting to go.

"Tell Royce I want to talk to him when he gets on his feet," he said.

"He'll never talk to a company man. He'll work it around so you'll get killed and nobody will know he had a hand in it. But you're too big a fool to ride out of the country. You'll stay and you'll come back here." She stood with her feet wide-spread, red lips shaping a cool smile, a graceful seductive figure. "You'll be back, but not to see him, and I'll go on trying to keep you alive."

He turned his horse into the road. He didn't look back, but he knew she was standing there, staring at him, and probably smiling. She would be a dangerous enemy. Or a friend who could never be fully trusted.

Nature had endowed Peg Royce with all the weapons in the feminine arsenal and taught her their use. Morgan knew how to fight men like Jaggers Flint and Rip Clancy, how and when to push. He didn't know how to fight Peg Royce.

He tried to put her out of his mind, but she clung there tenaciously, disturbing him and whipping his pulse to a faster pace. Buck Carrick had said: *Don't ever see her. She'll drag you through perdition. She's poison.* Now Morgan knew what Buck had meant, but the knowledge made no difference. She remained in his mind.

When Morgan was out of sight, Peg turned back into the cabin. A grave soberness had come into her face. For a long time she stared down at Pete Royce, bitterness and frustration flooding her consciousness.

"You've sold your soul to Ed Cole for a thousand dollars, Royce," she whispered. "You'll kill the best man who ever rode into the valley, but you can't have my soul to take to the devil with you. Not for all your thousand dollars!"

# VI

Leaving the Royce place the road was no more than two vague ruts cut through the sage. As Morgan followed it, a thousand memories crowded back into a mind already too full. He had not wanted to come here. This was one part of the valley he'd had no desire to see, but he had to talk to Jim Carrick.

Morgan thought again of his boyhood, of his

58

hound dog Tuck, the clean sound of axe on pine as his father and brothers had built the cabin, the first deer he had ever shot, the long trip north with the herd from California and his father's words: *There's room enough for us and the Clancys in this valley. Someday the settlers will come and we'll help 'em when they do, but right now we'll take what we can hold.*

But there hadn't been room enough in the valley, and the Morgans hadn't been able to hold a square foot. Morgan had never known what had started the fight, but it had been destined from the first. Broad Clancy and Josh Morgan had known each other years before, and the capacity for hatred was great in both of them. Clancy had won because he was the first in the valley and, with his greater wealth, he had been able to hire more men.

The last fight. The motionless bloody bodies of Murdo Morgan's brothers. The funeral. The hollow sound of clods on the pine coffins. His father's gray, frozen face. Broad Clancy had been there. Morgan had never understood that. It hadn't seemed right. Clancy or his men had killed his brothers, and then had come to see them buried.

They had left that afternoon, Josh Morgan and Murdo, taking a pack horse and a few things Josh wanted as keepsakes, one of them a tintype of Murdo's mother. Then that last look at the valley, the smoke plume rising from the burning cabins. Those were the things a man could never forget if he lived as long as the desert had been here.

Nor could he forget his father's words. *There's room for a thousand families down there where Broad Clancy runs his cattle. I'm goin' to bring 'em and I'll bust Clancy, which same ain't important. Givin' homes to hungry people is.*

But Josh Morgan had died too soon. This was another day and it was Murdo Morgan and not Josh who was here. Breaking Broad Clancy was less important to Murdo than it had been to Josh. Even saving the investment that Murdo had made seemed a minor thing. It was the thousand families that loomed big in his mind—giving homes to hungry people. Morgan had the power to do what his father had only dreamed about.

The Carrick cabin had been built on the ashes of the bigger Morgan cabin. The row of poplars that Josh had planted had been little more than switches when Murdo had left. Now they were tall, slender trees, throwing a shade laced with golden sunlight across the yard.

A huge fireplace centered the lodgepole pine cabin. The cabin winked brightly at Morgan from a thousand eyes as he rode up. When he was close, he saw that broken pieces of obsidian had been set among the other stones. Lilac bushes grew at the end of the cabin, their blossoms spreading a haunting fragrance in the air. It was a pleasant place, more pleasant than Morgan remembered. Emotions, long suppressed by the simplicity of his life, rose uninhibited.

East of the house the rimrock made a twenty-foot cliff, and a short distance to the north a creek spilled over the edge in a crystal waterfall. Beyond the creek was the fence that Josh Morgan had built around the graves. It was as tight as Josh had left it, the headstones were still here, the grass green and trimmed.

Two men were idling by the corral, a saddled horse standing behind them. They had been watching Morgan's approach. The dark-bearded one raised a hand in greeting.

"Light, stranger!" he called amiably.

Morgan pulled up beside them and, stepping down, held out his hand. "I'm guessing you're Jim Carrick."

"That's a plumb good guess," the bearded man boomed. He motioned to the slender man at his side. "My boy, Tom."

"I'm Murdo Morgan." He shook young Carrick's hand and dropped it. It was damp, and withdrawing as the man himself was withdrawing.

"Morgan!" Jim Carrick cried. "Say, you ain't kin to them three we got buried over yonder, I don't reckon?"

"Brother," Morgan said. "I was just a kid when it happened."

"You remember, don't you?" Tom Carrick demanded eagerly. "You came back to fight 'em, didn't you?"

"No. What's done is done. If it's a fight, Broad Clancy will make it."

Disgust stirred Tom's leathery face. "What kind of a man are you, totin' your iron that-away and talkin' like a pan of milk." He spat a brown ribbon that slapped into the dust and stirred it briefly. "Blue-john milk at that."

"That's enough, Tom," Jim Carrick said sharply. "You don't need to look for a fight all the time."

Young Carrick cursed bitterly. His was a barren, vindictive face. He wore a bushy mustache that was tobacco-stained, and his clothes were a cowman's, not a nester's. His bone-handled Colt was carried low and thonged down in the manner of a man who fights for pay. He was not a man to be found on a nester place, and Morgan, watching him closely, was puzzled by him.

Tom ran the back of his hand along his mouth. "If I had three brothers salivated like them Morgan boys was and I came back after all this time, I wouldn't look for a fight. I'd sure go out and make one."

Wheeling, he mounted and lined south along the rimrock.

"Mighty proddy, Tom is," Jim Carrick said worriedly. "He don't take to bein' pushed around by the Clancys, but I don't see no way of livin' on this range if you don't stand for pushin'."

Jim Carrick was as big a man as Morgan, with brown eyes that were both friendly and honest, and dark hair holding no more gray than his bushy beard. He pulled a pipe from his pocket and dribbled tobacco into it, great hands trembling with the bottled-up emotion that was in him.

"A man can stand so much pushing," Morgan said. "No more."

"Yeah." Carrick slid the tobacco pouch back into his pocket. "I heard old man Morgan died after Clancy ran him out of the valley, but didn't know he had a kid." He swung a big hand over the valley. "Enough graze here for two outfits. You'd have had a big spread if you could have held on. No sense of Clancy tryin' to be both Providence and the devil. Bein' the devil is enough for one man."

"A cowman's paradise," Morgan murmured. "Mild winters, plenty of bunchgrass, and good summer graze plumb over to Harney County. Dad used to say that."

Carrick scratched a match on the top corral bar and held the flame to his pipe. "That's right. I reckon Broad Clancy has made more money than he knows what to do with. Don't cost much to raise his beef 'cause his grass is here for the takin'. The herd he hazes south to the railhead in Californy makes the cattle they raise down there

63

look downright puny. Don't get the diseases up here they do in warmer climates."

"Dad used to say something else," said Morgan. "About cowmen pioneering the way into a new country, but the farmers always came later. He said in the long run a stockman couldn't use a million acres to support maybe a hundred men while a thousand families could make a good living on the same amount of land."

"Your dad was sure right." Carrick motioned toward the green strip that marked the creek. "You can raise mighty near anything here. Reckon it'd be a good fruit country, but that's just crazy dreamin'. There's a dozen of us nester families in the valley. We live where Clancy tells us and we live the way he tells or we've got trouble."

"That won't go on forever," Morgan said guardedly. "One of these days Clancy will stump his toe."

Carrick laughed sourly. "Looks to me like he's walkin' mighty good. I'm like Tom a little bit. I ain't proddy, but we've got to fight or get out and quit callin' ourselves men. I was hopin' you aimed to throw some lead Clancy's way."

"What are the nesters like?" asked Morgan. "The rest of 'em?"

"Pete Royce is a double-crossin' coyote who'd sell anything to anybody for an extra dollar. Arch Blazer is a barroom fighter and meaner'n

Royce. Some of the rest are the same way, just hidin', I reckon, thinkin' the law won't find 'em here. The others are like sheep, hatin' Clancy but kowtowin' to him all the same."

"By fall you'll see a thousand families living here," Morgan said. "Then Broad Clancy will sing a little low."

Carrick took his sweat-stained hat from his head and then wiped it with a bandanna. "If it wasn't so cussed hot, I'd laugh. What makes you think there'll be a thousand families in the valley by fall?"

"Because the Cascade and Paradise Land Company is selling acreage in the Middle West now. After the drought and grasshoppers those people have had, they'll be of a mind to buy and try it out here."

"I'll be hanged," Carrick murmured. "So the land company is finally goin' to do it. We'd heard the old bunch had sold out. . . . Pull your gear off your horse, Morgan, and I'll rustle a drink."

Morgan off-saddled, turned his black into the corral, and swung toward the cabin. He had to have some help, and Carrick was a better man than he could rightfully expect to find. Usually men who stood for pushing were, as Carrick had hinted, men who were willing to accept Clancy's rule in exchange for a place where they could live without fear of the law catching up with them.

Jim Carrick would do.

# VII

Carrick was waiting in the shade in front of the cabin, a whiskey bottle in his hand as Morgan came from the corral. The nester motioned toward a battered leather chair.

"Sit and have a drink," he invited. "I want to hear you talk. If the land company is what I think it is, you won't get more'n one drink from me."

Morgan grinned as he took the bottle. "It's a hard choice between Clancy and the land company, ain't it?"

"Plumb hard." Carrick sat down with his back to a poplar tree. "There ain't enough of us to fight Clancy. You can't count on men like Royce and Blazer nohow, but the worst of it is that all of us, including Clancy, are just squattin' here."

"If you made a deal with the company, you'd have a patent to your land," Morgan suggested.

Carrick reached for the bottle and took a long pull.

"You're talkin' crazy, mister. In the first place, nobody like us could deal with the land company. Money's all they want, and no matter what we've done to improve our places, we'll get our rumps kicked. In the second place, this grant was given to a company that never done a thing to earn it. I know. I was supposed to be on the road when

I came here, and it wasn't nothin' more'n a few stakes and five, six boulders rolled to one side. Road? Glory to Betsy, it wasn't no road at all! Just another dirty land grab."

Morgan could have pointed out that Jim Carrick had settled on the best farm site in the valley, not caring whether it was open to entry or not, but he didn't argue. His own father had done the same thing, and held the same low opinion of the company. So Morgan built a smoke, and shook his head when Carrick offered the bottle.

"You're sitting between a rock and the hard place, ain't you?" Morgan asked.

"That's right," Carrick said gloomily. "We furnish Clancy and his outfit with grain and garden sass and hay. That's free to him for lettin' us live here. Once a year he butchers and gives every family a quarter of beef. You'd think he was bein' plumb generous the way he acts. Might as well be livin' in the old days with a king pushin' you around. Got so you can't even blow your nose without ridin' over to the Turkey Track and askin' old Broad about it." He shook his head. "Now if the company moves in, we won't have nothin'."

"Might be you're wrong. Suppose a lot of people move into the valley. It'll bust the Turkey Track. You'll have neighbors working for the same thing you are. Won't be long till a railroad is built in and Irish Bend will be a big town."

"Crazy talk," Carrick jeered. "I'll lose this place, won't I?" He flung a big hand toward the Morgan graves. "You know why I kept 'em up? Clipped the grass and watered 'em? I'll tell you. Them boys died fightin' Broad Clancy. I never knowed 'em, but they stood for somethin'. I keep hangin' on, thinkin' more folks'll move in so we can give old Broad a fight and I want 'em to see other men have died tryin' to make this a free valley."

"Look, Jim," Morgan said suddenly. "I own the wagon road grant. Not somebody back in Boston in a soft-bottomed chair. I want families on this land. I hope to make money and I hope to bust Clancy, but mostly I want folks to develop this valley the way Dad wanted it done."

"I'll be blowed!" Carrick had started to lift the bottle again. He put it back, eyes pinned on Morgan. "Yes, sir, I'll be blowed!"

"This place is on an odd section," Morgan went on. "That makes it mine, but I don't want to shove you off. I've got a proposition. Interested?"

"You're danged right!" Carrick boomed.

"By September the valley will be full of settlers. They've got to be fed. We'll have to haul water for 'em. They'll need horse feed. Maybe there'll be a fight with the Turkey Track. I want your help. You give me that help, and the day the land sale is finished, I'll hand you a deed to your land."

"Mister, you've made a deal, and I hope there's some fightin'."

"What about the others?"

Carrick spat contemptuously. "Like I told you, Royce is no good, and that gal of his is a no-good. A Delilah. I like a pretty filly same as the next man, but I don't like to see 'em give a wiggle at every man that goes by. Maybe you'll find a few who'll back you up, but most of 'em will sell out to Clancy." Carrick sobered. "You're buckin' a pat hand, Morgan. All below the north rim know that the minute they start goin' ag'in' Broad Clancy, he'll send Rip and Jaggers Flint and a bunch of riders, and every nester in the valley will get cleaned out."

"I'll go see 'em," Morgan said promptly.

"Me and Tom and Buck will back your play no matter what it buys us," Carrick promised.

Morgan leaned back in the chair. He was more tired than he had realized. He felt like a man who has been in a whip-lashing gale and will go into it again in a moment, but now is in a pool of quiet. He looked across the valley toward the Sunset Mountains, rising swiftly above the nearly flat desert, the green pine-covering turned a hazy blue by the distance.

Here was an open land, a wide land bright with promise. For the moment Morgan let his dreams build. If they held the dark shadow of trouble, it was no more than he could expect. He could cope

69

with trouble when it came; he had been raised with it. He had always been alone; he would be alone now except for the Carricks.

A man could do no more than fight the thing that opposed him, regardless of the form it held. The fun came in the dreaming and the shaping of that dream into the hardness of reality. Someday he might not be alone. A woman gave a fullness to a man's life. He had never known his mother, but from the things his father had told him, she must have been beautiful and fine, the kind of woman a man sees in his mind, with little hope of finding.

He thought of Jewell Clancy, sweet and fine and practical, but set apart from him because she was named Clancy and he was a Morgan. There was Peg Royce, vibrant and alive, the thought of her enough to send a stirring through him. Carrick had called her a Delilah. Buck had said she was a poison. Still, she fastened herself in his mind. He remembered the fragrance of her hair, the thrill of her nearness when she had stood close to him.

Carrick sat in silence, watching Morgan soberly, as if sensing the younger man's thoughts.

"I ain't one to tell another fellow his business," he broke out, "but you'd better get one thing straight now. Don't have no truck with either Pete Royce or his girl. They'll sell you out and shoot you in the back. They'll . . ."

The clatter of horses' hoofs brought Carrick upright.

"Tom," he whispered. "He's bringin' Buck in. The boy didn't come home last night."

Buck was reeling in his saddle, his face powder-gray, blood a black patch on his shirt front.

"Got shot by Rip Clancy last night!" Tom Carrick called. "Pretty bad. Now you ready to go after him?"

Jim Carrick swayed drunkenly, a hand gripping a fence post.

"Let's get Buck in," he said harshly. "Then I reckon we'll ride." He swung to face Morgan. "Mister, no use puttin' this off. If you want our help, you sure as thunder better ride with us."

"That'll wait." Morgan helped Buck down. "Your boy won't."

They carried Buck inside. Buck was, Morgan saw, closer to death than he had at first thought.

"Doc Velie's at the Royce place," Morgan said grimly. "If Tom busts the breeze gettin' there, he can catch him."

"I ain't goin' after no sawbones," Tom said darkly. "I'm goin' after Rip Clancy."

"Then you'll have a dead brother," Morgan snapped. "That slug has got to come out of him."

Still Tom hesitated, his narrow vindictive face dark with the urge to kill.

"Go on," Jim Carrick said. "Morgan's right."

Tom wheeled out of the cabin. The thunder of

71

his horse's hoofs came and was slowly muffled by distance, then died.

"Kick up your fire." Morgan motioned to the fireplace. "Get a kettle of water on there and find some clean rags."

Jim Carrick obeyed. Buck lay on the bunk, eyes closed, body slack from weariness.

"Can't understand it," Carrick muttered. "Buck went to town yesterday. We've been workin' pretty hard gettin' some crops in. Tom . . . he ain't worth a cuss here. Hunts and fishes and rides all the time. Ain't no part of the farmer in him, but Buck had a night for howlin' comin' to him. Must have got drunk and jumped Rip."

"Tell him, Buck," Morgan said softly. Buck stirred, his eyes coming open. "Nothin' to tell," he muttered.

"You're forgettin' Peg," Morgan pressed.

It was cruel, but necessary. The one thing Morgan couldn't afford now was a showdown fight with the Turkey Track. If he rode to town with the Carricks, the only result would be a useless death.

"That Royce gal ain't got nothin' to do with his gettin' shot!" Jim Carrick bellowed. "You tryin' to say she did, Morgan?"

"Go ahead, Buck," Morgan urged, "unless you want me to tell it."

Young Carrick understood. He struggled for a moment with indecision before he said: "I met

Peg at the Smith shack. This *hombre* was there. Rip and his bunch was huntin' me. Peg came back and I lined out south, but Rip caught up with me at the lake. We swapped some lead and they got lucky, but I gave 'em the dodge. Fainted once and fell out of the saddle. Tom found me the other side of Morgan rock. Couldn't get back on my horse."

Jim Carrick was trembling with rage. He began to curse. "So you're seein' that cussed, double-crossin', no-good . . ."

Morgan came quickly across the room to him. "You trying to kill him, you fool? Tell him it's all right."

Carrick sleeved sweat from his forehead. He swallowed and cleared his throat. "All right, boy. It's all right."

Buck had closed his eyes again. "I love her, Dad. I'll run away with her if I have to."

Morgan jerked his head at the door. Carrick stepped outside, Morgan following.

"Now get this through your head, Jim. We can ride to town looking for Rip and get ourselves killed, which same won't do no good at all. Buck asked for his trouble. If you go off and leave him, he'll die."

"You said yourself a man can stand so much pushin' and no more," Carrick flung back. "I've had mine."

"There's no hurry," Morgan urged. "Wait till

Buck's on his feet. No sense in getting salivated if it doesn't do some good."

Carrick wiped a big hand across his face, a driving rage battling his better judgment.

"All right," he said at last. "We'll wait, but I won't have him seein' Peg Royce. You hear?"

"Don't tell me," Morgan said softly. "Tell Buck when he's able to listen."

# VIII

It was near sunset when Doc Velie rode in with Tom Carrick. Doc was an old man, close to seventy, white whiskered and gaunt with gray eyes that were unusually keen for a man his age.

"Been kicking things around for a fellow who's been in the valley less than twenty-four hours," he said as he shook Morgan's hand. "Old Josh Morgan's son, ain't you?"

"That's right."

"You won't live long," Velie said briskly. "Nobody backs Jaggers Flint down, growls at Broad, shoots Pete Royce, and peels Rip's hide off his back, and lives to talk about it. You just cut too wide a swath, mister."

Tom Carrick's dour face was momentarily lighted by a rush of admiration.

"I figgered you wrong, Morgan. From now on count me in. I want to see things like that."

"You'll see him die," the medico said brusquely. "Come on, Jim. Give me a hand. You other two stay outside."

While Doc Velie operated, Morgan told Tom Carrick why he was in the valley and what he hoped to do. Tom swore in delight.

"I'd have braced old Broad myself if I'd had the chance," he declared. "I ain't cut out for no farmer. Maybe I'll be a town marshal when Irish Bend spreads out."

"Maybe," Morgan said, and let it go at that. Tom Carrick lacked the cool judgment a lawman needed, but there was no point in telling him so.

Hours later Doc Velie came out of the cabin, with Jim Carrick behind him.

"It'll be close," the medico said. "He's lost a lot of blood and that slug was hard to get. Keep somebody with him all the time, Jim, and don't get him worked up over nothing. Might be a good idea to send for Peg Royce."

"She'll never put a foot in my house," Jim Carrick said darkly.

"All right. Let the boy die." Velie pinned his eyes on Tom who had come to stand in the patch of light washing through the open door. "If you want Buck to live, quit talking about getting square with Rip Clancy. No use of worrying him with your tough talk."

Without another word Doc Velie strode to

his horse, pulled himself into saddle, and rode westward.

"There goes the one man in this valley," Jim Carrick murmured, "who ain't afraid to tell Broad Clancy what he thinks. . . ."

The next week was slow and worry-plagued. Morgan or Jim or Tom Carrick was always in the cabin or within call. Tom fretted with the inaction, giving less time than either of the others, and the moment he was relieved, he would saddle his horse and thunder out of the yard without a backward glance.

"Always been that way," Jim Carrick said, with regret. "I've been a farmer all my life. Always will be. Like to have my hands on the plow. Like to have my feet in the furrow. Buck's like me." He shook his head, brown eyes turned dull by regret. "But Tom's got wild blood in him. Wants to ride out of the valley and hire his gun. Born to die with lead in him, I reckon."

It was not a wasted week for Morgan. He learned the names of the nester families, what each man was like, how far he could be depended upon. He trusted Jim Carrick's judgment. He felt a closeness and understanding the same as he instinctively felt distrust of Tom. Not of the boy's integrity or loyalty, but his stability, for Tom Carrick was the kind who would throw away his life on a sudden wild impulse, and bitterness over Buck's shooting was growing in him.

At the end of the week Doc Velie nodded with satisfaction as he made his examination of Buck.

"Give him plenty to eat and keep him quiet," he said. "All it takes is time." He winked at Buck. "That's what comes of living right." Outside, he laid a hand on Jim's shoulder. "I'm not one to meddle in family business, but Buck's not going to get back on his feet like he ought to unless he's got something to live for."

"If you're talking about Peg . . ."

"That's just who I am talking about," the medico snapped.

"He's got me to live for," Jim said sourly. "And Tom. He's got the place."

"Blessed if you ain't the stubbornest man outside the Clancy family there is in the valley. Jim, get this through your thick head. Buck has come close to dying. He loves you and Tom, sure. He likes the place even if it isn't yours, but there's something more than that in the living and dying of a man. I don't know what it is, but I've seen it time after time. I know it's something beyond what any doctor can do for a man. I reckon you'd call it the will to live. Put Peg Royce in this house for a few hours and you'll think it's a miracle. Don't send for her, and chances are you'll bury him up there with the Morgan boys."

It was the longest speech Morgan had heard the medico make.

"Jim," he said, when Velie was gone, "I've got to get some chores done. I'd like for Tom to notify all the north-rim nesters that there'll be a meeting tonight. Can he see 'em in time?"

"Sure."

"Where'll we have it? Here?"

Carrick shook his head. "It'd be a long way for some of 'em to come. Let's say Blazer's place. That's central, and it'd make 'em be there." He gave Morgan a straight look. "Be ready for the cussedest fight you ever had. A pair of fists is the only thing that'll make Arch listen."

"Then that's what I'll use." Morgan glanced up at the sun. "Get Tom started. You and me will head out of here 'bout noon."

As Morgan turned toward the corral Carrick called: "Where you goin'?"

"After Peg."

Morgan didn't look back. He had learned to know Jim Carrick well, and he measured him as a just man but a stubborn one. He was not sure whether Jim would rather see his son dead or married to Peg Royce.

Strangely enough, he never doubted that Peg would come, but when he reined up in front of the Royce cabin, doubts hit him like the rush of cloudburst waters roaring down a dry channel. Peg was standing in the doorway, black-haired head tilted against the jamb, the same confident smile on her lips that had been there the last time he had seen her.

"So, you came back, Mister Morgan." She walked quickly across the yard to where he sat his saddle. "Get down. Royce isn't here."

"You've heard about Buck?" he asked her.

She nodded, suddenly sober. "Doc stops whenever he goes by. He was worried about Buck for a while."

"He's still worried. When Buck was out of his head, he did a lot of talking about you."

Interest was keen in her dark eyes. "What did he say?"

"He loves you, but I guess you knew that. He's still pretty bad. We've got to be gone a day or two. Jim wants you to come over and stay with Buck."

She stared at him blankly for a moment before she caught the significance of what he had said.

"I gave up believing in fairies a long time ago, Mister Morgan," she said then. "I'd as soon start in now as believe Jim Carrick wants me in his house."

"It's true."

He had a bad moment then. He wasn't sure Peg believed him and he wasn't sure she would come. He thought of telling her it was her fault Buck had been shot, and knew that wouldn't do. He thought of offering her money, and immediately gave that up. So he sat looking down at her and saying nothing until she laughed, not the gay laugh he had heard before but a short, bitter one, as if something had hurt her and she was covering it with a show of humor.

"All right. I guess I'd better not miss seeing Jim Carrick's face when I walk in."

"I'll saddle up for you," Morgan offered.

"You could take me up in front."

"This animal won't carry double," he said quickly. "I'll saddle up."

She bit her lip, frowning. "I don't usually frighten men," she said.

"I scare easy," he said. Reining around her, he rode to the corral.

There was little talk on the way back to the Carrick place. Morgan watched Peg for minutes at a time, but if she was aware of it, she gave no indication. He had never seen, he thought, a prettier girl. Her firm chest rose and fell with her breathing. He saw the pulse beat in her white throat. When at last she appeared conscious of his gaze, she turned to him, smiling again, and he saw the dimples in her cheeks and the knowledge in her dark eyes.

"Are you going to draw a picture of me?" she asked.

"No. Just store one in my memory. You're Buck's girl."

Quick pleasure stirred her face, then she looked

away. "No, not Buck's girl. I'm doing this because you asked me. I thought you knew that."

Again they rode in silence until they reached the poplars in front of the Carrick cabin, and Morgan, stepping down, reached up and helped her from the saddle. Jim Carrick loomed in the doorway, his face set.

"Come in, Miss Royce," he said in a dry, precise voice. "Buck's expectin' you."

Morgan put her horse away and waited until Jim called him to dinner. He couldn't guess what had been said and he didn't ask, but there was a look on Buck's lean face that should have told Jim what Morgan already knew.

Jim and Morgan left for the meeting shortly after they ate, riding northwest across the valley so that they cut between the lake and the barren Alkali Flats.

The sun, its roundness unmarred by clouds, dropped into the western sky, and the wind, cooled by the high Cascades, touched them briefly and ran on, stirring the bunchgrass with its passage. To the south, Clancy Peak was a sharp triangle marking the skyline. The smell of the air was clean and sharp, a good smell rich with sage, a smell Murdo Morgan had almost forgotten, and a hunger to live his life out in the valley struck him.

For a time, he harbored a thought he was afraid to explore. He could have Peg Royce.

"Not many Turkey Track cows in the flat," Carrick said suddenly. "Clancy keeps 'em down in the winter, but his riders have been shovin' 'em to the ranch the last two, three weeks. Reckon he's brandin' now."

"How soon will he start them for the marsh?" asked Morgan.

"Any time. He'll take a while to get 'em there. Too much snow to take 'em up yet, I reckon. More snow last winter than any year since I've been here."

But Morgan's mind was not on Broad Clancy's cattle. "You think the nesters'll come tonight?" he demanded suddenly.

"Sure. They'll come to hear what you've got to say, or to see Blazer beat you to death. These boys have the notion that if they lick anybody who comes in, they can hold their places." Carrick cocked his head at the sun. "Let's kick up a fire and eat. A man can't fight on an empty stomach."

"How far yet?" Morgan asked.

"A mile or so. No sense hurryin'. You want all the boys there to see you handle Blazer." Carrick reined up and looked directly at Morgan. "You done wrong, friend, and so did I. We shouldn't have left that girl with Buck."

Morgan let it go without argument.

They built a fire and cooked supper. Then they waited until the sun was behind the Sunset

Mountains and dust flowed across the desert and laid its purple hue upon it. A quietness came with the twilight, a quietness that worked into a man's mind and called up a thousand thoughts and images and dreams.

Morgan gave no thought to the fight with Blazer. It was immediate, a little dirty job that had to be done before he could do the big job. He let his thoughts range ahead to the families that would be making their homes here in Paradise Valley.

Rising at last, Morgan tossed his cigarette stub into the fire and kicked it out. "Let's ride," he said.

Carrick had been squatting on the other side of the coals, face dark and preoccupied, and Morgan knew he had not shaken Peg Royce out of his mind. "All right," Carrick said.

Mounting, they swung around a rock finger that extended into the valley from the rimrock and saw the red tongue of Blazer's fire.

"Got a good light," Carrick growled. "Like to put on a show."

Blazer had built his fire in front of his cabin. As Morgan pulled up, he saw that the cabin was set hard against the cliff and was built of stone. Blazer, he thought, had an eye more for defense than for home comfort.

"Hello!" Carrick called.

There were a dozen men hunkered in a circle around the fire. Tom Carrick was withdrawn from the others and squatting by himself, eyes watchful, jaws working steadily on his quid.

A big man rose and made a slow turn. He said: "Light," his tone heavy with hostility.

Carrick and Morgan dismounted and came into the firelight. Carrick introduced Morgan to each man, holding Blazer back till the last, a gesture of contempt that all understood. When at last Carrick called Blazer by name, Morgan's eyes locked with the big man's, and he made a quick appraisal of him.

Arch Blazer was as tall as Morgan and heavier-bodied. His neck was short, his ears small and set tightly against his skull. His yellow eyes were reddened by dust and sun and wind. He stood with shoulders hunched forward, hands fisting and opening, his wicked temper showing on his dark face.

"So you're the company man we heard was comin' to kick us out of our homes," Blazer growled. "You ain't goin' to do it, Morgan. You try it and I'll stomp your insides out!"


# IX

Quickly Morgan made a study of the circle of men, thinking how well Jim Carrick had called it. A raggle-taggle outfit if he had ever seen one, scared and ragged and dirty. Hiding out from the law and picking up a precarious living from their farms, a living supplemented by deer and antelope and perhaps an occasional Turkey Track beef.

"You know how the valley is held," Morgan said. "Some of you are living on government land, and maybe you've filed on it right and proper. If that's the case I've got work to offer you and good wages. If you're on company land, I've got the same work to offer you and a proposition."

"We don't want no proposition," Blazer snarled. "All we want is to be let alone. We ain't leavin' our homes so some cussed land company can sell 'em, when the company stole the land in the first place."

Again, Morgan let it go, ignoring Blazer and keeping his eyes on the nesters.

"I'm the company," he said distinctly. "The offer I make now goes. It ain't a case of some fat rooster back East in a plush chair going over my head. By the First of September there'll be thousands of settlers here in the valley. If you men will help me feed 'em, haul water for 'em, and fetch horse feed, I'll hand you a deed to your land the day the sale is finished. No red tape. No monkey business. How about it?"

Blazer wheeled, a great hand motioning toward Morgan.

"Don't believe this lyin' son. How do we know

who he is or whether he'll keep his word?"

"I believe him," Jim Carrick said. "I'm done kowtowin' to Broad Clancy. If Morgan puts this land sale over, it'll bust the Turkey Track, and that's plenty of reason for me."

Blazer whirled on Carrick. "You always was soft as mush, Jim!" he bellowed. "I say to run this smooth-talkin' son out of the valley. I'll plug the first man who sets foot on my land and claims he bought it from the company."

"Then you'll be hanging for killing," Morgan said quietly.

Blazer threw back his great head and laughed. "Hangin', he says, for killin'. You won't be around to see it, bucko. You won't even be around. I'm goin' to bust you up. I'll teach the company to send in a long-tongued rooster like you, lyin' about ownin' it yourself."

Morgan jerked off his gun belt and handed it to Carrick.

"All right, Blazer. I never look for a fight, but if it comes, I'll finish it."

Again Blazer laughed, deep and scornful. "You'll never finish *this* one, bucko. I'll have my fun and I'll still be here when your friend Carrick is diggin' a hole for you."

"If you want fun, here's some," Morgan said, and came at the man fast, right fist cracking him hard on the mouth.

It was Arch Blazer's way to bluff as far as he

could, to scare a man and make him back up before a crowd and half win the fight before it started. He had never had a man bring the fight to him. Surprise and Morgan's blow half stunned him for an instant. He retreated a step. Morgan, catching him on the jaw with another short, wicked right, knocked him flat on his back.

"Boot him!" Jim Carrick called exuberantly.

From the other side of the fire Tom Carrick watched with cool pleasure, for he had long hated Blazer, but knew that he was not the man to do what Murdo Morgan had just done. The others came closer, silent and watchful, swinging which ever way the fight swung.

Blazer bounced up, a strangled curse breaking out of his bruised mouth. He drove at Morgan and struck him a hard blow on the chest. Morgan wheeled and let the weight of Blazer's charge carry him by. He was on the big man then. For an instant Blazer was off balance. Morgan ripped through his guard, punching him with rights and lefts, the big head weaving from one side to the other.

Blazer clubbed a fist at Morgan's face and closed with him, swinging a fist into his middle. Morgan was hurt. He threw his weight hard against Blazer, cracking him in the ribs, turned sideward as Blazer rammed a knee at his stomach. Catching the man's leg, he dumped him into the hot coals at the edge of the fire.

Blazer screamed and rolled clear. He came to his feet again and rammed at Morgan, but he was slower this time. The heart had gone out of his fight.

Sensing that this was the moment, Morgan came in for the kill. His fists, ringing on Blazer's head, flattened the man's nose and closed an eye. He saw the blood, tasted his own, felt the jar of each blow run up his forearm and wondered what held the nester up. Then, for no reason that he could understand, Blazer's knees became rubber and he curled to the ground.

Morgan stepped back, thinking Blazer was out, and instantly knew he had made a mistake, for Blazer had rolled away from the fire and had drawn a gun. Another gun spoke, the bullet kicking up dirt a foot from Blazer's hand.

"You're fightin' him fair!" Tom Carrick's angry voice cut across the space between them. "Curse you for a dirty polecat!"

Blazer dropped his gun. He squalled, "I'll get you Carricks for backin' . . ." Blazer didn't finish. Morgan fell on him, knees hard on the big man's ribs, grabbed a handful of hair, and twisted Blazer's head so that the fellow's chin was a clear target. Morgan swung his right, the sound of the blow a meaty thud of bone on bone.

He raised his fist to strike again, heard Jim Carrick call—"That done it, Morgan!"—and knew that Carrick was right.

He rose, a boot toe digging into Blazer's ribs, but there was no stirring left in the man.

"Thanks, Tom," Morgan said. He wiped a hand across his bloody, sweaty face, not realizing until then how much he had been hurt. "You boys heard my proposition. You interested?"

"Sure," one of them said without enthusiasm.

Some nodded, others stood staring at Blazer as if unable to believe they had seen him beaten.

"All right. If you carry out your end of the bargain, you'll get the deeds to your land." Morgan took his gun belt from Carrick and buckled it around him. "Blazer will never get a chance to pull another gun on me when I don't have mine. Tell him that when he's in shape to listen. Tell him he'd better start smoking his iron the next time he sees me 'cause I'll sure be smoking mine."

Morgan lurched to his horse and painfully eased into saddle. He rode around the finger of rock and presently the Carricks caught him.

"That's one of the things I wanted to see," Tom said jubilantly. "Blazer's run over everybody ever since he's been here."

"What about the others?"

Tom laughed shortly. "Blazer'll tuck his tail and run. He won't want to swap smoke with you, and, with him gone, the rest will be mighty happy haulin' your horse feed and water."

Jim Carrick shook his head. "I ain't sure about that, Tom. Not with Pete Royce around."

"I don't think I feel like riding back, Jim," Morgan said.

"There's a spring down here a piece. We'll camp there."

After they had made camp and Morgan lay with his head on his saddle, he gave voice to a question that had been nagging his mind.

"Some men just like to fight, but I'm not sure about Blazer. The proposition I offered him was fair. Why would he jump me thataway?"

"He's just an ornery cuss," Tom said.

"Might be more to it," Jim Carrick said. "He's plumb thick with Royce."

Presently the run of horses came to them.

"Some of the boys going home," Morgan murmured.

"I'll see," Tom said, and, mounting, rode away.

"Can't set still," Jim growled. "Had ants in his pants ever since he could walk. Ridin' most of the time. Knows more about what goes on than anybody else in the valley."

Morgan closed his eyes. There was no understanding how a man like Jim Carrick could have Tom for a son, but Tom was not one to change.

Morgan and Jim Carrick breakfasted at dawn and reached the Carrick place by midmorning.

"Go on in," Carrick said as Morgan dismounted. "I'll put the horses away."

"I'm in no hurry," Morgan said.

They walked into the cabin together. Peg was sitting by the bed, reading. She looked up when she saw them, carefully closed the book, and rose.

"How you feel, Son?" Jim asked.

"Fine." Buck grinned at Peg. "She's the right medicine for a man."

Peg wasn't listening. Her eyes were on Morgan, concern in them. "You had trouble?" she asked.

"He licked Blazer," Jim Carrick said. "That's all."

Peg picked up the scarf she had worn around her head. "I'll be going."

"Thanks," Jim said carefully. "I'll saddle up for you."

"You'll come back?" Buck asked in a low tone.

"Sure, I'll be back," Peg said easily, and left the cabin with Jim Carrick.

Morgan idled in the doorway, shoulder blades pressed against the jamb, feeling the soreness that would be days leaving him. He watched Peg mount and wave to him. He raised his hat and nodded, unsmiling. He was thinking again that he could have Peg Royce, and panic was in him with the rush of knowledge that he wanted her.

"Morgan!" Buck called.

Morgan walked to the bed and sat down. "Want me to read to you?"

"I told you she was poison," Buck said harshly.

"I said she was a fever that got into your blood. Remember?"

"Yeah, I remember. Why?"

"You ain't foolin' me no more'n a little. You're playin' smart, goin' after her and all, but you ain't foolin' me."

"What in thunderation are you talking about?" Morgan demanded sharply.

"You know all right." Buck's fists clenched above the blanket. "I saw the way she looked at you. I'm tellin' you, Morgan. Let her alone or I'll kill you!"

# X

Peg Royce did not sleep the night she returned from the Carrick place. Her lean-to room held the day's heat with grim tenacity; the smell of her straw tick was musty and stifling. She lay on her back, motionless, staring at the black ceiling. Tomorrow would be another day, the same routine, the same frustrations, the empty sagebrush miles all around, choking her, imprisoning her, walling her in from the world she had seen in her dreams. The staccato beat of her clock marked the slow passage of the minutes, while the gray ashes of discontent piled high in her mind.

Daylight wiped out the darkness in the corners

of her room. Royce was gone. She didn't know where. He was gone when she had come home the day before. It was that way most of the time, one of the few things for which she could be thankful.

She should get up and build the fire. Feed the chickens. Milk the cow. Water the horses. Cook breakfast. She would get a cursing if Royce came home and found her in bed. Maybe more.

Anger smoldered in her. No, nothing more. She'd had the last beating she would take from him. She reached under her pillow and pulled out the small pistol she kept there. No, she would never take another beating from Pete Royce.

She should get up, she told herself. She sat on the edge of her bed, took off her nightgown, and lay back. No hurry. What was waiting to be done could keep on waiting. If Royce didn't like it, he could stay home and take care of it himself.

The sun laid a pattern of black and gold across her bed. She propped herself up on her elbows and looked at her slim body. She might as well be a squaw. She had her choice of a cocky scrawny-faced kid who wanted her, but had never offered her the Clancy name, and Buck Carrick who had planned to kidnap her and take to Prineville to marry him, a nester whose father didn't even own the land they lived on.

Then she thought of Murdo Morgan. But then she had been thinking of Murdo Morgan all night.

Peg had never really known another woman. Her mother was a vague blurred memory. There were a few nester women below the north rim. Dowdy women broken to the daily labor of this land, women for whom the flame of life had gone out long ago. Then there was Auntie Jones in town and Jewell Clancy, who had left her strictly alone.

There had been men around as long as she could remember. All of them but Ed Cole had run to a type. Like Arch Blazer. Tough and dirty and smelling of whiskey and horses and tobacco and stale sweat. Men who had wanted to paw her, men that even Pete Royce did not trust with her.

She knew men, knew the urging of their desires. She had never met a man she could not have had if she had wanted him, even Ed Cole, until Murdo Morgan had ridden into the valley.

She had heard men talk lightly about love as if it were the same as desire. Probably it was with most men she had known. It would not be with Morgan, but what did he want in a woman that she did not have or could not give him?

Now, picturing his tall, hard-muscled body, his black hair and high-boned face, the powder-gray eyes that seemed to look beyond the limits of ordinary men's vision, she felt an undefined longing that she had never felt before. She asked herself if it was love, and suddenly regretted what she had said to him about holding the winning hand on the last deal.

Outside, a rooster crowed, a harsh sound that brought her upright in bed. She shook her black hair out of her eyes, slid into her worn slippers, and went into the other room. She built a fire, pumped water into the coffee pot, and set it on the front of the stove. The pine kindling was exploding with dry crackling pops when she went back into her room.

She sat down in front of her dressing table and began combing her hair. She had made her table as she had made everything else in her room except the mirror on the wall that gave back a waxy image of her face.

Her dressing table had been a huge goods box. She had built shelves into it, papered the inside with red wallpaper, and covered the top with a flounce of print. She had made the rag rug that covered her floor. It was hers, all of it, a sanctuary where Pete Royce let her alone unless he had work for her to do.

She combed her hair sleekly back from her forehead and tied it with a red ribbon. She dressed then, slowly, and was buttoning the last button when she heard horses. She ran out of her room, a wild hope in her that it would be Morgan. But it was Pete Royce. A moment later she recognized the man with him. Ed Cole.

Peg was slicing bacon when they came in. She

had the table set, the coffee boiling, and Cole stopped in the doorway, sniffing.

"Say, that smells good, Pete," Cole said. "This girl of yours is getting smarter all the time."

"Gettin' lazier, you mean," Royce grunted. "Ridin' at night. Wantin' to sleep all day. I'll have to tan her with a blacksnake so she won't forget who's boss around here."

Peg wheeled, balancing the razor-sharp hunting knife in her hand. "I've told you, Royce. I'm telling you again. You lay a hand on me and I'll kill you."

Royce dropped into a chair. "See how it is, Ed? The mountain men had the right idea. Marry a squaw and lodgepole her when she got out of hand."

He was under average height, a stocky man with shiny blue eyes set close together astride a flat nose that had been smashed under another's fist years before. He leaned back in his chair and, drawing a cigar from his pocket, slid it between dark teeth.

"A wildin', this filly," he remarked. "Why don't you marry her, Ed?"

Cole came across the room to where Peg stood at the table.

"You're lovelier every time I see you," he said. "You know your dad's suggestion isn't bad. How about going back with me? You'll like San Francisco."

"Royce said something about you marrying me," she said pointedly. "Is this a proposal?"

His smile was a quick, amused curve of his lips. "Of course, but it depends on breakfast. I'm hungry enough to eat a curly wolf."

"You can nibble on your fingers till I get the bacon cooked," she said.

"Couldn't do that. I'm no cannibal."

He went back to sit across from Royce. Peg moved around the table so that she could watch him while she stirred up the biscuits. At thirty-five Cole was the most handsome, perfectly-mannered man she had ever known. She had been attracted by him when he had been in the valley before. He had tried to kiss her once, and she had slapped him. She had never been sure why, and she didn't know what she would do if he tried again.

His eyes were blue, and as guileless as a child's. His hair was light brown and curly, his teeth white and perfect when he smiled. But Peg Royce understood him. He played his own sharp game. He had not said anything about taking her to San Francisco the other time he was here. He had his reasons now, or he wouldn't have made the offer.

Peg slid the pan of biscuits into the oven and, straightening, scratched her chin, leaving a daub of flour on it. It was her chance. Cole needed Royce and she could force a bargain from Cole.

San Francisco. The city of dreams. Why not?

But after breakfast Cole came to her and slid an arm around her.

"About this San Francisco deal," he murmured. "I've got to get right back, and I need you here. If I took you now, I wouldn't have time to show you the town."

"In other words, you don't want me to go." She jerked away from him and moved around the table. "That's fair enough. I didn't say I would go."

He stroked his pointed, carefully trimmed mustache, his smile confident. "You didn't say so, but you would. Any woman would."

"You're bragging," she murmured. "Why not take Jewell Clancy?"

"She's not as charming as you are. I take only charming women to San Francisco." He laid a pile of gold coins on the table. "Let's not lose sight of the reason I want you to stay here. I'm no gambler, Peg. I'm going to crack Murdo Morgan, and I want it a sure thing."

"She can't do nothin' I can't," Pete Royce said. He picked up the cigar he had been smoking before breakfast and lighted it again. "No use payin' her good money. She'll just blow it on duds."

"Your daughter has capacities you aren't aware of, my friend." Cole brought his eyes back to Peg's face. "Pete tells me you've met Morgan.

He's been riding with a lot of luck. If that lasts, I'll need you."

"He's got to the end of his luck," Royce said darkly. "He'll never lick Arch Blazer again."

Peg took a sharp breath. So, they knew about the fight. Cole was worried, or he wouldn't be piling gold on the table in front of her.

"Blazer won't give him another chance," Cole said. "When we see Clancy today, I have a notion old Broad will do the job for us." He picked up the gold coins and dropped them again. "Like the sound of that, sweetheart?"

"What do I do to earn it?" she asked.

"You're my ace in the hole. Suppose Clancy doesn't do the job? Or things don't work right for your dad to stop Morgan's clock? That's where you step in. You're persuasive, honey. You could wangle anything out of friend Morgan or even talk him into a foolish move."

"Like what?"

Cole shrugged. "Your dad or Blazer might want to know where he'll be at a certain time. Might even knock him on the head and throw him into the tules for the hogs. How's that, Pete?"

Royce chuckled. "It's a good idea."

"How about it, sweetheart?" Cole was watching her closely.

"I couldn't wangle anything out of Morgan," she said.

"You can get anything out of any man if you

try," he said impatiently. "Can I depend on you?"

"Certainly. And when it's over?"

"San Francisco. I'll have the most charming girl in the city."

She stood in the doorway as they mounted and rode west to Irish Bend, the gold clutched in her hand. Cole had kissed her again and this time she hadn't slapped him. He was playing his game and she was playing hers.

"I didn't tell you what you could depend on, did I, Mister Cole?" she said softly.


Murdo Morgan stayed at Carrick's until Buck was out of danger. The day he left, young Carrick was sitting on the porch, thin and filled with self-pity, his uncut hair shaggy long. It would be weeks before he was himself, but there was no more need for Morgan here, and he was beginning to feel the pressure of time.

Jim Carrick watched Morgan saddle his black, more solemnly visaged than usual.

"Tom rode off again this mornin'," he said. "He's goin' to find the trouble he's lookin' for if he keeps at it."

Morgan nodded. Tom was all right. It was Buck who worried Morgan. Peg hadn't been back after that one time. The truth was gnawing at Buck with terrible tenacity.

"Tom can take care of himself," Morgan said,

as he led his horse to the trough. "I ain't sure Buck can."

"I ain't neither," Jim said dully. "If it was any other girl . . . Oh, shucks, I ain't goin' after her again. You hear?"

"Going after her doesn't change anything," Morgan observed.

"What are you goin' to do?"

"I'm aimin' to see Broad Clancy first thing. I've got to get this business lined out so there won't be any trouble when the settlers start rolling in."

"Take more'n words to change Clancy's way of seein' things."

Morgan stepped into saddle. Jim Carrick was right, but if there was fighting to be done, it had better be done now.

"Thanks for giving me a hand, Jim," he said.

"It was you that give me a hand. If you hadn't sat up with Buck, I don't know how I'd made out. Tom wasn't no help."

"You gave me more of a hand than you figured," Morgan said somberly. "You're the balance wheel in the valley, Jim. I'm counting on you. So long." Morgan reined his black toward the road.

"Take care of yourself, son!" he heard Jim call after him.

Then sourness was born in Morgan. He raised a hand in farewell to Buck, but young Carrick made no answering gesture. Jealousy stamped a festering bitterness on his face.

Morgan wouldn't stop at the Royce cabin. He would ride on. Peg was Buck's girl. But when Morgan passed the Royce place, he saw Peg working in the yard. Coming to the road, she waved to him, and, despite his promise to himself, he reined over to her.

"It's my friend Murdo," she said. "Come in."

He lifted his hat, eyes on her. She had a firm curved body and a sort of straightforward daring that he liked. She stirred him now as she always did when he was with her.

"Howdy, Peg," he said soberly.

She studied him a moment, a smile striking at the corners of her mouth. It wasn't, he thought, as confident a smile as she had given him before. Something had happened to her, softening her.

"I've got a pot of coffee on the stove, Murdo. Come in. Royce isn't around." She seemed to sense instantly that she had said the wrong thing. "I don't mean you're afraid of him. He's just a nuisance."

He shouldn't go in. She was Buck Carrick's girl. He couldn't forget that. But he did go in and, as he drank the coffee, another thought struck him. Buck said she was his girl, but it wasn't Peg's idea. There was no mistaking what she was trying to tell him.

He finished his coffee and shook his head when

she reached for the pot. "I've got to be riding," he said.

"Ed Cole was here the other day," she said suddenly.

"Cole!" He stared at her, surprised that Cole was in the valley. "Does he know I'm here?"

She said: "Yes." Her face held an expression he didn't understand.

"Why didn't he see me?" Morgan asked.

"I guess he didn't want to."

Anger touched him. "I'd want to see a friend if I was this far from home."

"Friend?" She laughed shortly. Then, seeing his face, she shut her lips against what she had meant to say.

"Sure," he said. "I knew him in Colorado before I ever had a notion I'd own half the road grant."

He automatically reached for tobacco and paper and twisted a cigarette, puzzling over Cole's reason for being here. The Citizens' Bank had no interest in the grant unless Morgan failed to repay his loan within the specified time. But if Cole had come only out of friendship, he wouldn't have left without seeing him.

Walking around the stove, Peg stopped near Morgan. There was a new expression in her dark eyes as if something had disturbed her.

"I know what you're up against better than you do, Murdo," she said softly, "but there isn't much

I can do except to tell you to ride on while you're still alive."

"I won't do that," he said roughly.

"I know." She laid a hand on his arm, making a soft pressure there. She was watching him closely, as if wondering what she should say. "There is something else, Murdo. Don't trust anyone. They're all against you."

The cold cigarette dangled from a corner of his mouth. He fished a match from his pocket, but he didn't bring it to life. He held it there, half lifted in front of him, his mind trying to pierce the veil behind which she had hidden her thoughts.

"A man's got to trust somebody," he said. "You can't live alone."

She had told him all she would. A quick smile flowed across her face, warm and compelling. Her hand on his arm was soft.

"You wouldn't have to live alone, Murdo."

He dropped the match and tore the cigarette from his mouth. Gripping her shoulders, he jerked her to him and kissed her, her lips turning up to meet his. They were warm lips, filling him with ancient man hunger, the same as they had filled Buck Carrick and Rip Clancy. He let her go, the thought of the other two filling his mind with gray distaste.

She didn't move back. Her arms were around his neck, her lips parted. He saw that she was pleased with what she had done.

"That was what I meant, Murdo," she murmured.

"You've had your fun," he said roughly. "I guess that was what you wanted." He wheeled away from her and strode out of the cabin and across the yard to his horse.

She ran after him, suddenly fearful. "Murdo, didn't it mean anything to you?"

He didn't answer until he was in the saddle.

"Yeah, it meant something," he said then. "Made me think of what Buck said."

"What was that?"

"That you're a fever in a man's blood if he looks at you twice. I made that mistake. One look should have been enough."

"Murdo, this is different. I never promised Buck."

"You're his life," Morgan said soberly. "I've learned to know him pretty well the last few days. Why don't you go back and see him?"

"All right," she said. "I will, because you've asked me."

"Thanks."

Morgan lifted his Stetson and rode on toward Irish Bend, a vague unease in him. She was going to see Buck because Murdo Morgan had asked her to. That left him in her debt and that was not the way he wanted it.

# XI

The empty miles dropped behind. The lake and the tule-carpeted swamp were lost behind a ridge. A band of horses broke across the road and thundered on through the sage and rabbitbrush toward the pine hills to the south.

Morgan was hardly conscious of them. His thoughts were a tumbling white-frothed stream within him. Peg had wanted to tell him something, then had been afraid to say it, but when he tried to concentrate upon it, the memory of her kiss ripped through the pattern of his thoughts.

It was nearly noon when Morgan reached town. He racked his horse in front of the store, his gaze sweeping the street. It was the first time he had been in Irish Bend since the day he had come to the valley, but it was entirely different. Then the Turkey Track outfit had been in town.

Now Irish Bend was almost empty. A single horse stood in front of the Elite Saloon, head down, dozing in the sun. A short-legged dog padded down the middle of the street, ears proudly erect as if the town were his by conquest instead of default.

Turning into the store, Morgan asked for a pencil and sheet of paper. The storeman eyed him a moment speculatively before he slid a stubby pencil and a torn fragment of wrapping paper across the counter.

"That'll do if you ain't fussy," he said, his tone intentionally hostile.

Morgan drew a knife from his pocket and whittled a sharper point to the pencil. "Where is everybody?" he asked.

"It's always this way when the Turkey Track ain't in town," the storeman said. "The boys are winding up branding today. Reckon they'll be heading out for the high country. Be plumb quiet till they get back."

"Maybe not." Morgan began writing. "You'll have more business this fall than you ever had. Better get stocked up."

The man snorted, started to say something, then shut his mouth with a click of his ill-fitting store teeth. He held his silence until Morgan spoke.

"Hang this up where folks can see it."

"The devil I will!"

"I said hang it up." Morgan grabbed a handful of the man's shirt and jerked him against the counter. "This has been Broad Clancy's town, but it ain't going to be for much longer. I want that paper hung up."

"I'll hang it." The storeman turned the paper and read:

The Cascade and Paradise Land Company announces an auction of its land beginning

September First. Stockmen and settlers desiring to secure title to the company land they have been squatting on are advised to contact Murdo Morgan while he is in the valley.

Murdo Morgan<br>Cascade and Paradise Land Company

The storeman lifted his eyes to Morgan. "If they're going to contact you, friend, they'll sure have to hurry 'cause you won't be around much longer."

"That so?" drawled Morgan.

"You'll ride out or you'll get run out."

"Let me do the worrying, friend." Morgan shrugged. "Where you going to hang this paper?"

Growling, the storekeeper picked it up and jabbed it over a nail behind the tobacco counter.

"This is one place they all come." Morgan nodded. "Is there a lawman in town?"

The storeman's laugh was a contemptuous snort. "You wanting some protection?"

"You'll need the protection if you keep trying to be smart," Morgan said angrily. "It doesn't fit you, mister."

Humor faded from the man's eyes as if it had been slapped out of him. Fear touched him, narrowing his eyes, and bringing the self-hatred it does to a man when the veneer of his toughness has been stripped from him.

"Abel Purdy," he grunted. "Past the post office."

"Thanks." Morgan swung to the door and, pausing, looked back. "If that sign isn't there the next time I come in, I'll hang your hide up in its place, and don't you forget it."

The storeman's lips twitched, his sullen curses reaching Morgan only as incoherent growls. Grinning, Morgan turned into the street. Irish Bend had been geared to Broad Clancy's pleasure. The land sale would change that, along with everything else in Paradise Valley.

Purdy's office was beyond the post office, with a weed-grown vacant lot between. Morgan stepped through the doorway, and had a quick glance around, and said: "Howdy." There were three straight-backed chairs against the wall, a roll-top desk in the corner, covered with a litter of books and papers, and an ancient swivel chair. That was all except for the dust, the splinters of a broken stool in the corner, and Abel Purdy.

"Good morning." Purdy rose and held out his hand. "I'm Abel Purdy and I believe you're Murdo Morgan. I've heard of you."

Morgan shook the proffered hand. "I'm not surprised. A stranger gets talked about."

"You're like the new broom, Morgan. Sweeps up a lot of trash until somebody saws off the handle. It ain't much good after that." Purdy motioned to a chair. "Sit down. I never like to talk with a standing man."

Morgan took the chair. He liked Purdy, as he had instinctively disliked the smart-aleck storekeeper. Purdy might have been thirty or fifty. It was hard to judge his age. His head seemed to be entirely without hair and was ball-round. Then Morgan saw that he was wrong. Purdy had hair, but it was clipped short, and was so thin and light-colored that it took a second glance to realize it was there.

"Maybe nobody's going to saw this broom off," Morgan said.

"Somebody will try." Purdy removed his thick glasses and rubbed his eyes, red-streaked from too much reading, the pupils nearly as colorless as his hair. "Time always catches up with us, Morgan. Broad Clancy thought it never would, but things that happen in the rest of the country will sooner or later happen here. Half of the valley is owned privately. Ignoring a fact like that don't change the fact."

"Well," Morgan said, "I'm glad somebody around here knows that."

Purdy laid a marker between the pages of the book he had been reading and closed it.

"You're the law, aren't you?" asked Morgan.

"Yes, I'm the law." Purdy's smile was self-mocking. He wiped a sleeve across the shiny star pinned on his shirt. "That, of course, all of us here understand. I'm the marshal, the mayor, and the justice of peace. I preside over the town meetings. I arrest a drunk if he is a settler. Then I jail him." He motioned to a door behind him. "We have one cell. I sit as judge if a trial is necessary, but a trial is never necessary unless the arrested man is a settler. You understand?"

Morgan nodded. It was plain enough, the same as Broad Clancy's rule was plain to see everywhere that Morgan looked.

"But it's like you said a while ago. Clancy can't change facts by shutting his eyes. The company is selling the wagon road grant to settlers."

"Maybe," Purdy said skeptically. "It will take a lot to beat Clancy, and my experience with nesters tells me they won't stand against a show of force."

"This is different, Purdy. We're selling the land now to people in the Middle West. They pay ten percent down when they sign their contract and give a note for the balance, payable at the time of the drawing. I'm gambling they'll fight for what they already own."

Interest sharpened in Purdy's pale eyes. "It might work."

"Another thing. This isn't free government land, so we're bound to get a better class of farmers than the usual raggle-taggle outfits that show up every time there is a land rush."

"That might be," Purdy admitted thoughtfully. "Does Clancy know this?"

"I aim to tell him today. He wasn't of a mind to listen the time I saw him in the Silver Spur."

"Suppose you die?"

"Then I'll be dead, but the land sale will come off regardless."

"Clancy may have a different idea."

Morgan shrugged. "I aim to keep alive. I didn't come in here to talk about Clancy. What I want to know is this. When the settlers come . . . that'll be the middle or the last of August . . . will they get the protection of the law as fully as you can give it?"

Purdy reached for a corncob pipe, that self-mocking smile turning his mouth bitter.

"You'll have it, as well as I can give it. Notice what I say, Morgan . . . as well as I can give it. I'll explain that. I have a job. It pays a living. I don't know what I'd do or where I'd go if I lost it. Love of security does that for a man, and my security lasts as long as Broad Clancy lasts."

Purdy was making it as plain as he could without admitting his own abasement. The hard years had reamed the heart out of this man, leaving only the shell.

"I'll depend on that," Morgan said, rising. "Broad may not cut quite as wide a swath in another month or two as he does now."

"Time is a great sea washing in around us,"

Purdy murmured. "We'll see how well Broad has built his walls. And, Morgan, if you're going out to Turkey Track, watch this man Flint. Wounded pride can make even a coward dangerous."

# XII

A familiar sight greeted Morgan when he reached the Turkey Track, a sight that reminded him strongly of his Montana cowpunching days, for it was a scene that changed only in detail wherever cows were run. The constant rising dust cloud. The smell of wood smoke from the branding fire. Loops snaking out. Bawling calves and bawling cows.

It was a sort of organized chaos. Half a dozen Turkey Track irons in the fire. The rush of smoke as a hot iron burned through hair and into flesh. The smell of it, the smell of blood as knives flashed. Turkey Track run on the left side. Underbite off both ears.

"Rafter L from Dry Lake!" a buckaroo yelled.

"Nothin' but Turkey Track on this range!" Broad Clancy shouted arrogantly. "Put the iron on him."

Smell and sweat, pain and blood, dust and smoke, and over all of it that never-dying bawl of worried cows and scared calves, curses, and Broad Clancy's taunting laugh if a rope missed.

Throw him! Burn and cut him! Hot iron and steel blade! Drag up another! The cycle repeated until a buckaroo yelled: "This is the one we want!"

"I don't want him. Looks just like the last one to me."

"Sure. It is the last one."

Dusty, sweating faces grinning as men stretched and wiped sleeves across cracked-lipped mouths. Somebody kicking out the fires. Cleaning the irons by running them through the dust. Heads sloshed into troughs to come out snorting. Spitting water that was close to mud. A good job well done. Pride here among these knights of gun and horse.

Morgan, watching from the fringe of activity, understood and smiled. He would feel the same as Broad Clancy if he were in Clancy's boots. It was an old scene to Clancy, one that had been repeated every spring since he had ridden north from California with his herd. Today he had viewed it for the last time, if Morgan's plans went unchallenged.

If Morgan had been seen, no one gave the slightest hint. Riders were hazing the cow and calf herd away from the corrals. Broad Clancy, riding a chestnut gelding as only a man can ride who is a cowman born, grinned at young Rip and said something Morgan didn't hear. He motioned to Short John and Jaggers Flint and, as if by previous agreement, the four reined their horses toward Morgan and rode directly to him.

Morgan had remained away from Clancy because he knew that as long as the branding was going on, the little man wouldn't talk. He had been waiting until he found the moment that seemed to be the right one, thinking they had been too busy to note his arrival. Now he knew he had been seen from the first and ignored, a common treatment Clancy prescribed for unwanted guests, exactly as he had prescribed it for Morgan that first day in the Silver Spur.

Morgan had not come with the intention of fighting. He had avoided it in Irish Bend only by a show of toughness, but young Rip hadn't been there that day, and Rip was the most dangerous man old Broad had. Now, watching them come at him, Morgan had a moment of doubt. Triumph was on Rip's ugly face. Short John, out of place in this tough company, was afraid. Jaggers Flint's muddy brown eyes held the smoldering rage of a man who lacked the cold courage it took to make a play, and hated himself for that failing.

But it was Broad Clancy who surprised Morgan most. He reined up a dozen steps from Morgan, green eyes smiling from under the bushy gold-brown brows. He had shown a nervous fear that day in the Silver Spur when he had learned Morgan's name. He had not wanted to know

Morgan's purpose in coming, assuming it was revenge.

Perhaps he had never forgotten the Morgan kid who had left the valley sixteen years before. It might have been that his mind had held the shadowy fear of the boy's return, and he had been shocked by that fear when he discovered that the thing he had been afraid of had become stark reality, instead of a black dread held in the recesses of his mind.

Today Broad Clancy was a different man. Morgan saw no fear in him. There was pride, the dignity of a small man who feels his position, the old arrogance that Morgan had remembered most of all about him. He seemed entirely sure of himself and his own future, as if Murdo Morgan was nothing more than a bothersome gadfly that could be swept away with a motion of his hand.

"We're busy, Morgan," Clancy said crisply. "What do you want?"

"Trouble," Rip breathed. "Let's give him some."

"Shut up," Broad ordered. "Speak your piece, Morgan. Then get off Turkey Track range. This is wrong ground for you."

Rip was a stick of dynamite, a short fuse sparking. He was the one of the four to watch. Jaggers Flint was the next, but Flint would not start it. Short John wanted none of the trouble, and old Broad, for some reason Morgan did not understand, was filled with a confidence that his position did not warrant.

That was the way Morgan read it, and he hesitated a moment, uncertain what his own play would be. He could beat Rip to the draw and kill him. He was certain of that, and he was equally certain that if it happened, he would lose the last slim chance of a compromise peace.

"Rip's on the prod," Morgan said at last. "If he pulls his iron and starts smoking, I'll kill him, but that isn't what I want."

"Behave, Rip!" Clancy bawled imperiously, without looking at the boy. "Talk, Morgan. Cuss it, I haven't got all day to set here."

"You said I was on wrong ground," Morgan said evenly, keeping Rip within range of his vision. "It so happens I'm on my own ground."

Broad Clancy threw back his oversize head and laughed. It was a deep laugh, as if this was a moment to savor, to be enjoyed to the last full second.

"Look, Morgan," he said at last when he could talk, "you surprised me the other day in town. When you said your name was Morgan, I naturally figgered you'd come back to square up for what happened to your brothers. Since then, I've learned different. I know why you're here, and you don't scare me worth a hoot. I'll tell you why. You haven't got the chance of a snowstorm in Hades of pullin' this off. The Citizens' Bank will close you out, and I'll deal with them. . . . That all you've got to say?"

Questions prodded Morgan's mind. Clancy knew about the Citizens' Bank, so he must have found out through Cole. But what was back of it? There was no time to consider it now.

"Not quite all, Clancy," he said. "You've made a lot of money off a range that never belonged to you. I'll give you whatever credit you've got coming for fighting Paiutes and the other troubles you had, but those days are gone. You'd be . . ."

"We're still here," Clancy cut in tauntingly. "One blasted company or another has owned the wagon road grant for years, but my cows keep on eatin' company grass. I haven't paid a nickel for it and I never will. Now get out!"

"Not yet," Morgan said. "I had hoped to make a deal with you. I want everything cleared up before the settlers start coming in. If you want to buy the tract your buildings are on . . ."

"Save your breath," Clancy jeered. "I'll hold a patent to every acre of company land before I'm done."

"You've had your chance," Morgan said harshly. "You can save part of the Turkey Track or you can lose it."

"I'll save all of it and I'll bust you." Suddenly Broad Clancy was deadly serious, the last trace of good humor fading from his wrinkled face. His eyes were emerald slits, the corners of his

118

mouth working under the stress of emotion. "I let you alone after our ruckus in town because I thought you had sense enough to slope out. Now I can see you're short of savvy. You figger you're a tough hand. You got the jump on Rip at Royce's place, and you licked Arch Blazer. All right. You've used up your luck. Get out of the valley, or, by the eternal, I'll hang you with my own hands before I'm done."

"There is such a thing as law," Morgan flung at him. "That law recognizes the right of private property. You aren't as big as the law."

But no one was listening. Broad and Short John had ridden off after the herd. Rip's prodding laugh cut into Morgan's words. Then he and Jaggers Flint wheeled their horses toward the house.

There was no regret in Murdo Morgan as he sat staring after Broad Clancy and Short John. He had done all he could. Clancy's ears were stone.

But why was he so supremely confident? The only answer lay in his certainty of Morgan's failure, and he must have a better reason for that certainty than his belief in himself. Again Morgan considered Ed Cole, but failed to find the answer to his question.

Morgan smoked a cigarette, sitting his saddle there by the corrals. There was no sign of life about the big log-and-stone house. Rip and Flint had disappeared.

Morgan thought of Jewell Clancy. She had offered to help. She was the only one of the Clancys who had foreseen the inevitable pressure of time and what it would do to the Turkey Track. He reined his black toward the house. Since he was here, he might as well see Jewell.

Morgan had seen the Clancy house only at a distance. Now that he was here in front of it, he felt his admiration for it. Broad Clancy, coldly self-confident, had picked the spot beside a spring where he had wanted to build years before. The fact that it was company land and not open to entry had made no difference to him. Yet he had built well. Morgan, who had seen ranch houses from Yellowstone to the Río Grande, had never seen a better one.

Tying his horse at the pole beyond the row of Lombardy poplars, Morgan's gaze swept the house. It was east of the bunkhouse and cook shack. The barns and corrals were across the road and a short distance to the south. From the wide porch, the Clancys could look across the sage-floored valley to the pine hills and the sharp point of Clancy Mountain. Old Broad had named the peak. It had been his boast that he stood out among men the way Clancy Mountain stood out above the rolling hills.

The house was of stone, two stories high, the wings on both sides of lodgepole pine. There was no yard, but there was a row of red hollyhocks along the front of the house. Jewell's work, Morgan thought, an expression of a woman's love of beauty, the same as the yard in front of the Royce cabin was a mark of Peg's character.

Morgan crossed the porch and knocked. The door was open and he could look into the big living room with its tremendous stone fireplace on the opposite wall. Bear skins were on the floor, there was a scattering of homemade furniture, including a sort of divan covered with Navajo blankets, and a collection of firearms on the wall. A man's place, yet clearly marked by a woman.

There was no sound within the cool gloom of the interior. Morgan knocked again, louder this time. He heard the pad of feet and the Chinese cook shuffled into the room.

"Is Miss Jewell here?" Morgan asked.

"Missy out liding," the Chinese answered. "Back welly soon. You come in?"

Morgan nodded and stepped in. The Chinese pattered on across the room and disappeared.

Morgan twisted a smoke, his gaze swinging around the room. A huge picture within a carved walnut frame hung above the fireplace. Broad Clancy's and his wife's wedding picture, Morgan guessed. He had never seen Mrs. Clancy, but now, studying her face, he felt he would not have liked her. Lips too thin, too tightly pressed.

He grinned when he looked at Broad's picture.

Young, with a long curling mustache, the gold-brown brows not so bushy then, and hair. Plenty of it. But Broad didn't look entirely happy. Sort of disappointed, Morgan told himself. Morgan's grin widened. Maybe the picture had been taken after they'd been married.

Morgan swung around the room. There were other pictures, mostly of the children, but the one in the little office at the end of the long living room shocked him. The door into the office was open. On the wall above the desk was a picture that was startlingly familiar, so familiar that he thought for a moment it was his own mother. Then he wondered if it could have been her sister.

Taking the tintype of his mother from his pocket, Morgan studied it, then lifted his gaze to the picture on the wall. They were so alike it was fantastic. The only difference was a matter of age. The wall picture was that of a younger woman, hardly more than a girl.

A squeak on the floor brought Morgan around, the tintype still in his right hand. In that way he was disarmed, a fact that saved his life. The slightest motion for his gun would have brought death. Rip Clancy stood there, a cocked Colt in his hand, his thin face utterly wicked.

"I've been waitin' for this ever since you got lucky that day at Peg's place," Rip said with taunting malice. "You ain't as smart as Pap figgers, or you wouldn't have stepped into it."

Jaggers Flint took a step forward until he stood beside Rip.

"I'll take care of him, Rip," he said. "I've done a little waitin', too."

But a vicious cunning had seized Rip.

"Not yet, Daggers," he said. "Tie him up. Before we're done with him, he'll make a swap, his land for his life."

"Broad's got some fool notions about how to treat anybody while he's in your house," Flint objected. "He ain't goin' to like this. Let's take this huckleberry and dust out of here."

"Pap'll change his mind."

The sound of a horse's hoofs silenced Rip. He wheeled toward the door.

"It's Jewell!" he cried. "Tie Morgan up and dump him into my room. She won't go in there."

# XIII

Jewell had seen Murdo Morgan ride up to the branding when she was saddling her brown mare. She had hesitated, wondering what had brought him to the Turkey Track, and knowing the answer at once. This visit had been inevitable from the moment her father had refused to listen to Morgan in town.

For a moment Jewell had stood motionless beside the mare, watching Morgan sit his saddle outside the circle of activity. There might be trouble and it was not in her power to prevent it. Mounting, she had turned her mare toward the rimrock that formed the north wall of the valley.

She rode well, with the easy rhythm of one who had sat in leather before she could walk. A hot, dry wind thrust at her and brought her hair down her back and, catching it, straightened it out behind her, a filmy gold-bright mass in the sun.

Jewell knew every trail and road in the valley, in the pine hills to the south, in the Sunset Mountains to the west. Nature had endowed her with a throbbing restlessness that daily drove her out of the gloomy house and into the open where the air was thin and clear and pure. She had never understood it, but when the wind gave her its wings and the sunlight painted a distant and beautiful world beyond the far edges of the valley, when the strong sage smell was all around her and the sky was the only roof above her, the restlessness was gone entirely.

This was her land, and she was its child. But there were the passions of her family to mar perfection. The hidden fears, the huge pride, the false-rooted arrogance—all united to build a shame in her and wrench a protest from her that was wasted.

Usually Jewell rode to the rimrock and worked her way to the top along the snake-wide trail, but not today. She was remembering Ed Cole's visit, her father's grim laugh and growing sureness. Then she remembered Murdo Morgan, tall and squarely built, a dark-faced, black-garbed man with a dream greater than any Clancy had ever dreamed.

The old conflict boiled within her again, loyalty to a family she did not respect and did not understand, against the loyalty to a man she had met only briefly, the man whose dream had been her own unspoken dream, the man who, as a boy, had been in her thoughts through her growing years.

She reined up in the talus and stepped down. She idled among the boulders, her gaze sweeping across the gray flat to the pine hills, made hazy blue by the distance. There, standing as a memorial the Creator had made, was Clancy Mountain. Broad Clancy had committed sacrilege in stealing it.

Jewell had always been honest with herself. She knew how little love Broad Clancy had for her, but she did feel a closeness with Short John that she felt with neither Rip nor their father. There was one thing in common between them. They were out of place, tolerated rather than loved. Broad Clancy poured his affection on Rip, seeing in his youngest child much that was in himself. He didn't understand Jewell because he didn't understand women, and Short John wasn't tough enough for the position life had given him.

Jewell sat down, hands behind her, eyes on Clancy Mountain. Suddenly she realized, and the knowledge shocked her, that she hated the mountain. Beautiful. Symmetrical. Snow-covered until late spring. A sharp arrow pointing to heaven. She should love it because she loved everything that was beautiful, but she didn't.

Abel Purdy had said in a rare burst of frankness that time would consume all of them except old Broad, but the mountain would never allow him to be forgotten. It would be there as long as the earth itself was here.

In that moment Jewell made her decision. If Morgan died today, her hopes died with him. If he lived, he would have whatever help she could give him. Then, with a swift rush of panic, she realized she should have stayed at the branding. She might have prevented his dying.

She mounted and put her mare at a fast pace back across the valley. The branding was finished. Everyone was gone, but Morgan's big black stood in front of the house.

Jewell ran inside. Morgan must be here. He would never leave his horse.

The front room was empty. Disappointment knifed her. She had hoped to find him waiting. Then she saw Rip in the office.

"Where's Morgan?" she called.

"Morgan?" Rip took his boots off the spur-scarred desk and stood up. "How the devil should I know?"

"His horse is in front."

"Which same don't prove a thing," Rip said irritably. "Maybe he left his nag and took one of ours. If he did, we'll sure hang him for horse stealin'."

That was about as unreasonable a thing as Rip could say. There wasn't an animal on Turkey Track except Flint's sorrel that compared with Morgan's black, but Jewell chose not to press the point.

"You didn't have trouble?" she asked.

Rip laughed jeeringly. "Trouble with that big wind? 'Course not! He had something to say about Pap buying land, but Pap told him he'd dicker with the Citizens' Bank when the sign was right, like Cole said." He moved to the door. "I'll go look for that hair-pin, if you want to see him." His face suddenly turned ugly. "Say, you ain't sweet on him, are you?"

"I don't want him killed. There's enough Morgan blood on Clancy hands now without adding his."

Rip jeered another laugh. "I reckon there'll be some more 'fore long. Pap should have knowed that pup would grow into a wolf. Now we've got the wolf to kill."

Jewell watched Rip cross to the barn, questions thrusting themselves at her. Turning, her gaze swept the room. Morgan was here, somewhere. Maybe in the barn. Maybe Rip was going to kill him now. She ran upstairs for her gun. Then, in the hall outside the door to Rip's room, she saw Morgan's black Stetson.

Usually Jaggers Flint was with Rip, but she hadn't seen the gunman when she'd come in. She turned into her room and lifted her short-barreled revolver from the bureau drawer. She saw her hunting knife and, on second thought, took it. Jewell Clancy had never killed a man in her life, but she would now if that was what it took to free Morgan.

Then a thought paralyzed her with shock. That man might be her brother Rip!

Jewell slipped the knife into the waistband of her Levi's and left her room, a cold purpose ruling her. She moved with cat-like quiet along the hall, her gun cocked. There was a law in the Clancy house that a bedroom was never entered except upon invitation of its occupant, but Jewell didn't hesitate.

Gripping the knob of Rip's door, she turned it slowly and shoved the door open with a violent push. She expected to see Jaggers Flint there and she expected to kill him, but the gunman was not in sight. Morgan was on the floor, hands and feet tied, a bandanna gagging him.

For a moment, the room turned in front of Jewell. She gripped the foot of Rip's bed, shutting her eyes, faintly aware of an incoherent gurgle from Morgan. She had been keyed to a killing, and now that the killing was not necessary, she stood trembling, tears struggling to break through. Then she gained control of herself, eased down the hammer of her gun, and, lifting the knife from her waistband, slashed Morgan's ropes and gag.

He licked dry lips and flexed the muscles of his wrists. "I'm beholden to you," he began.

"Not here." She gripped his hand and pulled him to the door. "Rip will tear the house down when he finds you've gone."

Morgan was in the hall then, picking up his Stetson.

"Careless of Flint to drop it here," he said.

"Flint isn't smart and he was in a hurry, but I'd have found you anyhow. I got back sooner than Rip expected and saw your horse outside." Jewell opened the door of her room and pulled Morgan into it, smiling at his disapproving frown. "A woman's room is no different than any other room, Murdo. Just four walls."

"If Rip found me in here, he'd have some reason to drill me."

"He won't find you," she said, hoping Rip would respect the rule she had not. "This is my one island of refuge."

Morgan stood rubbing his wrists, eyes on her. He was, she thought, tough enough to finish this job he had started. This was a world of violent action and brutal force, of blood and dust and sweat. Morgan fitted that world, but, more than that, he had the capacity to adapt himself to any situation. If he survived, there would be another world of quiet and order here in Paradise Valley, a world of turned furrows and filled irrigation ditches and churches and schools. He would fit into that world, too.

"I don't savvy Broad," Morgan said. "He was plumb jumpy when I saw him in town. Wouldn't listen. Just wanted me to get out or get plugged in the back. Today he acted like he had the world by the tail."

"Ed Cole and Pete Royce paid us a visit," Jewell said quietly. "Dad knows why you're here."

"Cole and Royce?" Morgan started to reach for tobacco and paper. Then his hand fell away from his shirt pocket. "What did they want?"

"Cole told Dad that you owned the road grant and had borrowed money from the Citizens' Bank. He said the land was being sold in the Middle West now."

Morgan walked to the window and looked out upon the sage flat, the afternoon sunlight cutting strongly across his face.

"Why did Cole tell Broad that?" he asked in a wondering voice.

"His bank wants the valley and he thinks this

is a cheap way to get it. If you fail, the bank will close you out, and he said he knew how to make you fail, but if his plans didn't work, he wanted Dad to help."

"What's in it for Broad?"

"Cole promised to see that Dad got title to the land he needed in return for helping break you."

She saw the misery that was in him, saw it tighten his mouth and narrow his eyes, saw the beat of his temple pulse. Ed Cole had bragged that Morgan was a trusting fool who wouldn't suspect him because they were friends, and she sensed the hurt that was in Morgan. He was the kind of man who would give everything to a friend and, for that same reason, expected the best from those he called friends.

Jewell stood at the door, watching him and saying nothing, knowing that he had to work this out with himself. He had, she thought, expected trouble with some of the nesters like Pete Royce. He would have expected trouble with the Turkey Track, but he would not have anticipated this fight with the man who had negotiated his loan and called it an act of friendship.

Morgan turned suddenly to face her. "I came to the house to see you, but I guess there isn't anything you can do. Long as Broad figures he's got me on the run, none of us can do anything. I might as well drift."

"You can't go now!" she cried. "Flint and Rip

are outside and you haven't got your gun. Wait till dark. I'll find your horse and you can go out through this window."

He gave her a queer grin that might have meant anything. "I've been in some tights that looked pretty tough, but I never saw one so tough I had to sneak out through a woman's window."

Crazy, but that was the way Murdo Morgan *would* feel. She moved quickly to stand against the door, searching for something that would make him stay.

"How did Rip happen to get the drop on you?" she asked.

He was halfway across the room when she asked that. He stopped as if suddenly remembering something.

"I was looking at a picture on the wall of Broad's office. She looked a lot like my mother."

"She was your mother," Jewell said quietly.

He rubbed the back of his neck, staring blankly at her while his mind grappled with what she had said.

"How did Broad get it?" he asked.

"I told you there were two sides to this thing," she said. "Dad loved your mother in California, but your father won her. Dad never forgave him. He married right after that, but he didn't love my mother. They quarreled all the time. That's about all I remember of her."

"Then that's the reason Broad and Dad hated each other."

"Most of it. The rest was Dad thinking your father came here to flaunt his victory. Dad left California to get away from the Morgans and try to forget your mother."

Outside, a man called: "Where's Morgan?"

Morgan wheeled to the window, with Jewell a step behind him. Tom Carrick stood there with the sun to his back, slim and arrow-straight, hand splayed over gun butt. Rip stepped out of the house and paced slowly toward Tom. Jewell gripped Morgan's arm. She sensed what was coming, and she knew Morgan did.

"The fool," Morgan muttered, "had to keep looking for his trouble till he found it."

"What do you want Morgan for, you yellow-livered clod-buster?" Rip called tauntingly.

"Don't call me yellow!" Tom Carrick bellowed. "There's Morgan's horse. Abel Purdy said he was comin' out here."

Morgan tried to raise the window, but it was solid. Jewell handed him her gun. He took it and wheeled toward the door, but it was too late. Rip had pulled his Colt, confident of his superiority over this brash nester.

Jewell opened her mouth to scream, but no sound came. Something gripped her throat. Rip had made the wrong guess. Tom Carrick's gun spoke before Rip's was clear of leather, and Rip

Clancy, his Colt unfired, folded into the hoof-churned dust.

Morgan whirled back to the window when he heard the shot. That was when Jaggers Flint, shooting from the barn across the road, cut Tom Carrick down with a shot in the back!

# XIV

Kicking out the window, Morgan had Jewell's small gun in his big fist. "Stand where you are, Flint!" he shouted. "You'll hang for killing!"

Jewell glimpsed the gunman's upturned face squeezed tight with the panic that Morgan's voice had stirred in him. He tilted his gun and fired.

Morgan pushed Jewell away. She fell across the bed and, coming back to her feet, saw the splintered slice that Flint's bullet had made along the edge of the window casing. She heard her gun in Morgan's hand, and smelled the burned powder.

Morgan wheeled out of the room. "Stay here!" he called. "I'll get Flint!"

She came back to the window just as Flint swung aboard his sorrel and broke out of the ranch yard in a wild run. She heard Morgan pound down the stairs and across the living room, heard her gun talk again, and saw that he had missed.

Outside, Morgan stooped beside Rip, felt of his wrist, and seeing his gun in the dead man's waistband, lifted it and slid it into holster. He knelt at Carrick's side and, turning, waved for Jewell to stay inside. She knew then that both were dead.

"Flint will head for the lava flow!" Jewell screamed.

She didn't wait for Morgan to ask where it was. She walked out of the room slowly, her legs stiff and without feeling, an emptiness in her. When she reached the front porch, Morgan was in his saddle and cracking steel to his horse.

Jewell stood watching him, worry a sharp pain in her chest. She knew that only one would come back. Then she moved off the porch and through the dust to Rip. Oddly enough, her thoughts fastened upon her father. She wondered what he would do now that Rip was dead. . . .

Morgan pulled his black down after the first hundred yards. Flint's horse was faster, but at the reckless pace the killer was taking, he would kill the sorrel. There would be time then for the reckoning.

They reached the rim, the distance steadily increasing between them, and crossed the plateau between the foothills and the valley. The sun was behind the Sunset Mountains then, and by the time they reached the fringe of timber, black night gripped the mountains. Morgan swore bitterly.

He had been sure his horse could overtake the sorrel, but Flint had disappeared in the scattering pines that seemed to stretch endlessly ahead.

The big black was more important to Morgan than Flint. No horse, not even the sorrel, could take many hours like these. Somewhere ahead of him, perhaps in the lava flow, Flint would be on foot. Morgan, knowing that time was on his side, reined up. Making camp in the protection of a fifty-foot cliff, he waited out the long night.

This was strange country to Morgan. He had come into the valley several miles to the north. He had heard of the lava flow when he was a kid, but knew where it was only in a general way. It would be, he knew, a perfect place for a hide-out, filled with caves and steep-walled depressions where a man could hide and wait for his pursuer.

That would be Flint's way—the way he had killed Tom Carrick. With that thought, hatred gripped Murdo Morgan. There would be no turning back until Jaggers Flint was dead.

Daylight showed gray, then sharply red, shadows reluctantly fading from the hills and draws. Hawk's Nest, a rugged point of rock that Morgan had seen from the valley, rose above the gently sloping hills and made an unmistakable landmark ahead of him. The lava flow was not far beyond.

Morgan saddled and rode west, slowly now, for he was sure the sorrel could not have gone much farther. A sense of danger made a growing uneasiness in him. What Flint did depended on how panicky he had become, but, unless he had completely lost his head, he would hole up and ambush Morgan. His kind of killer seldom changed.

Sunlight crawled along the hillsides and down into the draws, and slowly warmed, baking the chill of the long night out of Morgan's muscles. The lava flow loomed ahead, a black, twisting ridge that had been spewed out of some nearby crater in prehistoric times as a savage molten mass. Cooling, it had formed this nearly lifeless desert in which only a few stunted trees found precarious footing.

Flint was close. The nearness of his presence sent a warning impulse along Morgan's nerves. He drew his Colt, his eyes scanning the lava, the million places along that ragged ridge where the gunman could hide while he laid his sights on the man he wanted to kill.

Something had warned Morgan and his mind sought the source of that warning. It might have been the chattering of a squirrel or a jay, or a deer bounding through the timber. Then he caught it, the faint reflection of the sun on a rifle barrel poked through a hole in the lava ahead of him.

Morgan went out of his saddle in a long leap, trying for a pine to his left. He heard the rifle, heard the snap of the bullet, and lunged for the tree. The second bullet got him in the shoulder and knocked him flat. Flint should have killed him then, and would have if his third shot had been less hurried. As it was, the slug kicked up dirt and pine needles just beyond Morgan's head. He fell into a depression behind the tree and for the moment was out of Flint's sight.

Morgan pulled breath into his aching lungs, a little sick with the realization that death had missed by inches. Then he felt the blood from his shoulder wound and knew the sickness had a more tangible cause than relief.

Boots scraped on the lava. Rocks loosened by a man's feet clattered down the steep slope. Flint was coming after him. Morgan's first thought was that Flint's action was utterly senseless. Flint would be smart to ride on.

Morgan eared back the hammer of his gun, ears keened for sound of the man's movements. Then he understood. Flint was going downslope toward Morgan's horse.

Morgan struggled upright, swaying uncertainly until he laid the point of a shoulder against the trunk. Flint, hurrying toward the black, did not see him.

"Turn around, Flint!" Morgan called.

The gunman must have thought he had killed Morgan or had at least hit him hard enough to take him out of the fight. He wheeled, shocked into immobility, lips parted as he stared at

Morgan. He dug for his gun, lunging forward in a wild leap. He got in one shot, a hurried desperate one, far wide of its mark.

Morgan's first bullet knocked him off his feet. Flint fought back to his knees and tilted his gun. Morgan fired a second time. Flint's body gave with the impact of the heavy slug. He went flat, the power of self-movement forever gone from him.

The hillside seemed to buckle before Morgan's eyes. He dropped his gun and clutched the pine trunk for support. Then his fingers gave and he fell, his blood forming a slowly spreading stain on his shirt, shoulder aching with steady hammering throbs.

Morgan lay there a moment, an inner warning beating along his spine. When he tried to get up, he found that his left arm was useless. He realized vaguely that he had to stop the blood, and worked his bandanna out of his pocket.

Rolling it into a ball, he slid it inside his shirt against the wound. He lay there a moment, gritting his teeth against the pain that was rocketing through his body.

The warning still tugged at his foggy consciousness. Then he knew what it was. Horses! Coming upslope. He picked up his gun and fumbled two loads into the cylinder. Old Broad and some of his men probably. He lay with his back against the side of the depression, trying to hold his gun steady, and knew it was no use. He couldn't hit anybody if he had a shotgun.

"Murdo!"

It was Jewell Clancy's voice. He didn't try to understand why she was here. He accepted the fact that she was.

"Here . . ." He tried to shout, but the word came from his throat in a hoarse whisper.

He heard her steps then, saw her looking down at him, her face grave with concern. He tried to get up, but the world was falling apart. Her words—"Quick, Doc!"—seemed to come from a great distance and he fell sideward into an aching void that was without bottom. . . .

It was dark when Morgan came to.

He lay helpless for a time, aware of a throbbing pain, of thirst. He tried to remember what had happened. It came to him slowly, but he wasn't sure whether it had happened in reality or in a nightmare. Time made a slow unmeasured passage.

"Jewell!" he called.

He heard her come to him, felt her cool hand on his forehead. She made him swallow something, and he fell back and was asleep again.

They were strange, weird days. He twisted in a fever, found Jewell beside him when he called to her. Sometimes Doc Velie was there. Days and night were the same. He dreamed, wild aching dreams that always held a monster called *failure*. Broad Clancy had won.

Slowly, reason returned and the world settled back into reality. Jewell told him she had brought Doc Velie from town and they had hidden in a cave while Clancy and his men searched, Clancy believing that Morgan had killed Rip.

"I guess nobody knows about this cave but me," Jewell said. "I come here lots of times. Stay overnight when I can't stand home any more. That's why I always kept food here. We won't starve, Murdo."

He lay looking at her, weak, but not so weak he couldn't admire her, even here in the gloom of the cave. He owed her his life, but he could do no better than say: "I'm beholden to you."

"If you do what you plan, Murdo," she said, "I'll be beholden to you."

"You're Broad Clancy's girl . . . ," he began.

"I can't help where life put me," she said bitterly, "but I can help staying there. I've talked to Doc and Abel Purdy and some of the others. They hate Dad, and they hate what he's done, and what he's doing to the valley, but Doc's the only one who has the courage to tell him. I think Purdy will someday. He says the valley could support hundreds of families and that's the way it will be. That's the dream I've had, Murdo. I guess Purdy gave it to me. Or maybe I couldn't forget the day you and your father left because of what Dad had done. I was just a little girl, but it made too deep an impression for me ever to forget it."

"Looks like we dream the same kind of dreams," Morgan said. "Broad had his chance, but he wouldn't take it."

"He isn't big enough to deal with a Morgan," Jewell said, "and he isn't a man to settle for half. When it's over with, he'll still run the valley or he'll be dead." She rose and looked down at Morgan, troubled. "Don't judge all the Clancys by Dad," she said, and went out for wood.

Doc Velie came after dark, and when he had finished examining Morgan, he said with satisfaction: "Tough as a boot heel, Morgan. You'll come through in good shape if you've got enough sense to listen to me."

"Don't know 'bout that," Morgan said.

"Then you'll be dead," Velie snapped. "I've got a letter for you that I took the liberty of opening. In case you didn't know it, I'd like to see this land sale come off the way it ought to. No sense of Broad Clancy acting like he was a combination of man, Creator, and devil. I want him trimmed down."

"Read the letter," Morgan said.

"It's from a gent named Grant Gardner. Says here . . . 'Dear Morgan. I am glad to report that the sale of your land is progressing faster than we could reasonably expect. I can safely promise that every contract will be sold by August First.

I will be in Irish Bend within a few weeks and we will make definite plans at that time for the drawing. If you want me to, I'll take charge of the details, since it was an old story to me. As a matter of fact, I have already given orders for my men to be in Irish Bend in time to get everything set up before the First of September. There will be nothing for you to do but see that the peace is kept.' "

Doc Velie laid the letter down. He kicked more wood on the fire. He looked at Morgan and cleared his throat.

"Son, I don't know all that's going on," he said bluntly, "but I do know that keeping the peace is going to be a big chore."

"Go on," said Morgan. "What else does the letter say?"

Doc Velie picked it up, and went on reading: " 'I am happy to say that I am much more optimistic about the success of your venture than I was at the time we talked in my office. One reason for my optimism is our unprecedented success in selling your contracts. That can be accounted for by several dry years and the resulting crop failures in much of the Middle West. The second is your own record. I have checked it thoroughly. Even if this project fails, I hope you will consider a job with my organization. Cordially, Grant Gardner.' " Velie raised his eyes from the paper. "Who is this Gardner?"

"A millionaire a few times over. If he likes the valley, he'll build a system of ditches and reservoirs for us."

"Then we'd better make him like the valley. Now get this straight, Morgan. You're well enough to take care of yourself. Jewell had better go back with me. Broad's in town, catching up on his sleep and taking on more supplies. If Jewell shows up, he'll think you're dead or she couldn't find you. Then he'll call off his dogs. Jewell knows these hills better than anybody else. If she can't find you, he'll know well enough he can't."

"Sure, I'll get along," Morgan said.

"But, Doc . . . , " Jewell began.

"Now shut up!" Velie bellowed. "Listen, Morgan. This is more than your fight. If you lose, things go back the way they've been for years. If you win, this valley can be made the paradise Broad named it for. You go back in a few days and you don't live ten minutes."

"I reckon I won't be going back right away," Morgan admitted.

"I mean for you to make yourself scarce till the middle of August. I wrote to Gardner to hustle up here. Told him you'd been shot. He can do everything that needs to be done, can't he?"

"Yes, but . . ."

"No buts. He said your job was to keep the

peace. All right. It'll take a well man to keep the peace in this valley when the settlers start rolling in. You won't have your strength before the middle of August. Maybe not then."

Morgan rubbed a stubbly dark cheek, knowing that what Velie said was right, and at the same time feeling the pressure of his pride.

"I've got to see Jim," he muttered. "I let Tom get killed."

"No, you didn't!" Jewell cried. "You were gone from the window when it happened. Rip drew first."

"I should have hollered to him," Morgan said bitterly.

"It wouldn't have made any difference. Flint was behind him. He'd have shot Carrick in the back no matter what you did."

"They had Tom whipsawed all right," Morgan said. "You tell Jim, will you?"

"I've already told him," Velie said. "I've told him where you are, and how bad off you've been. Now are you going to promise you'll stay out of the valley, or am I going to have to send Jim up here to make you stay?"

"I'll stay," Morgan murmured. He brought his gaze to Jewell's face, troubled by the knowledge that Broad Clancy had built a wall between them. "No way out of it. Maybe me and Broad are both wrong. If it works out so Broad . . ."

He stopped, failing to find the words he wanted,

145

but Jewell nodded as if she knew what he wanted to say.

"You've got to win, Murdo. I won't apologize for Dad, and I know he won't change. Do what you have to do. . . ."

# XV

Morgan rode back into Irish Bend before the middle of August, the uncertainty of what was happening and the pressure of what had to be done driving him into action. His wound was healed, the soreness gone, and strength was back in his whip-muscled body. Yet there was a difference in him that went deeper than the beard covering his face and the hungry leanness that gave his features a mild resemblance to those of a brooding hawk.

He was a forward-looking man, never one to waste time in regrets. Still, Tom Carrick's death weighed heavily upon him, a weight that the killing of Jaggers Flint had not removed.

Racking his black in front of the barbershop, Morgan had a shave and haircut and sent the barber to the store for a new shirt while he had a bath. He was not certain whether the barber knew him or not, but the man was coolly distant, so he thought he had been recognized.

It was no different now, and it wouldn't be until

they saw that Clancy was beaten. Then Murdo Morgan would have friends. Dozens of them.

Morgan was leaning back in the zinc tub lathering his long body when he heard steps cross the barbershop toward the back room. The word was out that he was in town. He had left his gun belt over a chair within easy reach, an instinctive precaution that he had taken without thought.

He lifted his Colt from holster, soapy thumb slipping on the heavy hammer as he tried to cock the gun. He cursed, wiped his hand on the towel, and had the hammer pronged back when the door opened.

It was Doc Velie and Grant Gardner.

"A fine note when a man can't take a bath without being busted in on, isn't it?" Velie asked complacently.

Gardner paused in the doorway, suddenly embarrassed as if, in his anxiety to see Morgan, he had not thought how it would be.

Morgan grinned. "Howdy, Doc." Letting down the hammer, he laid his gun on the chair and held out a wet hand. "Howdy, Gardner."

"A fine note when a man greets his friends with a cocked gun, too," Velie complained. "Isn't it, Gardner?"

"From what I've seen since I got to Paradise Valley," Gardner said soberly, "I'd say it was a good idea to greet anybody with a gun until you know who it is."

Morgan laid his gaze on the capitalist's face. "What's happened?"

"Nothing," Velie said quickly. "Broad decided you're dead. Jewell had a row with him and moved to the hotel, but he's got a man watching her. That's why she didn't come out to see you."

Gardner lifted a cigar from his pocket. "I'm used to situations like this. Fact is, I've had to do a little fighting on my own hook when I started carving up a cowman's range." He fished in his pocket for a match. "But this one's the toughest deal I've been on. You're still on top, Morgan, but a man's luck doesn't last forever."

"A man makes his own luck," Morgan said. "I'll make mine. Like you said in your letter, my job is to keep the peace."

"And a tough job it is with most of it still ahead of you," Gardner stated. "Mine's about finished. Every contract's been sold. Next week we'll put up the big tent and we'll have a field kitchen for the settlers who aren't equipped to cook their own meals. The hotel is far from adequate, so we'll have to put up another tent for them to sleep in."

"Springs and mattresses, I reckon," Velie grunted.

Gardner waited until he had his cigar going. "Hay on the ground and they'll be glad to get it. There is another problem, Morgan. Whenever you get a crowd like we're going to have, you

148

get several drifters and gamblers who have to be handled. I have a feeling you'll be busy enough without taking care of the riff-raff."

"There's a lawman here named Purdy," Morgan said.

Velie snorted. "Don't figure on Purdy."

"A little confidence might go a long way with him," Morgan murmured.

"Purdy thinks too much," Velie growled. "Reading and thinking don't give a man nerve. Confidence don't either."

"We'll try him," Morgan said sharply.

Gardner shook his head doubtfully. "The barber's back, Doc," he said. "We'd better let the man dress."

"Nothing's stopping him," Velie snapped. He slid exploratory fingers over Morgan's shoulder. "Don't get the idea we came in here because we were so glad to see you. Just professional interest. Mmmm. I did a good job on you. Healed up fine. Surprising, considering you had to eat your own cooking after Jewell left."

"I didn't stay there all the time. Rode over to Prineville. Then spent some time on the Deschutes."

"Couldn't stay put, could you?" Velie's eyes smoldered with anger. "Well, now that you're back, see if you can stay alive. Blazer and Royce have been hanging around the Elite. Talking about what they'll do to you if you show up.

They never did take to the yarn that Flint had tagged you and you'd crawled off to die."

Morgan got out of the tub and reached for the towel. "See you later."

Gardner left the room, but Doc Velie paused in the doorway, eyes speculatively on Morgan.

"Shut the door!" Morgan howled.

"Shucks, you're not so pretty," the medico grunted. "I told you Jewell's at the hotel."

"I heard you. Shut the door!"

Growling something that didn't reach Morgan as words, Velie slammed the door and left the barbershop.

Morgan dressed and buckled on his gun belt, thinking with grim reluctance that Gardner had been right in saying the job of keeping the peace was a tough one, and that most of it was still ahead. He wondered how accurate Velie had been in his harsh judgment of Purdy. If the medico was right, he, Morgan, was wrong, but if Purdy had even a small part of a man's natural heritage of pride, Murdo Morgan was right and Velie was wrong. He would have to know before the crowd came.

Leaving the barbershop, Morgan paced along the front of the saddlery, eyes on the street. It was nearly as deserted as it had been the day he had seen Abel Purdy, but an apparently deserted town could be a dangerous one. Both Royce and Blazer, like Jaggers Flint had been, were the kind of men who would shoot him from a hiding place if they thought the law was too weak to handle them.

By this time the news of Morgan's presence would have swept the town like a prairie fire before a high wind. Pausing in front of the hotel, Morgan remembered there had been two horses racked before the Elite when he had ridden into town. Now the hitch pole was empty. He turned into the lobby, pondering this, but failing to see any danger in the incident.

Jewell was not behind the desk. Disappointment built a gray uneasiness in him. He had not realized until he swung into the dining room how much he had counted on seeing her. When he had eaten, he asked for her at the desk.

The clerk eyed him with the same veiled hostility he had sensed in the barber.

"She ain't here, mister. Out, I reckon."

Morgan wheeled out of the lobby. He built a smoke as he moved along the walk to the corner, stopped in front of the Stockman's Bank and, scratching a match across its front, lighted his cigarette. He stood there, considering, tobacco smoke a shifting shape in front of his face. As long as Blazer and Royce were in town, they were as dangerous as a pair of rattlesnakes in a man's bed.

Decision made, Morgan slanted across the intersection to the store, his gaze fixed on the front of the Elite. He had to kill Blazer and Royce or drive them out of the valley. Both claimed to be settlers, and for that reason either was capable of doing irreparable damage when the contract holders arrived in Irish Bend.

It wasn't until Morgan reached the post office that he saw the newly lettered sign hanging in front of what had been an empty building east of the Elite.

OFFICE OF
CASCADE AND PARADISE
LAND COMPANY

He grinned as he turned into Purdy's office. Gardner, he thought, was a good man to be running things.

Purdy blinked behind his spectacles. Then he rose and gravely held out his hand.

"Greetings from a mortal to one in the other world. I understand you're dead, with Flint's bullet in you."

"It's a lie. The slug went on through."

Purdy laughed and motioned to a chair. "Sit down, Morgan. I'm glad to see you."

Morgan shook his head. "I've got business in the Elite. I hear Royce and Blazer are all set for me."

"They've done some wild talking," Purdy admitted.

"I'm giving those two a chance to show how much is wind, which same brings up another point. Gardner says we'll have some toughs in town when the crowd gets in. Are you going to handle them?" It was a blunt question, brutally put. Purdy looked down at his star, holding his answer for a moment. He was afraid. Morgan saw that in the sudden squeeze that fear put upon his features, but instinct did not force a quick refusal from him. His pride, then, was not dead, and Morgan knew his confidence had not been wasted.

"I'll try," Purdy said at last.

"Good." Morgan nodded as if there had never been any doubt. He lifted his gun, checked it, and slid it back into leather. "Come on over to the Elite. Might as well see the fun."

Purdy hesitated, then turned to his desk. Picking up an ancient Navy Colt, he slipped it into his waistband.

"I wouldn't want to miss it," he said.

# XVI

Doc Velie was coming out of the company office as Morgan and Purdy angled across the dust strip toward the Elite. He stared in the way of a man who sees something unreal take the cloak of reality. Then he ducked inside.

They reached the walk, crossed it. "I just want a fair fight," Morgan said. "See that I get it." He put a shoulder against the batwings and pushed through, hand on gun butt.

Except for the droopy-mouthed barman, the place was empty, but hoof thunder sounded from the alley and faded as distance grew.

"They're not here," Purdy said, as if this evident fact was something he had hoped for but had not expected.

Morgan moved directly to the bar. "Where's Royce and Blazer?"

The barman laid down his towel. "Don't know. They went out the back door when you two left Purdy's office. Reckon they've made some dust by now."

"I've been in town two hours," Morgan said. "How come they got in such a hurry all of a sudden?"

"They knowed you was here," the barman said. "They aimed to gun you down the minute you showed your nose in the door, but they got another notion when they saw Purdy. Funny how a star can change a fellow's mind."

Morgan grinned at the astounded Purdy. The pale-eyed man had discovered something new concerning the dignity of a lawman's badge.

"We'd better have a drink on that, Abel," Morgan said. "I'm a little put out. I figured it was me that had them *hombres* worried."

"You did." The barman set a bottle and glasses on the mahogany. "That was why they wasn't takin' any chances on you, but they didn't figger on the law, so they got spooked when they saw Purdy."

Morgan took his drink and jingled a coin on the bar. "See you later, Abel," he said, and left the saloon.

The building that housed the company's office had been a store, but the owner had lost an argument to Broad Clancy and left the valley. It had been filled with broken chairs and boxes, a long counter, dirt, and innumerable cobwebs.

Morgan paused in the doorway, amazed by what he saw. The place now was clean, the débris cleared out, and the smell of fresh paint lingered in the air. There were several desks in the front of the room behind a railing that marked a line of demarcation between clerical workers and a waiting room for visitors. Two small office rooms had been built in the back, one marked GRANT GARDNER, the other MURDO MORGAN.

Gardner saw Morgan and bustled out of his office.

"Been looking for you. I wanted you to see what we've done."

"Looks fine," Morgan stated. "Never thought I'd have my name on an office door."

Gardner flushed with evident pleasure. "This is part of my contribution to a worthwhile endeavor,

Morgan. I'm no good on the fighting end, but I know this part of the business." He pointed to rows of filing cabinets along the wall. "Duplicate copies of the contracts that have been sold. My office crew will be in from Alturas tomorrow. Lot of work yet for all of us. I want you to go over a map of the road grant with me. We'll mark off the tracts according to the size you want them sold. All this bookkeeping and the cost of taking care of our customers and the traveling expenses for those who represent twenty or more contracts will cut into your profit, but in the long run it will pay."

Gardner swung his hand around the room. "Show stuff, maybe, but it impresses folks. A lot of them will want to come in and talk, and we'll have to take time off. If we can keep them in good humor and hold their confidence, the drawing will go off like clockwork." He opened the door into Morgan's office. "How do you like that?"

A new swivel chair, roll-top desk, brass spittoon on the floor, three chairs. Morgan chuckled and, sitting down at his desk, ran his fingertips across the varnished wood.

"Well," he whispered, "I'll be hanged."

Gardner began fishing for a cigar. "A few more things to tell you," he said casually. "This valley is far superior to what I had expected to see. Your friend, Jim Carrick, tells me that the soil is good and the water is here if reservoirs are built to hold it. I intend to do that if the settlers are the solid citizens my salesmen say they are. Back there, they've been blowed out, dried out, burned out, and starved out. They're looking for a place where there is water, good soil, and a moderate climate."

Morgan leaned back in his chair, boots on the desk top. "We've got those things," he said, and waited.

Gardner bit off the end of his cigar and dug into his pockets for a match.

"Folks like a show," he commented. "We're selling land, and after that I'll sell them water. I've got a surveying crew in the hills now. We've got to live with them, so we want to start off right. The thing we've got to do is avoid letting them get any idea that the drawing is crooked. Knowing Ed Cole, I'm sure he'll work on that end."

Gardner found a match, struck it, and fired his cigar. Still Morgan held his silence, knowing from Gardner's round-about approach that there was more to come.

"I've been pounding my brain until I got the right idea." Gardner blew out a long smoke plume. "Pretty girls always appeal to a crowd of men, so I want you to line up two pretty girls to help with the drawing."

This was what Gardner had been working up

to. Morgan took his feet off the desk and stood up. Jewell Clancy and Peg Royce were the only pretty girls in the valley as far as he knew, and he couldn't ask either one of them.

"I won't do it," Morgan said angrily. "Peg's dad is Pete Royce, and Jewell's is Broad Clancy. You know how both of them stand."

Gardner waved his cigar at Morgan. "That's the reason we want them. The settlers can't accuse us of being crooked with those girls doing the drawing."

"I won't do it!" Morgan said again, hotly. "You're crazy to think I would."

Gardner's chubby face reddened. "I was crazy to contract with the Sneed boys to butcher wild hogs so we'd have pork for our customers. I was crazy to ride out to Broad Clancy's camp and ask him for beef. I suppose I was crazy to come up here at all!"

"What are you talking about?"

"We contracted to furnish water, fresh meat, and horse feed during the drawing and for a week before to those who got here early. I heard through this man, Royce, that there were wild hogs in the tules. He said he butchered them all the time, so I got the Sneed boys to butcher enough to keep us in fresh meat until we get Clancy's beef to the settlers."

"You asked Broad Clancy to furnish us with fresh meat?" Morgan demanded.

"Why not?"

"Nothing, except it don't make sense for him to do it. I can't understand why he didn't pull a gun on you when you went up there."

"He was very courteous," Gardner said stiffly. "Abel Purdy went with me. He introduced us, and the instant I told Clancy what I wanted, he said he'd sell us all we needed. I told him we'd pay top price and save him a drive to the railhead."

"It doesn't make sense," Morgan said stubbornly. "You don't know Clancy. He was ornery before Rip was killed. He'll be twice as bad now."

"You've got him wrong," Gardner muttered. "He sees the handwriting on the wall, and he's smart enough to read it."

Morgan let it go at that, but he knew Clancy was not a man to look for handwriting on the wall. He would use his beef as a lethal weapon to wreck the land sale, and there was no way to counter his move unless Morgan could find out what his plan was.

Gardner fidgeted at the door, puffing fiercely on his cigar and eyeing Morgan.

"I didn't think you'd get your neck bowed over asking those girls to help," he finally said. "We've got to figure every corner, and it's my guess trouble will pop in a few days. I've already told the girls you'd ask them."

So, he was committed. Morgan said: "All right." Then he sat down at his desk again, feet cocked in front of him.

He didn't notice when Gardner left. Resentment died in him. Gardner was a good man, with savvy for his part of the business, the kind of savvy that Morgan didn't have, but Gardner lacked the understanding Morgan had about men like Broad Clancy. Trouble would pop all right, and probably over Turkey Track beef.

Morgan was still at his desk when the rumble of a heavily loaded wagon brought him to the street door. Jim Carrick was bringing in another load of hay. Buck was lying on his back behind him with his hat pulled over his face.

Morgan hesitated, knowing this was something that had to be done. He should have ridden out to Carrick's place. Now that Jim was in town, he had to see him. He went back for his hat, and when he reached the street, Carrick had turned at the intersection and pulled in behind the Silver Spur Saloon.

The wagon was stopped beside a half-formed stack when Morgan reached it. "Howdy, Jim!" he called.

Carrick stepped away from the load, saw who it was, and let out a great squall.

"Well, cuss me if it ain't Murdo! Where you been, boy?"

Morgan gripped the farmer's hard hand. His

fear had been groundless. Jim Carrick held no bitterness toward him.

"Getting over a bullet hole Flint gave me," he said.

"Doc said you'd been shot, but I couldn't keep from thinkin' you'd be back, so I went ahead on this hay deal. Gardner's took over and that's what he said to do."

"That's right." Morgan swung a hand toward the finished stacks. "That's a lot of hay. I don't have any idea if we'll use all of it."

"Better to have it on hand. Tried to buy some of Royce's old hay, but he wouldn't let it go."

"We'll have enough. Some of them will come by stage or horseback. Soon as the drawing is over, the majority of them will scatter and figure on coming back in the spring."

"Buck's up on the load," Carrick said, as if suddenly remembering. "Buck, Murdo's here."

Young Carrick shoved his face into view, dislike stamped upon it.

"Yeah, I heard him. Kept hopin' you'd cashed in, Morgan,"

Jim's eyes hardened. "You're too old and too big to have to lick, but I'll do it if I hear any more of that out of you."

Buck grunted an oath and drew back.

"Let it go," Morgan murmured. "He's still in love."

"Don't make no difference," Carrick said

bitterly. "He's been seein' that Royce girl. She came over a time or two after you left. Soon as he could stay in a saddle he rode over there, but she won't marry him."

"About Tom." Morgan dug a boot toe into the dirt. "I was there when he was killed. Maybe there was some way I could have . . ."

"None of that talk," Carrick said sharply. "Doc told me how it was. I talked to the Clancy girl, too. Tom just had to keep lookin' for trouble till he found it. Headed for town soon as he got back the day you left. Allowed there'd be fightin' and he was goin' to side you."

"If I'd known that, I'd have talked to him," Morgan said. "Maybe he'd have stayed in town."

"No sense blamin' yourself. You plugged Flint and got yourself shot up to boot. What's done is done. I ain't seen old Broad since it happened, but they tell me he's about loco. Keep your eyes on him, son." Carrick paused, his gaze on somebody behind Morgan. He muttered: "There she is."

"Murdo, I heard you were back!"

It was Peg Royce, panting from her run, her dark eyes afire with pleasure. Morgan started to say something, but didn't, for Peg threw her arms around his neck and pulled his lips down to hers.

There was no reserve about her, no holding back, no subterfuge. She had never made any secret of her want of him, and now she told the world. Even then, with the sweet taste of her lips upon his, with the heat of her kiss burning through him, the thought of Jewell Clancy was a quick repelling force in his mind.

"All right!" Buck Carrick slid off the load to the ground.

Peg stepped away from Morgan, composed and unabashed.

"Hello, Buck. I told you the bullet hadn't been molded that could kill him," she said.

"I wish it'd been me instead of Flint that had that chance." Buck took another step toward Morgan, his great shoulders hunched, his fists balled in front of him, his handsome face turned ugly by the fury of his rage. "I'm goin' to bust you, Morgan! If I had a gun, I'd kill you!"

Indecision gripped Morgan. He stepped back, thinking of Tom Carrick, of Jim, and how much he owed him, and knew he couldn't fight Buck.

"Don't try it," he said. "I've got nothing to fight you for."

Buck's laugh was a taunting slap. "I sure have got somethin' to fight you for."

"Which same don't make a girl love you," Morgan said.

He went back another step, heard Peg cry: "Don't Buck! If you love me, don't!"

But Buck didn't stop. Weeks of smoldering hate exploded in him now, taking him beyond the edge of reason.

"You was sweet on her all the time!" Buck bawled. "I ain't been fooled a little bit. She'd've married me this summer if it hadn't been for you. Now I'm goin' to fix that mug of yours so she won't do no more kissin' on it!"

One of Buck's great fists swung out. He had strength. Nothing more, and Morgan knew he could cut him down with half a dozen driving blows. Still he couldn't do it. He ducked the fist and retreated, still searching for something that would stop the boy. Peg was at Buck's side, beating at him with her fists.

"He doesn't want to fight you, you fool!" she was crying. "I'd never marry you! I never would have!"

But it was Jim Carrick, letting it play out this far, who drove sense into his boy. Gripping his pitchfork, the tines shining in the sunlight, he brought it forward in a quick jab, slashing Buck in the rump.

Buck let out a howl of pain and, throwing his shoulders back in an involuntary motion, grabbed his seat.

"Get back on that load," Jim said hoarsely. "If I have to do that again, you'll be eatin' off a high shelf for the rest of the summer."

Buck sidled back toward the wagon, the fight gone out of him. But the bitterness was still there, a hatred that would fester with time until he became a madman capable of killing.

164

Without a word, he climbed back on the load.

Peg gripped Morgan's arm. "I want to talk to you," she whispered.

Nodding at Jim Carrick, Morgan turned away, deeply troubled. He respected and liked Carrick as he had respected and liked few men. He would be largely indebted to him for whatever success he had with the land sale, but life was dealing off the bottom of the deck. First, he had been indirectly to blame for Tom's death. Now Buck was working himself into a killing frenzy.

"I've been looking for you," Peg said hurriedly. "Every time I came to town I asked Gardner. Why didn't you let me know?"

"I didn't think you'd worry. Doc thought it was better if nobody knew."

"You knew I'd worry," she said hotly. Then bitterness touched her face. "You were right. Pete Royce is my father. I couldn't be trusted."

"It wasn't that," Morgan protested. "No one knew."

They rounded the Silver Spur and went on across the street.

"Let's have supper in the hotel, Murdo," Peg said as if she had only then thought of it. "Royce hasn't been home for a long time and I'm tired of eating alone."

"All right," Morgan grunted, not wanting to because he hadn't seen Jewell, and he didn't want to meet her with Peg on his arm. But if Peg felt his lack of enthusiasm, she gave no indication of it.

"Royce and Blazer are hanging around to kill you," she said, "if you turned up alive. Cole will be here for the drawing. I wanted to tell you about him the last time, but I couldn't. You thought he was your friend."

"I know. He saw Broad Clancy. Jewell told me what he was trying to do."

"Jewell told you!" She bit her lip, not letting her sudden flare of anger show. "What are you going to do when he comes back?"

They reached the hotel and went in. "I don't know," Morgan said.

He had known it was a situation he would have to face. Cole would come back to see if Murdo Morgan had been destroyed, and Morgan honestly didn't know what would happen then. He shrank, even in his thoughts, from killing this man he had called friend.

"It's good to see you on your feet, Murdo."

It was Jewell, coming down the stairs beyond the desk. She was wearing a blue bombazine dress with long sleeves. Morgan had not seen her in that dress before, and his eyes, taking in her small figure, showed his appreciation. He lifted his hat.

"It's good to be on my feet," he told her.

Jewell nodded to Peg. "How are you, Peg?"

For an instant Peg had no answer. She stood

tall and straight beside Morgan, her hand still possessively on his arm, her head high, as she fought for self-control. Morgan, turning his gaze to her, saw the pulse beat in her throat, the quiver of her lips. She had, he guessed, sought this meeting, and now that it was here, she couldn't bring it off the way she had planned.

"I'm fine, Jewell," Peg murmured. "We're having supper. Won't you come with us?"

"Thank you, but I've had supper."

"Gardner said he'd told you girls I'd ask you to help with the drawing," Morgan said bluntly. "That isn't right, knowing how your folks feel."

"I'll be glad to," Peg said quickly.

Jewell hesitated, and she was the one about whom Morgan was most concerned. Pete Royce was no good. Everybody in the valley knew that. Peg hated him, and she would help with the drawing to spite him, if for no other reason. Broad Clancy was something else. Morgan knew Jewell didn't agree with him, but she didn't hate him.

"Broad won't like it," he said.

"She'll do it, Murdo," Peg breathed. "It's the least she can do. Gardner said it would be a big help to you, because everybody would know it was an honest draw."

A smile touched Jewell's lips. "Of course, I'll help, Murdo."

167

Peg's answering smile was quick and lip-deep. "I thought you would."

Morgan looking from one to the other, did not fully understand. He only knew they were women, facing each other, fighting with claw instead of fist, one tall and dark and full-bodied, the other small and slim, with wheat-gold hair afire now, with a slanted ray of sunlight falling across her head. There was this moment of tension, spark-filled. It was steel pressed against a whirling emery wheel, and Morgan, striving desperately to find something to say to break the tension, could do no better than say: "Doc says it healed up fine."

Jewell brought her eyes to Morgan. "I've worried about you. You were so weak when I left you."

Morgan felt Peg stiffen.

"You were with him when he was shot?" she asked coldly.

"No, but I found him afterward. I guessed Flint would head for the lava flow and Doc and I were close enough to them to hear the shots. I stayed with Murdo until after his fever broke."

"And you left him when he was still weak?"

"Doc thought I should. Dad was looking for him, and we thought that if I came back and said I couldn't find him, Dad would pull in his men, thinking that if I couldn't find him, he was really gone. It did work that way."

Peg's breath was a long sigh. "If I had been taking care of him," she whispered, "I'd have stayed until he was well."

"He should have sent for you," Jewell said.

"I was all right," Morgan cut in.

A sob came out of Peg, startlingly sudden. "You wouldn't send for me, would you, Murdo? You couldn't trust me like you could her."

Whirling, she ran out of the lobby and on through the dust of the street to her horse. Mounting, she quit town at a wild, reckless pace.

"I'm sorry," Jewell said contritely. "I shouldn't have done that. I don't know why I did."

Still Morgan did not fully understand it. He only knew that women clash in a different way than men, that Jewell had struck back in self-defense. He turned toward the dining room, then swung back to say: "I don't want to bust you and your father up."

"You won't. I've already left home. Now go get your supper. . . ."


# XVII


Gardner had figured the uncertain element of time as accurately as a man could. His office crew came north on the stage from Alturas, fast wagons bringing their equipment. Empty water wagons creaked across the desert to make the long haul from the creeks around Clancy Mountain, where the water ran clear and cold in a swift lacy pattern. Lumbering freighters, starting earlier, brought food supplies, blankets, a heavy stove for the restaurant, tents, and, from Lakeview, lumber for the platform in the big tent, and tables and benches for the dining room.

Morgan, watching idly because there was nothing for him to do at the moment, marveled at the military precision with which Gardner's men worked. Saws bit through pine. The ring of hammer on nail was a constant racketing noise. Canvas was stretched, stakes pounded deep into the earth, ropes tightened. Within a matter of hours, Irish Bend had reached out across the flat to triple in size.

Gardner, flushing with pride, slapped Morgan on the back.

"We're ready. Let 'em come!" He grinned in sudden embarrassment. "You know, Morgan, I've kicked myself for not taking a partnership in this deal. I misjudged the land and I misjudged you. I thought the valley was too far from a railroad, and I didn't believe you could take care of yourself against the opposition you'd have."

"We're a long way from a railroad," Morgan admitted, "and there's still plenty of opposition."

170

"Steel will come," Gardner said confidently. "And as for the opposition, Cole hasn't showed his face, Blazer and Royce have stayed out of town since you called their bluff, and it looks like Clancy is convinced we mean business."

Gardner might be right about the railroad, Morgan agreed, but he was dead wrong about the opposition. Morgan's mind turned to Clancy's beef agreement as it had continually during his waking hours since he had heard about it. The deal had been made. There was nothing to do but let time bring Clancy into the open.

"I couldn't have put this over if you hadn't given me a hand," Morgan said. "I didn't have any idea there would be this whoopdeedoo when I bought the grant."

Gardner showed his pleasure. "Glad to do it, Morgan. Fact is, I'll be a partner when I get the ditch system in. Funny about me. Some men get pleasure out of whiskey or women. Bringing farmers onto good land where they can own their home is mine." He chuckled. "Only this time somebody else is taking the risk. If the sale doesn't go off, you'll lose your shirt. If it does, you'll be a rich man."

"If it doesn't go off," Morgan said grimly, "you'll be digging into your pocket, because my shirt won't pay for all this."

Gardner took a fresh grip on his cigar. "Guess we'd better see it goes over." He squinted up at

171

the bright sky. "If the good weather holds like it has, we won't need to worry. Let them come. We've taken care of everything but the weather, which is one thing you just have to leave for Providence."

# XVIII

They did come. By stage. By horseback. By buggies. By buckboards. And in covered wagons loaded with household goods, ready to stay through the winter, echoes of their passage singing across the sage and bunchgrass. All roads led to Irish Bend. There the trail ended, the human tide piled up, and chaos had to be hammered into order.

It was the same drama that had been enacted and reënacted through the centuries, the drama that had made America. Explorers driven on by the deathless urge to see beyond the skyline, to see where the rivers were born.

Missionaries, men of God, their Bibles under their arms, risking their scalps to tell the howling, blood-lusting, brown skins of another world and their soul's salvation. Mountain men, buckskin-clad, fringe a-sway, Indian wives and half-breed children, taking the savages' way of life, driven into the empty land of the great silence because a neighbor had built within sight of them, the smoke from his chimney corrupting the horizon.

Miners and prospectors, haunting the bars and gulches, urged on by an inner hunger for the yellow metal, building boom town after boom town, climbing above timberline where ten times out of nine, they said, you'd find silver. Cattlemen, land pirates, harking back to the feudal days of chivalry with the chivalry so often missing, hiring the knights of horse and rope and gun, an aristocracy taking what it wanted without a by-your-leave of anyone, holding to what they claimed by any means they had, surrendering only to death or the tidal wave of those whose best weapon was the plow.

Every wave also brought the others. Hangers-on. Tradesmen. Lawyers and doctors, preachers and teachers, blacksmiths and carpenters. Women, the virtuous and the tinseled; those who followed their men because theirs was a love and devotion that went beyond human analysis; those who merely followed men, accepting their sordid profession through choice or perhaps driven to it by the exigencies of life.

Bad men and good, outlaws and law-abiding, the strong who shaped life and the weak who were shaped by that life. Bunco artists. Grifters. Con men.

All of them were here in Irish Bend, and Abel Purdy grew with the needs of the day.

Three men tried to hold-up the Stockmen's

Bank. Purdy caught them from one side, Morgan from the other, and the three of them died in the deep dust of Irish Bend's street while gunfire racketed between the paintless false fronts.

A shell game operator set up his board in front of the Silver Spur. Purdy invited him to leave. The invitation was accepted. A drunk accosted Jewell Clancy on the street. Morgan rammed his way through the crowd and knocked the man down. He spat out a tooth, wiped blood from his mouth, and bawled,

"You own the town, maybe, but you don't own the women!"

Morgan hauled him to his feet, knocked another tooth lose, and told him to leave town. Invitation again accepted.

It was rough and tough and turbulent, but Abel Purdy and Murdo Morgan held down the lid, and some of the turbulence died. Good men, these farmers. Driven by land hunger and a dream. Freckle-faced kids. Sunbonneted women. Weather-darkened men with hands curled to fit the handles of their plows. Kansans and Nebraskans, and east to the Appalachians.

"Good men," Gardner said. "That's why I'm aiming to build your irrigation system."

Good men, Morgan knew. Men with enough money to buy their land and still have some left for the hard years ahead. The raggle-taggle, the visionary, the seekers of something for nothing would come later, to settle on free government land. Maybe they would prove up. Maybe not. But these men were different. They would give the land a fair trial. If it beat them, they would lose the stake they had spent half a lifetime making. If they lost, they would move on and start again.

Jewell's hotel and Gardner's tent with its hay beds were filled. The store sold out and left the owner cursing because he had lacked faith and failed to build up his stock. The hotel dining room never had an empty table and the tent restaurant was always full as well.

At night campfires were stars stretching across the flat south of town. The haystacks the Carricks had built melted like snowdrifts before a burning sun. Kansas men gathered together. Nebraska men. Iowa. Missouri. Illinois. Visited and dreamed and stared at Clancy Mountain and allowed there might be deer up there.

In every group, leaders lifted their heads above the others, were listened to and toadied to, and grew deep-chested with attention. Clay Dalton, from the Nebraska sandhills, shook Morgan's hand with respect. He turned his head and spat a brown ribbon that plopped into the wheel- and hoof-churned dust of the street.

"Never seen a purtier valley, Mister Morgan. Had some misgivin's, comin' so far on the big gab of men you sent out to sell your land.

Figured it might be just another rush, aimin' to take the bark off our backs, but I reckon if you give us a fair sale next week, we'll be mighty well satisfied."

Good men. Excited a little by the crowd and a new land. Everything new. Talked to the old settlers, like Jim Carrick. Asking him this and that. What were the winters like? Were the summers always this cool? What could you raise? Would fruit grow here? Satisfied, solid men riding out over the valley, scratching shoe toes through the dirt, picking up a handful and letting it dribble between their fingers, finding the spots they hoped to draw.

Overnight, sleepy old Irish Bend, the cow town, was gone. A new Irish Bend throbbing with boom-town life, more canvas than wood, mushroomed among the clumps of sage and rabbitbrush. The old inhabitants scratched their heads and rubbed their eyes, and could not believe this thing they saw.

Some cursed Murdo Morgan. Some looked at him with new interest and admitted that maybe Broad Clancy was finished. He hadn't showed up. He hadn't turned a hair. By this time, he knew that Murdo Morgan was alive and in Irish Bend. It wasn't like Broad Clancy, and nobody understood. Not even Jewell. Not even Murdo Morgan.

Then Ed Cole rode the stage in from Prineville.

176

Morgan was in his office, visiting with Clay Dalton and some of his Nebraska friends, when his door opened.

"Ed Cole's here," Gardner said.

Morgan rose, a pressure on his chest making it hard for him to breathe. "I'll go see what he wants," he said. "Don't reckon I'll be long."

He stepped into the main office, the clattering typewriters annoying him. He strode into Gardner's office, gritting his teeth against the clamor that drove a shivering spasm down his spine. Ed Cole was standing at the corner of Gardner's desk, an easy smile on his lips, his blue eyes as guileless as they had been the day he had sat in his San Francisco office and told Morgan he would see about the loan.

"How are you, friend Murdo?" Cole said in a soft courteous voice. He held out his hand. "I came to watch the drawing. Looks like it'll be quite a show."

Gardner stepped in behind Morgan, closing the door after him. Morgan ignored Cole's hand. His breathing sawed into the quiet, air coming from the bottom of his lungs as he fought his anger.

"That isn't the reason you're here," he said, dropping his hand, the mask of courtesy stripped from his face.

"This is a fine way to greet a friend," Cole said harshly.

177

"Friend?" Morgan turned to Gardner. "Wonder what he'd say an enemy was?"

Cole slipped his hands into his coat pockets. There might be a gun there. Morgan wasn't sure.

"Let's have it, Morgan," Cole said. "We've known each other a long time. You wouldn't be where you are now if I hadn't negotiated your loan for you."

"I'm not so sure of that, but what you said about knowing each other is right. I'm remembering the time a bunch of miners had you cornered in Ouray. They claimed you'd crooked them in a poker game. I didn't believe it then, but I do now. You were mighty glad I was around."

Cole licked dry lips. "Sure, Murdo. You saved my life. I returned the favor by helping you get a loan. Now why . . . ?"

"No use in lying about it, Ed. You got me that loan because you thought I was a cinch to lose out in this land sale and your bank would get the wagon road grant for the price of the loan you'd made me. A blasted steal, which makes you a robber same as if you'd held a gun on me."

Color bloomed in Cole's cheeks. He chewed a lip, eyes not so guileless now as they whipped to Gardner and back to the raging Morgan. Suddenly he was afraid. Morgan remembered the way he had looked that night in Ouray. He saw the man now as he was, handsome and smooth-mannered, but with neither love nor respect for anything or anybody but himself. He was like a tree covered by sound bark, but utterly rotten inside.

"Who's been lying to you?" Cole asked in a vain attempt to bluff it through.

"Nobody. Jewell Clancy told me about you being out there to see Broad. You made a deal with him. If something went wrong so your back-shooting gundogs didn't get me, Broad was supposed to do the job and you were going to deed him the land he needed when your bank got the road grant. You never intended to keep that bargain, did you, Ed?"

"You've been lied to!" Cole screamed.

"Then why did you come to the valley after I got here?" Morgan demanded. "If you were on the level, why didn't you come see me? You're doing the lying, Ed. You put Blazer and Royce on my tail. Then you tried to make it a sure thing by seeing Clancy. Peg Royce said . . ."

"Peg wouldn't say anything. She took my money. . . ." Cole caught himself. It was admission enough. Dull red crept over Cole's face and on around to the back of his neck. There was this moment of struggle within him before he made a futile effort to keep his self-respect.

"I'm not going to stand here and be called a liar!" Cole raged, and started for the door.

Morgan grabbed a handful of his shirt and jerked him to a stop.

"Coming here was your idea," Morgan said.

179

"Now you can answer a question. Why did Broad agree to sell us beef?"

"I don't know." Cole tried to pull free. "I haven't seen Broad."

Morgan shook him. "You paid Royce and Blazer to kill me, didn't you?"

Cole struck at Morgan, a fist stinging his cheek. Morgan hit back, a wicked right that slammed Cole against the wall. He wiped a sleeve across his bleeding nose, then his hand dropped to his pocket and he pulled a gun. Morgan jumped at him, gripping Cole's right wrist with his left hand, twisting until Cole dropped the gun. He kept on twisting, bringing Cole's body around until he cried out in agony. He kicked at Morgan, tried to hit him with his left.

"If I didn't make myself clear, I will now," Morgan said.

He hit Cole again, driving him back against the wall. Cursing, Cole lowered his head and drove at him. Made wild by fear and pain, Cole forgot anything he had ever known about fighting. He tried to stamp on Morgan's toes. Drove a thumb at Morgan's eye. Lifted a knee to get him in the middle. Nothing worked. Morgan was nowhere and everywhere, letting Cole's charge wear itself out.

When the wild fury in Cole had blunted itself on the hard rock of failure, Morgan sledged him on the point of the chin. Cole dropped his hands and shook his head. Then his knees gave and he fell. The door to Gardner's office had been opened. Clay Dalton and his Nebraska friends stood knotted there.

"Boot him, Morgan!" Dalton called. "Bust his ribs in."

Cole groaned and drove a foot at Morgan's shin. Pain laced up Morgan's leg. He caught Cole's foot and dragged him out of Gardner's office, the crowd breaking to let him through. He went on, with Cole cursing and twisting and trying to jerk free. His head rapped on a desk, and he cried out in pain again. Morgan took him on through the gate in the railing and out through the front door. He let the foot go then and, pulling Cole to his feet, swung him to the edge of the walk and cracked him on the jaw.

Cole sprawled into the dust of the street. He sat up, sleeving dirt, blood, and sweat from his bruised face.

"All right, Morgan," he said thickly. "I'm licked, but you never made a bigger mistake in your life."

"Get out of town," Morgan said.

Cole came to his feet, lurching like a drunk, and reached a horse racked in front of the Elite. He tried to get up into his saddle and failed. He stood there a moment, trembling, hanging to the horn, knees weak, oblivious to the curious crowd that watched him. He tried again, and this time succeeded in getting a leg across the leather. Reining around the saloon, he took the north road out of town, slumped forward, reeling uncertainly with each jolting step of the horse.

"Who was he?" Dalton asked.

"A gent who thought he was tough," Morgan answered.

Dalton laughed. "Never seen a man take a worse beatin'. I'd sure hate to be on the other side from you."

"We're on the same side, Clay."

Morgan wiped a hand across his face, a sickness crawling through him. There had been no satisfaction in beating Ed Cole. He pushed through the crowd and tramped back to his office.

Gardner came in, eyes worried. "That wasn't good," he said. "Cole won't forget it. You'd better stay in town."

"I'm soft," Morgan muttered. "I should have killed him."

Gardner nodded sober agreement. "Before this is over, you will, or he'll kill you. . . ."

Overnight the temperament of the camp changed. The day Morgan had his fight with Cole the settlers were optimistic and good-humored. The next morning, they stood in thick knots along the street, scowling, a sullen anger upon them.

Gardner, taught by long experience to react instantly to a crowd's mood, felt the change, and started looking for Morgan. He found him having breakfast in the hotel dining room.

"Trouble's loose," Gardner said worriedly. "The settlers are standing around with their lower lips hanging down so far they'll trip on them."

"First time I've seen you worried," Morgan said, reaching for tobacco and paper.

"First time I have been. You don't reckon they'd listen to Cole?"

"He's not their kind, but they would listen to Royce and Blazer. We'd better get the drawing started."

"We can't. We advertised the First of September, and that's what it's got to be."

"What's biting them?"

"I don't know. Looks like they'd come in if they had a kick."

Morgan sealed his cigarette and slid it into his mouth. "Let's go talk to them."

"We can't risk a fight. That bunch could turn into a mob in a minute. We've got to find somebody we know to tell us what's wrong."

"Let's get hold of Dalton."

They left the hotel, the crowd on the board-walk making a path for them. Morgan spoke to some he knew. They nodded, saying nothing, faces sullen and resentful, the pressure of their hostility pushing at Morgan.

"You're right about these boys," Morgan muttered. "Wouldn't take much to turn them into a pack of wolves."

# XIX

Gardner and Morgan found Dalton at the bar with his Nebraska friends. Dalton's face was showing his resentment.

"You played hob, Morgan," he said darkly. "Didn't think you was that short-sighted."

"All right, Clay," Morgan said mildly. "Let's have it."

"I had it for supper," Dalton growled. "I don't want no more of it."

"Blast it!" Gardner cried in a frenzy. "What are you talking about?"

Dalton snorted and reached for a bottle. "Don't give me that pap. I figured you was a straight-shootin' outfit. Now I'm givin' you some advice. You run a straight draw or you'll get a neck stretchin'."

Gardner looked at Morgan helplessly. Morgan's cigarette had gone cold in his mouth. His searching mind could find no clue in what Dalton had said.

"It'll be an honest draw, Clay," he said patiently,

"but there's something we don't understand. What was it you had for supper?"

Dalton gave him a look rich with scorn. "Them hogs, you fool. We took one of them critters and cooked some of it. We couldn't eat it. Nobody else could, neither. The meals in the tent restaurant weren't no better."

Morgan looked blankly at Gardner. "What hogs?"

"I told you about them," Gardner said defensively. "I contracted with the Sneed boys to butcher some wild hogs. I saw one of the loads they brought in yesterday. The meat looked all right."

"Sure, it looked all right," Dalton snorted. "You try eating any?"

"No, but I tell you the meat looked all right."

"I said did you eat a hunk of it?" Dalton bellowed. "Tasted like you'd fed them hogs onions."

"Royce said they ate wild hogs all the time around here."

"So, Royce gave you the idea," Morgan said thoughtfully. "I don't know much about the Sneed boys, but they're north rimmers, too."

"I know what Royce is," Gardner began, "but it seemed like a good . . ."

Morgan waved him to silence. "Clay, I don't know just what's wrong, but I'll find out. There's several *hombres* around here who don't want the land sale to come off. This hog business is part of the deal."

Doubt struggled through Dalton. "I'd like to believe you, Morgan, but these fellers who came around last night talked mighty straight. They said we was suckers to come out here. Claimed you'd crook us on the draw. Good land would go to the Clancys. It was part of a deal you'd made with 'em last spring. They said you was pushin' them hogs off on us 'cause it was the cheapest meat you could get."

It made sense now. Fresh meat that nobody could eat after enjoying the anticipation of it. Then some of the valley settlers showing up and fanning a smoldering fire into a blaze.

"Who were those men?" Morgan asked.

"Didn't catch their names, but they live in the valley."

"What'd they look like?"

"One was big. Kind of pig eyes. Other one was smaller. Flat nose. Blue eyes set plumb close together."

"Royce and Blazer!" Gardner cried.

"Those are two of the valley men who want us to fail," Morgan said.

"Why?" Dalton asked skeptically.

"Several reasons. One is that they'll be dispossessed as soon as somebody draws their location. You boys are playing their game when you believe them. Now I'm going to lay my cards on the table. I need your help. We've bought some Clancy beef, but they haven't got the herd down from the hills yet. I'll go see Clancy today, but we haven't got anybody to do the butchering."

"We'll do it for you," Dalton said.

"Then that's fine. Pass the word along what I'm doing. And, Gardner, ride out to the lake and see what's wrong with that pork."

Grumbling, Gardner followed Morgan outside. "Clancy will kill you if you go up there."

"I'll take Purdy. Get now! Split the breeze."

Still grumbling, Gardner turned toward the livery stable. Morgan angled across the street to Purdy's office, feeling hostile eyes upon him. There was no overt act. Just sullen silence like the moments of sticky stillness before the heavens empty upon an earth made dry by a torrid sun. Morgan had seen mobs form; he knew the signs, and he didn't like what he saw this morning.

Purdy was pacing the floor of his office, fingers working restlessly through his short hair. He waved a hand toward the street, and, without greeting, said: "What's the matter with those men?"

When Morgan told him about the pork, he smiled thinly. "Nobody can eat a hog that's been feeding on tule bulbs. It's like Dalton said. They taste like they'd been eating onions."

"But Gardner said the meat looked good, and

the Sneeds claimed they butchered wild hogs every year."

"Sure, the meat does look good, but the nesters always drive a batch of hogs home and fatten 'em on grain before they butcher. Besides, I'd say the Sneeds were on Cole's side."

It was done. Nothing that Morgan or Gardner could do would change the settlers' temper except to get Turkey Track beef in today and start Dalton and his friends butchering. It was touch and go, a question whether even good meat could satisfy the contract holders.

Morgan looked around Purdy's office. It seemed no different than it had the first day Morgan was here, but it was different, and the difference lay in Abel Purdy himself. Doc Velie had been wrong about the man, and Morgan had been right. A miracle had been performed. Morgan's confidence had restored the heart to this shell of what had once been a courageous man.

"Gardner contracted with Broad Clancy for some beef," Morgan said. "I'm riding out there today."

This was Abel Purdy's test. Rodding a brawling boom town was one thing, but facing Broad Clancy was something else, for Clancy had owned Purdy the same as he had owned the storekeeper and the barber and the stableman and the rest in the town. Like Purdy, they could have said they wanted security, and that security lasted only as long as Broad Clancy did.

But the metamorphosis was complete. Purdy glanced at his star and slowly brought his eyes to Morgan. "I'll go along for the ride, Murdo. If you have any relatives who want to hear from you, you'd better take time to write to 'em."

"I don't," Morgan said. "Let's ride."

They left town fifteen minutes later, skirting the white city of tents and covered wagons, ignoring the sullen stares that followed them out of town. Black clouds were rearing threatening heads along the southwestern sky and a cool damp wind was breaking through the gap between the Sunsets and Clancy Mountain.

"We're in for a change of weather," Purdy said.

"A storm would play the devil with those *hombres*," Morgan grumbled, "with their tempers screwed up like they are now."

Purdy turned his pale eyes on Morgan. "The world is a more mixed-up business than most of us realize if we live just for ourselves. Remember me saying that time is a great sea washing around us?" When Morgan nodded, he went on: "I said we'd see how well Broad Clancy had built his walls. Now we know. Not high enough. I saw that before the invasion hit the valley. I knew it the minute you walked into my office after Flint had shot you. We'd been thinking you were dead.

When I saw you, I knew you'd take a heap of killing."

"My hide isn't that tough," Morgan said.

"You may die this morning, of course. What I meant is that men like you believe in something strong enough to fight for it regardless of the interests that bring changes about and batter down the walls that the Broad Clancys build. This is the same fight that has gone on since the beginning of time, just a skirmish, but the same fight . . . and we'll always have it."

"Doc Velie said you thought too much," observed Morgan.

Purdy smiled meagerly. "Maybe. Funny thing. I've wanted to be the kind of man Doc Velie was. He was the only one in the valley before you came who wasn't afraid of Clancy. When I heard what you and Doc and Jewell had done, I knew Broad was licked and I was going to help. Security for me wasn't important. The right to get up and howl when I wanted to was."

"You shoot mighty straight for a gent who wears glasses."

Purdy flushed with the praise. "I see all right." He squinted at the spreading gloom of the clouds. "Let's set a faster pace, Murdo."

They held their direction south across the slowly lifting sage flat. Then they were among the buttes, where the junipers were bigger and more thickly spaced than in the valley. Morgan, staring thoughtfully at the sharp point of Clancy Mountain, wondered if old Broad intended to keep his word. If he didn't, and the cattle were still in the marsh behind Clancy Mountain, there would be no fresh meat for the settlers today or any day.

They circled a butte and, breaking over a ridge, looked down upon a large Turkey Track herd. The cattle were being held in a pocket carpeted by bunchgrass, with a creek cutting through the center. Rimrock around three sides made a natural corral so that only a few riders were necessary to hold them. All but two of the cowpunchers were idling around a fire directly below Morgan.

"We won't need that many," Morgan said musingly. "Wonder why he fetched that big a herd?"

"That isn't the question," Purdy said. "I'm wondering why he brought any."

"He's down there." Morgan pointed to a rider angling toward the fire from the grazing cattle. "We'll ask him."

They dropped down the slope toward the fire, causing a stirring among the buckaroos when they were seen. One called to Broad Clancy who looked up, saw Morgan and Purdy, and brought his horse to a gallop. By the time Morgan and Purdy gained the flat, Clancy had reached the others and dismounted. As Morgan rode up to the fire, he had a feeling that this was what Clancy had expected and planned.

"Howdy," Morgan said civilly as he reined up.

Clancy did not return the greeting. He stood between the fire and Morgan, his spindly legs spread wide. Short John and the rest of the crew were behind him and on the opposite side of the fire. Clancy did not ask Morgan and Purdy to step down. He stood in cold silence, a sober, bitter man, with his eyes smoldering emeralds under bushy brows.

There were five men behind Broad Clancy, Short John on the end. Good men for their job, salty, loyal, and ready to fight, but Morgan didn't think it would come to that. A deeper game was being played, and Morgan could guess the reason. Like Ed Cole, old Broad didn't want killing laid to his door if trouble brought an outside lawman to the valley. It meant, then, that Broad had a better idea for achieving the same end.

"Broad," Purdy said sharply, "if you're planning on burning powder, you'd better get both of us because I'll take you in if you kill Morgan."

Clancy didn't laugh as he would have two months before. He had forgotten how to laugh, and Morgan, staring at him, realized only then how much Broad Clancy had changed. Rip's death had done it, but Morgan could not judge the depth of the change.

"Why haven't you fetched the cows Gardner bought?" Morgan asked.

Still Clancy said nothing. His green eyes stabbed Morgan, probing for something he didn't know. He seemed older and frailer than when Morgan had seen him in the Silver Spur that first day he was in the valley, so frail that it looked as if his bow legs would crumple under the weight of the heavy gun on his hip.

"Did you kill Rip, Morgan?" Clancy asked suddenly.

"No." Morgan understood it now. Clancy hadn't been sure. Perhaps that was the reason he had called off the hunt when Morgan was wounded. "Tom Carrick did."

"That was what Jewell said," Clancy muttered. "I never knew her to lie, and I don't reckon Josh Morgan's son would lie."

"We want some beef," Purdy cut in.

"Shut up, you double-crossin' weasel!" Clancy was suddenly angry, terribly angry as his stare cut Purdy. He brought his gaze again to Morgan. "What'll happen if you don't get any beef?"

"I'll have trouble," Morgan said frankly. "But you promised Gardner."

"Yeah," Clancy breathed, "and I keep my word. I'll have 'em within a mile of town tomorrow night."

"The boys are on the prod," said Morgan. "I've got to have some today."

"They've got to rest up," Clancy said. "Good grass here."

"Then have your boys cut out twenty head and me and Purdy'll haze them to town. You can bring the rest tomorrow."

Clancy rubbed his narrow chin as if weighing a decision. The men behind him relaxed. Even Short John, who had always looked scared whenever Morgan had seen him, now appeared relieved.

"All right," Clancy said finally. "Slim. Rory. Cut out twenty head. Push 'em down the creek."

Then, for no understandable reason except that he had held it back so long, fury gripped the little cowman. It painted his face purple, brought his gnarled fist up to threaten Morgan.

"Curse the woman who gave you birth, Morgan! If I thought you'd killed Rip, I'd gun you down, but I'm lettin' you live because I want to see your clod-busters put a rope around your neck. Now get out of here!"

"We don't need that many cows," Morgan said.

"You'll get 'em whether you need 'em or not!" Clancy screamed. "And you'll eat your beef in perdition. I said to vamoose! Get, 'fore I plug you!"

Morgan and Purdy swung their horses down the creek.

"How do you figure it, Murdo?" Purdy asked.

"I couldn't figure out in the first place why

he promised to let us have the beef, and I can't now." Morgan twisted a smoke, frowning at it. "And I can't figure out how he's going to get the settlers to hang us, but he was confident, Abel. Mighty confident."

# XX

Hard as Clancy was, he kept his promise. The herd bedded down within a mile of Irish Bend the night after Morgan and Purdy had brought in the twenty head.

"Kill as many as they'll eat," Morgan told Clay Dalton. "I don't want them to think we're trying to save money, and you'll have to send some beef to the hotel and Gardner's tent restaurant."

It worked better than Morgan could have hoped. The old friendliness and optimism did not return, but the sullen suspicion was gone.

"They figure to wait and see," Dalton said. "Depends on the drawin'. Some of 'em want a lottery. Take out the fool idea of biddin' on each tract."

"Can't," Morgan told him.

Morgan rode every day, knowing that if Cole and his bunch were in the valley, trouble was a constant possibility, but he could not find them.

"They've pulled out to wait until the drawing,"

Morgan told Jewell the night before the land sale started, "but they'll be on hand tomorrow. The trouble is I don't know who's going to be on my side when the shooting starts."

"You have more friends than anybody else in the valley, Murdo," she said.

"And more enemies. But it's the friends a man likes to think about. I wouldn't have got this far if I hadn't had some."

"Nobody ever did anything worthwhile alone, but you've got to keep watching, Murdo. Dad's a careful man. He has a trick that he's sure will work or he wouldn't have let it go this long." She stood looking at him, her full-lipped mouth sweetly set. "Do what you have to do. This valley is better for people than for cows."

Morgan thought about it that night and he was still thinking about it the next morning when he woke. He would do what had to be done, no matter what it did to him and Jewell Clancy.

He was shaving when he heard a tap on his door. He called: "Come in!"

Gardner opened the door and motioned a stocky man into the room. "Morgan, meet Post Office Inspector Bartell. He got in on the late stage last night."

Morgan shook hands with the man. "Glad to know you, Bartell." He indicated a chair. "Sit down. I'll be done in a minute and we'll go down for breakfast."

Gardner paced to the window. "Mean day," he said sourly. "Sticky. We're in for a thunder shower. Weather's as jittery as a nervous woman. Tempers ruffle easy on a day like this."

The inspector smiled as he lighted a cigar. "Then they'll have to ruffle. We can't change the law."

Morgan turned from the mirror. "What law?"

"The government prohibits land allotments by lottery. That's why I'm here."

"I know that. So do you, Gardner."

Gardner shuffled uneasily. "I haven't told you, you riding and looking for Cole like you've been doing, but the contract holders elected trustees Saturday . . . Dalton, Jale Miller, and Hugh Frawley. Yesterday those trustees got hold of me and demanded that the drawing be made a straight lottery. No bidding. They claimed that by allowing the bidding, we're opening the way for Clancy to buy his buildings and anything he wants. They don't have much money. Clancy does, so he can outlast them. In other words, they claim they should get each tract for the contract price of two hundred dollars."

"Why, it says right on the contract that there'll be a chance to bid on each tract before it's knocked off!" Morgan exploded. "I told you the first time."

"I know," Gardner said gloomily, "but Frawley and Miller were pretty hostile. Been listening to

Royce and Blazer again, I guess. Frawley and Miller said they couldn't guarantee that the men would stay in line if Clancy bid in a few choice tracts."

For a moment, there was no sound but the steady scratching of razor on stubble. This was the trick on which Clancy was depending, the reason for his holding back. There had been no violence, although he could have led his buckaroos into town and brought about a reign of terror. He could not be blamed for what would happen today, and there would be no trouble for him even if the governor sent a special investigator to the valley.

There was no talk until Morgan finished shaving. Gardner fidgeted by the window; Bartell sat motionless, pulling steadily on his cigar. Morgan put on his shirt, buckled his gun belt around him, and slid into his coat.

"Let's have breakfast," he said.

"What are you going to do?" Gardner asked.

"Nothing," Morgan said flatly. "They'll abide by the contract."

After breakfast Morgan waited in the lobby for Jewell and Peg who had ridden into town the night before. They came down together, both smiling when he said: "Good morning." He could not tell from their composed faces that anything had passed between them.

"This is your last warning," he said. "That

platform won't be the safest place in town today."

"It'll be a good place to watch from if there's trouble," Peg said.

Morgan looked helplessly at Jewell who smiled as if this were an ordinary day instead of the most special one that Paradise Valley had ever known.

"I wouldn't miss it," she said.

"All right," he said. "We'd better get over there."

They followed the boardwalk to the Stockmen's Bank, angled across the intersection to the store, and moved around it to the big tent. Purdy was waiting outside. He motioned to Morgan and stepped back.

"Broad Clancy ain't here, but Short John is," Purdy said when Morgan joined him. "He's got six cowhands with him. What do you think he's up to?"

"I'm guessing he'll make a bid on a tract of land," Morgan said. "Then all tarnation will blow up in our faces. I didn't figure it out until this morning. Gardner just told me the trustees want to make it a lottery."

Purdy thought about it a moment, staring across the sage flat, troubled eyes blinking behind thick lenses. "Cole's in there with the Sneeds, Blazer, and Royce," he said. "Pretty close to the front and on the other side of the tent. I thought of arresting 'em, but I don't have any real charge and I was afraid of what the settlers would do."

199

"That's right," Morgan agreed. "I've got a hunch I can stop them. I had an idea when I was shaving. Come on up to the platform."

Purdy nodded, and, turning back to Peg and Jewell, he moved beside Morgan up the middle aisle. Every bench was filled and men were packed around the sides and back of the tent. There were a thousand settlers here, Morgan guessed, perhaps more.

He spoke to some he knew, and they spoke back civilly enough. There was no evidence of the sullen anger he had felt the week before. He thought they had, as Dalton had said, decided to wait and see. There was hope in that, but the material for an explosion was still present.

Morgan stepped back when he reached the platform, motioning for Peg and Jewell to go ahead. He mentally cursed Gardner for insisting on them being here. It was not going to be the kind of show Gardner had anticipated. Morgan climbed to the platform, while Purdy remained on the ground.

"Eight o'clock," Gardner said.

Morgan nodded, his eyes sweeping the platform. The bulk of Gardner's office crew had moved over here. There was a jumble of tables and chairs, books, boxes, and record sheets, and Morgan wondered if any kind of order could be kept once the drawing was under way. Gardner had seated Peg and Jewell behind a table at the front of the platform, with two boxes in front of them. The trustees were on the other side of the table. The post office inspector beyond them.

Stepping to the front of the platform, Morgan felt a sudden chill down his spine. Ed Cole's handsome face stood out in the packed mass. He was smiling, a contemptuous smile, as if this were the moment he had long enjoyed in anticipation. It was Morgan's moment, too, but now that it was here, he wished he were a million miles away. His head was a vacuum. No words came to his tongue.

"Get it started," Gardner whispered.

Morgan licked dry lips, eyes turning to Jewell. It seemed to him he could hear her say again: "You've got to win, Murdo. Do what you have to do." He swung back to that ocean of faces. The chill was gone from his spine. He knew what he had to say. This had to go. It was too close to the end to miss now. It had to go!

"On behalf of the Cascade and Paradise Land Company," Morgan began, "I welcome you and wish you prosperity and happiness in your new homes. Some of the land that will be drawn is good only for grazing and will go out in thousand-acre tracts. The better land has been cut into smaller tracts, ranging from one hundred and sixty acres down. The ten-acre tracts are all located south of the lake where irrigation is not necessary. You'll find no better land out of doors,

201

and I know you won't find another place in the West where you can get a clear title to a good farm for twenty dollars an acre or less.

"I have no promises to make about a railroad, but history tells us that steel will be laid to any place in the United States where the production is big enough to make it worthwhile. That production depends on you. One thing I can promise. Grant Gardner will see that you have water." Morgan turned to Gardner. "Want to say something, Grant?"

Gardner came to his feet and stepped up beside Morgan.

"When Morgan came to me several months ago," he said, "I was frankly pessimistic about his project. When I saw this valley, I changed my mind. I promised him I'd build the reservoir and ditch system if the type of settlers who came here looked like men who would work. Well, boys, you do. I'm an old hand at this business. I know I didn't make a mistake in you, and you didn't make a mistake in trying this valley. I'll make a promise now. By next spring work will start on the ditches and as many reservoirs as we find necessary."

The clapping was perfunctory. Morgan waited until the scattered applause died. The feeling was wrong. Suspicion rose from this closely packed crowd of men and pressed against him. Dynamite was here, and the fuse was attached.

Cole's contemptuous smile was a steady, constant thing. His face was a magnet that drew Morgan's gaze. Morgan's lips tightened. Jaw muscles bulged. He was too close to the fulfillment of a dream to let it die.

"One more thing before we start the drawing," Morgan went on. "The matter of doing away with the bidding and making this drawing a lottery was brought up by the trustees. We're willing to grant your request, but Uncle Sam ain't." He motioned toward Bartell. "We have a post office inspector with us who will remain for the length of the drawing. The minute we take away the right to bid, he'll close us down, so I have a request to make. Don't take advantage of the opportunity to bid. Accept your tract of land as it is drawn. We don't want more than the price of your contract. If there is bidding and the prices run over two hundred dollars, the balance will be divided and refunded to you."

Cole jerked forward, suddenly sober, the scornful smile swept from his lips. A sense of triumph surged through Morgan. He had cut away much of the ground from which Cole had expected to launch his attack.

"The procedure of the drawing has been explained, so I won't repeat it," Morgan hurried on. "We have two ladies on the platform . . . Miss Peg Royce and Miss Jewell Clancy . . . who will make the drawing. Grant Gardner will do the auctioning. We promised to pay the traveling expenses and give twenty-five dollars for your living expenses while here to any of you who represent twenty or more contracts. If you've got that coming and haven't collected, visit the cashier in our main office and you'll be paid."

# XXI

Sensing a change sweep over the crowd, Morgan paused. Despite the doubts and suspicions that Royce and Blazer had planted, these men wanted to believe in the inherent fairness of the company, and Morgan had convinced them.

Cole, Morgan saw, sensed that same intangible tide sweeping the crowd. He was hunched forward, his gaze fixed on Morgan, his eyes bright and wicked and entirely lacking their usual guile.

Swinging to Gardner who had stepped back, Morgan said: "All right, Grant."

Morgan stepped down from the platform and joined Purdy. The lawman laid a hand on Morgan's shoulder.

"I didn't know you were a public speaker, Murdo."

"Shucks, I'm not," Morgan said sheepishly. "For a minute there I couldn't have told you my name."

Purdy laughed softly. "I saw you look at Jewell, and everything came back. I think you licked Cole on that business of bidding."

"He looks licked," Morgan said, and turned his gaze to Gardner.

"You have your clearance receipt, men," Gardner was saying in crisp business-like tones. "As soon as your name is called, or if you are acting for an absent contract holder, make your bid for two hundred dollars. If I knock the tract off to you, come around to the back of the platform, pay the balance you owe the company, and you will be given your papers.

"Yesterday we had a conference with the trustees. They requested that if any errors are found in the titles, they should be corrected at company expense and that the company make the deeds to the contract holders instead of the trustees as stated in the contract. The company has accepted those changes."

Gardner moved around Jewell's chair and stood between her and Peg.

"In one box, we have slips of paper with the number and acreage of each tract," he said. "They have been well shaken, but it won't hurt to give them another mixing." He handed Peg's box to Frawley. "Shake yourself a good piece of land, Mister Trustee, and hand the box on to Mister Dalton."

"Why now," Frawley said, "if I shake myself

a good piece of land, Dalton there will shake it back down."

A man in the front row laughed, a tight, high laugh, the kind of laugh that comes out of a man when his nerves have become so taut they must have release. It became a contagion, sweeping through the crowd like a spring wind. Men roared and slapped each other on the back and wiped the tears out of their eyes.

"It wasn't funny," Purdy observed. "It's just men getting their feet on the ground after being up in the air. A good study of how crowds act, Murdo."

Gardner took Peg's box and handed Jewell's to Frawley. Peg said something, and for the first time Frawley seemed aware of her. He shook the box and handed it to Dalton, his eyes on Peg, frankly admiring her.

Dalton and then Jale Miller shook the box, and Gardner finally placed it in front of Jewell.

"All right, Miss Clancy." Gardner paused dramatically. "Make the first draw."

Jewell's hand slid through a small opening in the side of the box. She drew out a slip and read: "Hans Schottle."

"Hans Schottle!" Gardner called, motioning for a secretary behind him to write the name on a long sheet of paper. "Now the tract, Miss Royce."

Peg drew a slip and read: "Tract Number three

thousand, nine hundred and fifty-six . . . twenty acres."

"Tract Number three thousand, nine hundred and fifty-six . . . twenty acres!" Gardner called. "Make your bid, Mister Schottle."

A paunchy man near the middle aisle rose and called: "Two hundred dollars!"

"I am bid two hundred dollars," Gardner intoned. "Two hundred dollars. Two hundred dollars. Two hundred dollars for twenty good acres. Are you all done?"

"No." Short John Clancy was standing on the left side of the tent, his buckaroos forming a tight knot behind him. "I bid one thousand dollars."

Murdo Morgan stepped away from the platform, confidence washing out of him. This was Broad Clancy's trick, and Cole and his bunch were here to see that it worked.

Silence gripped the crowd. One thousand dollars! Broad Clancy had that kind of money. None of the settlers did. Fear gripped them. Then bitterness. The things that Royce and Blazer had said were right. Clancy would use his money to secure title to the land he had used for years.

For that one short moment Morgan didn't know what to expect and he didn't know what to do. He took an uncertain step along the platform, hand on gun butt.

"Mister Clancy," he heard Gardner say, "isn't

that bid out of line with the value of the tract?"

"No!" Short John bawled. "It's got our house on it. I ain't sittin' here and lettin' a clod-buster named Hans Schottle have it!"

"You're mistaken, Mister Clancy," Gardner said. "Tract Number three thousand, nine hundred and fifty-six . . ."

Blazer was on his feet, bull voice roaring down Gardner's: "We told you boys what the company was! A thievin' bunch of coyotes!"

Royce jumped onto a bench and was shaking a fist at Gardner.

"Look at him! Fillin' his pockets with honest men's money like he always has. Fixed it with the Clancys so you boys won't get the good spots the cattlemen want. You're just farmers. The company and the Clancys are in together."

"What about it, Schottle?" Blazer bawled. "You goin' to stand for it?"

Morgan had started through the crowd toward Cole and his men, shoulder smashing a path, gun gripped in his right hand. He couldn't shoot in this packed mass, but if he could get to the men who were making the trouble, he would silence them.

"Sure we're in cahoots with the company!" Short John was yelling. "A pretty penny it cost us, too. You saw it was my sister who pulled Schottle's name out!"

There wasn't any sense in what Short John was

saying, but it wouldn't take sense to turn these men into a pack of howling wolves.

"I'll get a rope!" Blazer was yelling. "Swing 'em and let 'em dance!"

Gardner was trying to talk from the platform. The trustees were beside him, but their voices were lost in the rumble that rose from a thousand throats. Morgan got through the first two rows of men, and no farther. The settlers closed up into a solid wall and began pushing toward the platform.

Blazer and the Sneeds, with Cole and Royce behind them, were jamming their way to the end of the benches toward the canvas.

"Wait'll I get a rope!" Blazer was bellowing.

Morgan couldn't reach them. He was being pushed toward the platform, the distance between him and Cole steadily widening.

Through a sudden lull in the roar of the crowd Morgan heard Jewell's voice: "You were lying, Short John! Tell them you were lying."

Morgan looked back at the platform. Jewell was on the ground trying to reach Short John. As Morgan looked, she went down.

In that moment Murdo Morgan became a madman. He wheeled toward the platform, his gun barrel a terrible slashing club. Men spilled out of his way, cursing and crying out in agony. He was in the clear then.

Dalton had seen Jewell and was bellowing:

"Look out, you fools! You'll tromp the girl to death."

Morgan jumped to the platform and raced along it. Gardner and his office crew had picked up chairs and lined the edge of the platform to hold the settlers back, a thin line that would have broken under the mob's weight the minute it surged across the platform. Dalton and Frawley were fighting their way toward Jewell when Morgan took a long, flying leap into the crowd, the swinging gun barrel opening a path for him.

"Look out for the girl!" Dalton kept crying.

Something stopped the forward push of the crowd. Morgan never knew what it was. Dalton's voice or his own gun barrel or the fact that Blazer was not there to urge them on. The settlers stood motionless, bewildered, those in front of Jewell breaking away from her.

Then Morgan saw that Purdy was already there, with Jewell on the ground below him. The sheriff's face was battered, his nose was bleeding, his glasses had been torn from his eyes, but his gun barrel had been as formidable a weapon in his hands as Morgan's had been. Somehow, he had kept them away from Jewell.

"All right, all right!" Dalton and Frawley were shouting. "Sit down. We'll see if anything's wrong."

Slowly the crowd fell back. Men looked at each

other, not sure why they had done what they had. Morgan lifted Jewell's still form in his arms, his high-boned face squeezed by the passionate fury that was in him.

"I'm taking her to the doc!" he called. "If she isn't all right, I'm coming back. You and all the land in the world aren't worth her little finger!"

That finished it. Jewell's head rested against Morgan's chest, her face white, her wheat-gold hair cascading around her face. Shame was in them then. They sat down, the only sound in the big tent the shuffling of feet and squirming of bodies as they found their places on the benches.

"Clancy," Purdy said evenly, "you're under arrest for inciting a riot."

Morgan was striding down the middle aisle, carrying Jewell, when he heard Gardner call: "Clancy, tell these men you were lying when you said you were in cahoots with the company!"

"All right, I lied." Short John's voice was high-pitched and laden with fear. "We fixed it with Ed Cole for . . ."

That was all Morgan heard. He was out of the tent, running around the back of the store and across the street and along the front of the Silver Spur to Doc Velie's office. He kicked the door open, and Velie rushed out of the back.

"What the devil's going on?" he bawled. Then he saw Jewell. "Here Morgan," he said, "on this cot. What happened?"

Morgan told him while the doctor made his examination.

"No bones broken," Velie said then, "and I don't think she's hurt. I'd say she got cracked by somebody's fist and was knocked cold. You never know what happens in a mess like that."

"Do something!" Morgan cried. "Don't stand there like a fool!"

"All right," Velie said crustily. "I'll do something if you don't shut up. I'll hit you over the head and let you see how you come out of it."

Morgan subsided. He looked down at Jewell's white face, a great emptiness opening inside him. She was breathing softly and evenly. Then she stirred and her eyes came open.

"You're all right?" Morgan bent over her, hand touching her face. "You're all right?"

"I'm all right," she breathed. "Is it . . . ?"

"Everything's fine." Morgan choked and turned away. "Keep her there, Doc. She's not doing any more drawing."

The drum of running horses came to Morgan when he reached the street. He raced along the boardwalk to the Silver Spur. He saw them on the road to the north rim—five riders, with the dust rolling behind them. Ed Cole and his bunch, their horses on a dead run.

Morgan started toward the stable for his black and knew it would take too long. There were horses racked along the street. He had wheeled toward a buckskin when Purdy came around the store with Short John Clancy in front of him, a gun prodding his back.

Morgan's place was in town. This was what it would take to set old Broad off.

"You're raising old Nick," Morgan said, swinging in beside Purdy.

Purdy peered at him, pale eyes blinking. "I aim to," he said. "You know how close that was?"

"I know how close it was for Jewell," Morgan said bitterly. "You saved her life, Abel."

Purdy didn't say anything until the cell door was locked behind Short John. He fumbled in his desk until he found another pair of glasses and put them on. He sat down as if suddenly and terribly tired.

"Nobody needs to thank me for what I've done," he said then, "but I've been wanting to thank you. Broad Clancy didn't build his walls high enough. Time caught up with him. Nothing can stop the land sale now. Cole and Blazer and the rest came back with ropes, but they were mighty surprised when they looked into the tent. They turned around and vamoosed without a word."

Purdy wiped blood from his face and wadded up his handkerchief. "I was in torment when you came, Murdo. Lost my nerve. Sold out to Clancy like the rest of them, but the difference with me was that I knew better. Jewell and I used to talk about things before you came." Turning in his swivel chair, Purdy reached for his pipe. "I'll never be the same again. Neither will the valley. I wasn't proud of myself six months ago. I am now. I've quit telling myself I'm doing the only thing I could. Security!" He laughed shortly as he dribbled tobacco into his pipe. "It's a bad bargain when anybody sells out for something they think is security. Now you get over to the tent and stay in town. This ain't finished."

"What about the Turkey Track hands who were with Short John?"

"Rode out. Went to tell Broad how it went, I guess."

# XXII

Not fully understanding what had gone on inside Purdy, but feeling a little of the new pride that was in the man, Morgan walked back to the tent. Gardner was on the platform, talking in a low, tense voice, but it was so quiet that his words came clearly to Morgan in the back.

"That's the story of Josh Morgan and his boys who are buried at Jim Carrick's place. It's the story of what Murdo Morgan has tried to do for you, but that part of the story won't be finished until your hands are on the plow handles and you've turned the soil of this valley. You've repaid Morgan by suspicions and . . . Well, I don't need to tell you what you've done. If you'd boiled over this platform a while ago the way you intended, and messed up our records and maybe hanged Morgan and me, you'd have finished the land sale. That was what Ed Cole and Broad Clancy have been working for. They played it smart and took you for suckers. Now let's get one thing straight. What's it going to be from here on?"

Frawley faced Gardner.

"There will be no more trouble of our making, Mister Gardner," he said without hesitation. "Let's get on with the drawing."

"That's what I want to hear." Seeing Morgan in the back, Gardner called: "How's Miss Clancy?"

"Doc said she was knocked out. She'll be all right."

"Then we have something to be thankful for. Frawley, one of you trustees will have to draw in place of Miss Clancy."

"I will," Frawley said, and took the chair beside Peg.

"Clancy withdrew his bid on Tract Number three thousand, nine hundred and fifty-six," Gardner said. "Are you all done? Sold to Hans Schottle for the contract price of two hundred dollars. Schottle, come to the rear of the platform, pay the balance, and receive your papers. All right, Frawley."

215

Frawley lifted a piece of paper and read: "Joseph Ramsay."

Peg drew and called: "Tract Number eight hundred and ninety-nine . . . forty acres."

"Two hundred dollars!" a man in the back shouted.

"I am bid two hundred dollars for Tract Number eight hundred and ninety-nine," Gardner intoned. "Two hundred dollars. Two hundred dollars. Two hundred dollars for forty good acres. Are you all done? Sold for the contract price of two hundred dollars. Who is the buyer?"

"Joseph Ramsay."

"Come to the back of the platform and pay your balance and receive your papers. Next, Mister Frawley."

Morgan turned away. From now on it would go like clockwork. He walked back to Velie's office.

"She's all right," the medico said. "She went over to the hotel."

Morgan drifted aimlessly along the street, watching the clouds rush in from the southwest, smelling the pungent sage scent that was swept in by the damp breeze. It was raining now in the Sunsets and probably on west to the Cascades.

At noon Morgan met Peg and took her to dinner in the tent restaurant.

"Dalton took my place while I'm eating," she said.

"You don't need to go back. Not after what happened."

"I told you the platform was a good place to watch from." She spooned sugar into her coffee, her eyes not meeting Morgan's. "I'm glad it happened. I've got some things straight now. You see, I've never liked Jewell. She had the things I didn't, and they were the things I thought I wanted." She raised her gaze to Morgan's face. "Maybe I had more fun than Jewell did, but fun isn't so important. I could have gone to San Francisco with Cole. I took his money, but I robbed him because all the time I was loving you. It's all right, Murdo. I didn't get the winning hand, but I got a good one. I'll marry Buck. I'll make him happy, and I'll make Jim like me."

Purdy had said: *Time is a great sea washing in around us.* He might have added that it changed people as it washed in. These months since Morgan had returned to the valley had been violent ones, twisting and shaping and melting human souls in life's hot crucible, but no one had changed more than Peg Royce.

Looking at her now, Morgan felt an admiration for her he had never felt before. She was smiling as if pleased with herself and her life. She had no regrets.

"What happened to you?" Morgan asked.

"Two things," Peg answered. "I know Jewell

217

now, and I like her. I like courage in anybody, and she had all the courage in the world when she headed into that crowd."

"The other thing?"

"I saw your face when you crossed the platform to her. She's your final woman, Murdo. Don't let her go."

"Her father happens to be Broad Clancy," he said bitterly.

"You crazy fool! It doesn't make any difference who her father is if you love her."

Maybe he was a crazy fool, but it did make a difference. That was the way life had dealt the cards, and it was beyond his power to change the deal.

Morgan went back to the tent with Peg, watched the drawing, and drifted away. Finding Ed Cole was his job, and he didn't know where to look. The man wasn't finished. He wouldn't be finished until he was dead. Cole would find Clancy, and the Turkey Track man would throw his crew in with Cole's.

Putting himself in their position, it seemed to Morgan that the natural move for them to make would be to break Short John out of jail. Likely the next would be an attack on the settlers' camp. The situation had become critical for Clancy and Cole, and they were the kind of men who would make a desperate move now that failure had blocked their progress.

• • •

The drawing was closed at nine o'clock, the money locked in the safe of the Stockmen's Bank.

"They'll try the bank, Morgan," Gardner said. "If they can get your money, you can't pay the Citizens' Bank, and it will get the grant."

"By that time the land will be sold," Morgan said. "If that was Cole's idea, he'd wait till the finish, but we'll put the Carricks in the bank just to be sure."

Morgan cruised the street, tense, ears keening the night breeze for any sound that was wrong. He wanted to see Jewell, but he had kept away from her after she had gone to the hotel. If he saw her, he would tell her he loved her, and he shouldn't. Not yet. Not until it was finished. Perhaps he never could. Not if Broad Clancy died before his gun.

It was black dark now except for the transient veins of lightning that lashed the sky. Clouds had wrapped a thin moon and the stars in a thick covering. Thunder was an irregular rumble, growing louder with the passage of time. By midnight the settlers were asleep, their fires dull red eyes in the night.

Jim and Buck Carrick were guarding the bank. Purdy was awake in his office, an array of rifles and handguns on his desk. The waiting pressed Morgan, tightened his already taut nerves until every sound in the darkness made him jump, hand dropping to gun butt.

It was nearly dawn when Morgan stepped into Purdy's office.

"I'll be singing to myself if this doesn't crack," he growled. "And I don't sing worth a hoot."

Purdy leaned back in his chair, forehead worry-lined. "Why are you so sure they'll move in tonight?"

"I know Broad. Cole is the kind who might quit, but Broad won't. It's like Jewell says. It's all or nothing with him."

"But why tonight?"

Morgan jerked a thumb at the cell door. "There's your answer. Broad's got patience. He's let it play along, gambling that the ruckus at the drawing would do the job, but it didn't work. Now Short John's in the jug. That's too much for a Clancy."

Purdy nodded. "I told you this morning it was an interesting study. Do you know why that bunch didn't rush in like Cole and Clancy expected?"

"No. I've wondered about it all day. They acted like they were only half convinced."

"That's it. You swung 'em your way when you made your talk. They couldn't swing back fast enough. If Clancy and Cole could have pulled that off sooner, it would have been a different story."

"It was time we had luck." Morgan turned to the door. "I'm going to ride out to the camp. I should have told Dalton to put out a guard."

Morgan got his black from the stable and rode around the Silver Spur and past the haystacks to Dalton's wagon. The three trustees were crouched around the fire, and when Morgan rode up, they rose.

"Get down, Morgan," Frawley said. "I couldn't sleep, thinkin' about what happened when you started the drawin', so I got Jale and Clay out of bed. We'd like to make it up."

A gun cracked to the south. Then another. Men yelled and thunder rolled into the man-made racket. Morgan's head lifted. A new noise washed in on the night wind, a noise he had not heard for years. The rumble of many hoofs beating into the dirt.

"Stampede!" Morgan cried. "Get everybody out of bed."

He swung his black around the wagon and cracked the steel to him, fear for the settlers' safety freezing his insides. This was Broad Clancy's ace in the hole!

A sliver of pale sky showed where the clouds broke away from the moon. Then it closed and it was completely dark again and thunder came with gun-sharp nearness. It began to rain, great slapping threads that plopped into the earth. Lightning scorched the sky as Morgan swung

221

his black toward the leaders of the stampede.

He could not think or plan. He could only pray that he could turn the herd, for at such a time man is a puny thing, dependent for life on heaven above and the horse between his legs. Four thousand hoofs! A million pounds of bone and muscle and horns! A wave of destruction, sweeping toward the settlers' camp!

There were women and children, men who had followed a dream half the width of a continent, men who had committed no greater crime than to challenge Broad Clancy for the land he had used, land he did not own, land for which he had not even paid a paltry rent.

The last bit of restraint went out of Murdo Morgan. He'd had opportunities to kill Broad Clancy, and now he regretted those chances that had been lost. But he had never thought Clancy would become a wholesale killer. Yet Clancy must have planned this from the first, or he would not have brought a herd of this size to the valley from the summer range.

Morgan was in close now, the black's speed matching the speed of the steers. Morgan's gun bellowed, powder flame streaking into the night, the noise of the explosion lost in the thunder above and the thunder of hoofs beside him, the blazing ribbon lashing from gun muzzle no more than a match spark in a world lighted by crackling flashes above.

Pull trigger. Throw bullets into the lead animals. Load and shoot again until the gun is empty. Build a row of dead steers. Press and push and hope that the raging line of destruction can be turned away from the camp. Hope that the black will not find a hole and fall, for nothing but death awaited a rider who went down beneath those driving hoofs.

It was wild and primitive, a world without order, chaos that had broken its bonds, death rolling across an earth that trembled under those hoofs with only a single man to avert that fate.

Then the miracle! Other men rode out of the night. More guns to flash, more men to yell and strike with coiled ropes and press the end of that heaving black horde, more men to turn them into the empty land where they could run until they couldn't run, more men to bind and lash this chaos into order. There would be safety only when breath was gone and hearts could no longer pound movement into those lumbering bodies.

The pressure was enough. The line was turned, the direction changed. Not much, but enough. Away from the canvas-topped wagons, away from campfires that had been replenished with dry wood and raced upward into the rain with long sizzling banners of flame, away from the agonized cries of mortal terror as women and children tried to flee to safety.

The wagons flashed by. The town was behind.

Somewhere out there the steers would stop when they could go no farther.

Morgan reined away and stopped. He stepped down from his heaving horse and loaded his gun. Daylight was washing out across the valley now. It had not been long since the stampede had started, but each minute had been an eternity, minutes when hundreds of lives had depended upon every crawling second.

There was no direction to Murdo Morgan's thoughts as he stood there in the rain. Only a consciousness of guilt for letting Broad Clancy live, but Morgan would not be guilty much longer. Most of the riders were staying with the herd. They were not pressing the leaders, but had pulled away and slowed their mounts. Later the steers would be brought back, but two men had turned and were riding directly at Morgan.

For a time, Morgan thought the riders were Broad Clancy and Short John, but the light was thin in the misty air, and when they were close, he saw that they were not the Clancys. They reined up.

"Put up your gun, Morgan," one said. "You'll have no trouble with us."

"Where's Clancy?" Morgan asked.

"Short John's dead," the rider said—a Turkey Track rider, Morgan realized then. "Maybe Broad is by this time."

Morgan was silent for a moment, his mind gripping this and failing to understand it.

"What happened?" he asked.

"We broke Short John out of jail," the buckaroo said. "Purdy got tagged, but he'll live. We left town when we heard the stampede, and ran into Cole's bunch at the edge of the camp. Broad cussed Cole for startin' it, and Cole said they aimed to smash the nester camp. Broad called it killin' and pulled. Pete Royce got him. There was some shootin'. We got the Sneeds and one of 'em drilled Short John. Cole sloped out with Royce and Blazer. Broad told us to turn the stampede away from the camp."

# XIII

Rain was lashing Morgan's face as he stared at the men. Slowly his gun slid back into holster. It made less than sense, but the Turkey Track man was telling the truth. Morgan saw it in his face. There was no reason now for him to lie.

"We'll slope along," the rider said. "If we saw you, Broad wanted us to tell you. He's in town now, I reckon, if he ain't cashed in. A couple of the boys took him to the hotel."

"Thanks," Morgan said.

Mounting, he let the black take his own pace to town.

• • •

It was full daylight when Morgan reached Irish Bend. The storm was over except for a drizzle that was more mist than rain. He rode slowly along the street, saw Broad Clancy's chestnut racked in front of the hotel, and tied beside him.

There was a strange stillness upon the town. Morgan remembered the hot spring day when he had first returned to the valley, a day that now seemed years ago. There had been silence then, the hostile silence with which Broad Clancy's Irish Bend used to welcome strangers. This was different. It was a brooding silence, filled with human fears.

Morgan stepped through the mud to the wet walk and stood there a moment. The sun, low over the Hagerman Hills to the east, broke through the shifting clouds and gave a hard brightness to the street. Steam curled up from the soaked earth and roofs and boardwalks, and strong and pungent desert smells flowed around Morgan.

No one else was on the street. No horses were racked along it but the two in front of the hotel. A rooster crowed from somewhere back of Doc Velie's office, the shrill sound beating into the silence. Then the stillness was upon the town again. It was as if Nature, outraged for so long by the plots and counterplots of scheming selfish men, had decreed that this would be the end.

Morgan paced toward the bank and stopped. Peg Royce stepped out of the hotel.

"Murdo!" she called. "Come inside before they shoot you!"

He didn't move. "Where's Cole?" he asked.

"In the Elite. Blazer's with him. Royce is dead. Jim Carrick got him. Jim's hit, but he'll be all right."

The Elite was straight ahead, past the bank and across the side street. The minute Morgan rounded the front of the bank, they would cut him down. Still he waited, considering this.

"Where's Buck?" he asked.

"Still in the bank."

That would have been like Jim Carrick, to stay where he had been stationed until the danger was over. It wasn't Buck's way, and Morgan didn't like the idea of young Carrick being behind him, but it couldn't be helped. He started on. Peg ran after him and caught his arm.

"They'll kill you!"

He shook her off and kept on until he reached the corner. There he pressed against the bank wall and called: "Cole! Come out, or I'm coming after you!"

"Wait, Murdo." Peg stepped behind him and into the bank. "Buck, Morgan needs help."

There was no answer from inside the Elite. Morgan drew his gun and sent a shot through the side of the saloon.

"Come out, Cole! You, too, Blazer!"

Behind him, Buck Carrick laughed. "Why'n thunder should I help Morgan? You got things plumb wrong, Peg."

"I won't marry you unless you help him, Buck."

Morgan heard young Carrick's long breath. "You'll marry me if I help Morgan?"

"I promise."

"Don't, Peg!" Morgan said without turning. "I'll wait them out."

"Shut up, Morgan," Buck snarled. "I'll make my own bargain. Peg, I thought you loved Morgan."

"Not any more. Buck, you'll never regret it. I promise. Jim won't either."

"Don't, Peg!" Morgan cried out. "Don't throw yourself away on a man you don't love." Then he lunged across the street, gun in his hand. He was in the open, mud sloshing under his boots. He was across to the other walk then, and Blazer and Cole were stumbling through the door. Morgan didn't understand it. He fired once. Blazer's gun was lifted, but the hammer didn't fall. He bent with Morgan's bullet in his stomach. He swayed uncertainly, hanging to life with grim tenacity, then the last of his life went into the trigger pull, his shot spilling wildly across the street.

Ed Cole was jerking frantically at his gun. It came out from under his coat, pathetically slow, for this was not his game and he was scared. He had depended on Arch Blazer, and the big man had failed him. There was no guile now in his blue eyes or on his handsome face. There was a wolfish rage in him, and the fear of a wolf that had been separated from his pack and can run no longer.

Morgan's gun was lined on Cole, finger slack against the trigger. Thoughts slid through his mind, thoughts of this man he had called friend, thoughts of the past when they had fought side by side, of his visit to Cole's San Francisco office and the loan Cole had obtained for him.

"Shoot him!" Peg screamed. "There's nothing worth saving in him!"

Cole's gun was in his hand now. Morgan thought of the stampede, of the women and children in the settlers' camp. He had seen stampedes. He had seen the bloody shapeless things that had been men before they had gone down under thundering hoofs.

It was enough. He pulled trigger, felt the breath of Cole's bullet on his cheek. Then Cole dropped his gun, hands gripping his shirt front. He wanted to say something. His lips framed a word but the sound that came from his throat was not a word. The agony of death was in his face and shock and disbelief as if he had been sure through all of it that he would never be brought to this place. He fell across the walk and his blood made a dark pattern on the wet boards.

Then Morgan understood. Dalton and Frawley and Gardner and a dozen settlers boiled through the door to form a circle around the bodies.

"We were forted up behind the saloon," Dalton said, "waiting for some more of the boys. Then we saw you cross the street and knew we had to do somethin', so we broke in through the back door." He scratched his chin, staring down at Cole. "Queer, ain't it? Both him and Clancy had all they needed, but it wasn't enough. Now they've got nothin'."

"Why did Cole stop to fight?" Morgan asked.

"He couldn't get away," Frawley answered. "Royce got hit when they tangled with Clancy's bunch, and they brought him to the doc. Jim Carrick blowed Royce's brains out and we circled the town. Cole and Blazer holed up in here."

Perhaps it was that way, but Morgan knew how it was with a man after he had schemed and failed and run. Any man can run so long. Then he can't run. It had to be ended, one way or the other, and Ed Cole had died like a man.

"Thanks," Morgan said.

He put his gun back in his holster, suddenly tired and sleepy and a little bitter. These men didn't understand. They never would. Not until this morning had they tried to fight, but fighting was what he was made for. There would always be the little men who needed their fighting done for them. That was the way the world moved forward. Only now and then would he find a Jim Carrick or an Abel Purdy who had within his soul the courage to stand and fight.

"Why," Frawley said, pleased, "I guess you've got no reason to be thankin' us. Not after what you done."

"We'll get the drawing started, Morgan," Gardner said.

It didn't seem very important to Morgan then. The important part had been done.

"Take care of them," he said, nodding at the bodies, and turned away.

Buck Carrick was standing in front of the bank, his arm around Peg.

When Morgan crossed the street to them, Buck tried desperately to hold his dignity.

"Why didn't you wait, Morgan? I'd have given you a hand."

"I do my own snake stomping," Morgan said. He stared at Jim Carrick's son who had hated him since that night at the Smith shack. Now Morgan felt sorry for Peg, he felt sorry for Jim. "She's got no call to marry you, Buck, if she doesn't love you. She deserves something better."

"Now hold on . . . ," Buck began.

"I had some things wrong," Peg broke in. She stood tall and straight, as cool and beautiful as carved ivory. "I lost my head about you, Murdo. Let's forget that. It was different this morning. I helped you because I wanted Buck to own the land he lived on, the land I'm going to live on." She smiled, but it was not the confident smile Morgan had seen on her lips before. "Broad died a little bit ago. Jewell will want to see you."

Morgan, looking closely at Peg, knew it was all right with her. Yesterday she had said she would make Buck happy and she would make Jim like her. She had meant it then and she meant what she said now.

He went on, the desire to sleep a million years pressing him, but he couldn't sleep yet. Jewell wanted to see him. Funny, the way it had gone. All the time he had thought he would have to kill Broad Clancy. Then Jewell would be beyond his reach, for that was a thing even love could not bridge. But Clancy had died before the guns of Ed Cole and his men.

He was in the hotel lobby then and Jewell was behind the desk as she had been that first day he had seen her. He paused and looked at her and thought of the things he had noticed then—of the eagerness in her blue eyes, her quick-smiling lips, her throaty laugh. But nobody had laughed much lately in Paradise Valley. The years ahead would be different. He might do some laughing himself.

"Dad's dead," she said. "Everything he had wanted was gone, but he said to tell you he didn't hate you. He hoped you didn't hate him. He brought that herd down to run through the big tent if everything else failed. He would have burned the town and your records and he aimed to kill you and Gardner, but he couldn't stand for Cole stampeding the cattle into the camp. He said he had never fought women and children. He was honest in what he believed. You believe that, don't you, Murdo? Can you forgive him for what happened to your father and your brothers?"

"I didn't come back to get square, Jewell."

She hadn't been crying, but now there were tears in her eyes. She rubbed them away.

"I know, Murdo," she said a little angrily, "and I'm not crying for him. I'm crying because of what he might have been, and what he might have done. I think he saw it himself that last minute. He said he had lost Rip. He had lost me. Then he made Short John come to the drawing to do what Rip would have done if he had been alive, and he lost Short John. He didn't care if he lived or died. It was too late."

Morgan thought briefly of his own father who had dreamed his dreams to the last. He thought of Abel Purdy who had said that time was a great sea washing around them. Now everything was different. He looked at this girl who had missed so much of the goodness of life.

"It's not too late," he said.

"What will you do now?" she asked.

"I kept back a piece of the butte land south of the valley. We could homestead the quarters between my land so we'd have patent to enough to know we could hang on no matter what happens. Seems like this valley has got a big chunk of me. I'd like to stay here. Would you?"

"Yes, Murdo. That's what I'd like to do."

He came to her and she moved away from the desk to meet him. He kissed her and her lips were warm and rich. She had never given the fullness of her love to anyone, but she gave it now, and Morgan, holding her in his arms, had a brief glimpse of the years ahead. They were inviting years, as winey and head-stirring as the cool thin air of the valley.

She pulled her lips away and clung to him, her body hard against his, and in all the changes that the great sea washing in around them had brought, none was as fine as this.

# THE FENCE

# I

Jim Hallet could look back upon a series of decisions, bitter, sometimes brutal decisions, which had influenced the course of his life, all of them building toward the stand he must take that day. Now, his hard-muscled back pressed against the doorjamb of the sheriff's door, the hot summer sun winking back from his star, he watched the Wyatts approach town, thinking of what he would say to Boone Wyatt. He had made his decision after a worried sleepless week, knowing what it would cost him, and knowing he could not change it.

There was no other family like the Wyatts in the Stillwater country, nor, for that matter, in all of eastern Oregon. White-haired, old Latigo Wyatt, as slim and arrow-straight at seventy as he had been at twenty, always rode in front with his granddaughter, Kitsie, when they came to town. Latigo's son Boone, Kitsie's father, forked a roan behind him, Kitsie's twin brother Stub at his side. They were the Wyatts, the royal family of the valley, proud of their name, their wealth, and of Wagon Wheel, the biggest spread in that corner of the state. All of them were certain of their high destiny, and all but Kitsie intolerant of opposition.

Gramp Tatum, younger than Latigo and looking ten years older, lurched along the path from his shack in the sagebrush west of town, reached the boardwalk, and stumbled toward Jim's office. He sat down in the doorway as if the last of his strength had seeped out of him. He said: "I sure need an eye-opener, son. Can't seem to get waked up this morning."

Usually Hallet sent the old man on about his business which was mooching drinks in the Bonanza saloon, but today was Saturday and Gramp's luck hadn't been good lately. "Go get your eyes opened," Jim said, dropping a dollar on the walk in front of the old man.

Gramp picked it up and slid it into his pocket. He muttered—"Thanks, son."—but he didn't stir. His eyes were on the dust cloud to the south. He said with deep sourness: "There they come just like they've been coming for twenty years. You could set your watch by 'em. Ten o'clock every Saturday morning, and for why? Just so folks will bow and scrape in front of 'em. Sure makes Latigo feel good."

Jim said nothing. He wished Gramp would move on. He had no sympathy for the old man. Gramp had made his decision years before when he had refused to fight back. Latigo had stomped on him and broken him and beaten the pride out of him. It was Latigo's way with any man who stood in front of him, but some had fought and died. That, to Jim's way of thinking, was better than crawling, belly-down, through the dust. For the third time that morning he lifted his gun and checked it and slid it back into his holster. He would not surrender, even for Kitsie.

"Yeah, bow and scrape and forget you was ever two-legged and walked like a man," Gramp said with more violence of feeling than Jim thought was in him. "That's what I've been doing every Saturday just to get a damned lousy drink out of Latigo or Boone."

Then the old man did a surprising thing. He brought an ancient cap-and-ball revolver out from under his ragged coat, fondled it for a moment as a small girl might fondle her favorite doll, and put it back. He looked up at Jim, lips pulled away from toothless gums in a wicked smile. He said without the slightest trace of braggadocio: "Someday I'm gonna kill that old rooster."

"They hang old men for murder," Jim said.

Gramp got up, faded eyes staring at Jim from under hooded brows as if arguing the sheriff's intent. He was as sober as Jim had ever seen him. "Here's one old man they'd never convict of murder," he said. "I ain't sure it'd be murder salivating a Wyatt nohow."

Gramp lurched on toward the Bonanza in his peculiar stilt-like walk, rheumatism and whiskey having combined long ago to stiffen his legs. Jim watched him until he disappeared into the saloon, wondering if his unexpected threat of violence was perhaps symbolic of what lay ahead.

Jim was still there in the doorway when the Wyatts reached town and turned eastward along Main Street.

Latigo nodded and called courteously: " 'Morning, Jim."

" 'Morning, Latigo," Jim said, and lifted his Stetson. " 'Morning, Kitsie."

She smiled in a cool, impersonal way, saying: "How are you, Jim?" Neither of them thought that Latigo or her father, Boone Wyatt, guessed their feeling for each other. The four of them rode on to rein up in front of the bank and rack their horses. Boone and young Stub had not even glanced at Jim. There was an understandable pride in Latigo that was never offensive. In his son and grandson, it became snobbish arrogance. They might have spoken condescendingly to Jim if he had spoken first, something Jim would never do.

Still watching, Jim saw Latigo go into the bank where he would have a long conference with Zane Biddle. They would decide, Jim thought with biting sourness, which of the Poverty Flat ranchers would lose their spreads and which one Biddle would let go another year. Latigo would do the deciding, and he would reach his decision on the basis of how each one of the Poverty Flat boys had treated him.

Kitsie went into the Mercantile where she would examine the new dress goods that had come in. Later, she would drop over to Nell Craft's place. Nell made her dresses, and her kitchen was the one sanctuary where Kitsie and Jim could meet.

Stub went into the Bonanza where he would drink too much. Then he'd get into a poker game and lose anything from $50 to $1,000 to Chris Vinton, the only Poverty Flat rancher who consistently paid his interest at the bank when it was due. Usually Boone trailed along with his son, obligingly paying his losses when the game folded.

It was Boone's habit, while young Stub was throwing good money away over the green-topped table, to spend his time at the bar, drinking sparingly and basking in the respect given him by the Poverty Flat boys. But today Boone did not follow Stub into the Bonanza. Instead he came directly toward Jim, a scowl lining his face, thick legs driving hard against the boards of the walk in sharp, echoing cracks.

Latigo Wyatt, for all of his pride and restlessness, was a likable man, but Jim found nothing likable in Boone. He was in his middle forties, heavy-shouldered and bull-necked, and anything but constant yessing brought his temper to an instant boil. He had spoiled Stub, had tried to make a boy out of Kitsie, and, failing, piled dislike upon her, except when Latigo was around. Kitsie, in manners and disposition, was a throwback to her grandfather with none of Boone's truculence in her.

Jim stepped out of his office and strode toward Boone, knowing that this was the moment in which he must take his stand. A year ago, he had been riding for Wagon Wheel when the sheriff, Bill Riley, had been killed by a dry-gulcher's bullet. Latigo had secured Jim's appointment, and everybody, except Jim himself, conceded that he was a Wyatt man, a mistake he had found no occasion to correct until today.

Boone was ten feet away from Jim when he bawled: "What kind of a damned ninny of a sheriff are you, Hallet?"

Boone Wyatt bullied everybody except his father who he feared and his son who he pampered. Others took it, the Poverty Flat cowmen. Zane Biddle, and the rest. Even Jim had taken it because of Kitsie, but all the Stillwater folks had been pushed nearly as far as they could be pushed and Jim was quite a bit ahead of the others.

"I'm a good sheriff," Jim said clearly, spacing his words so that each hit Boone Wyatt like the slap of an open palm. "What kind of a damned cheap thief are you, Wyatt?"

They had stopped a pace apart, and for an instant Boone looked as if he had ceased breathing. He stood spread-legged, head tipped forward, his face as set and hard as if it had been worked out of granite. Morning sunlight beat upon it, and in that sharp unrelenting light Jim saw doubt flow across the full-jowled face, saw arrogance wash out of him. It was, Jim thought, the first time since Latigo Wyatt had brought his herd and family north from California a generation before that a Wyatt had been talked to like that.

There was this moment of silence between them while Boone made up his mind. It was not fear that troubled the man, Jim saw. It was a case of battered pride, of mental struggle while Boone decided upon the best way of holding his shattered dignity, and Jim knew that regardless of what happened to them, he would receive from this moment the full force of Boone Wyatt's soul-deep hatred.

"Reckon I didn't hear right," Boone said.

"You heard. Or maybe you want me to repeat it."

"Once was one time too many. Write out your resignation, Hallet. We'll have no sheriff in office who tries to cover his incompetence with insults."

"I won't do that until the county court asks me for my resignation," Jim said flatly. "You can get them to call a special meeting. Maybe they'll fire me, but if you call that meeting, I'll tell them what you tried to do to Ernie Craft. I'll write the story and take it to the newspaper. I'll send it out to the Portland dailies. I'm calling the Wyatt hand, Boone. What are you going to do about it?"

Fury grew in Boone Wyatt, the kind of fury that insulted dignity raises in a man. It showed in the squeezing together of his meaty lips, the corded jaw muscles, the beat of his temple pulse. For a moment Jim was afraid that he had gone too far, that Boone would draw his gun. Then Boone shrugged casually as if the affair was of no importance.

He said: "Why should I do anything, Hallet? I get madder'n hell when a fly buzzes in my ear, but I never heard of a fly hurting a man."

Boone swung on his heel and strode along the boardwalk to the Bonanza. Jim, staring after the man, felt doubt stir in him. He had declared his independence. He had protected Ernie Craft against a phony rustling charge, something Bill Riley would not have done. Riley had been a Wyatt man. When Latigo or Boone wanted a settler moved away from the edge of Wagon Wheel range, Riley could always find a way if the banker could not. Now the Wyatts knew how Jim Hallet stood, and the answer to what they were going to do would not be long in coming.

The sheriff loitered in front of Hoke Foster's saddlery, rolling a smoke and lighting it, letting his presence show his defiance to Wyatt rule. He saw Kitsie leave the Mercantile and walk around the corner. She would go, he knew, to Nell Craft's house, and impatience tightened his nerves.

Jim smoked his cigarette, tossed it into the dust, and crossed to the hotel. Again he paused, gaze raking the street. Boone had disappeared into the Bonanza. Stub was still inside, and Latigo had not come out of the bank. Usually Jim waited an hour or more before he followed Kitsie to Nell's house, but he didn't wait today. He had made his decision. Kitsie must make hers.

He paced along the boardwalk, turned the corner, and went directly to Nell's house. It was a white cottage set behind a picket fence, the yard in lawn, a tall row of red hollyhocks along the front, the only house in town that showed pride of ownership.

# II

He pulled the bell cord and waited. A moment later he heard Nell's quick steps. She opened the door, stepping aside and saying: "Jim, you're early." She was a small brown-eyed woman, almost forty, who had somehow missed marrying in a land where women could take their pick, but although she disdained romance for herself, she did all she could to further Kitsie's.

Jim followed Nell into the kitchen, doubt

crowding him again. He stood in the doorway looking at Kitsie. Stetson in his hand, a tall slender man with a strong chin, a thin beaky nose, and smoky-gray eyes that said things to Kitsie he could not put into words. Kitsie, turning from the sink where she was peeling potatoes, smiled to tell him she understood.

"Aren't you running a big risk coming here so soon?" Kitsie asked. "And through the front door?"

"I aimed to run a risk," he said with unusual violence.

She put down her knife and gave him a straight look. Jim took a long breath. No matter what she said or did, or what the rest of the Wyatts did, he would never stop loving her. She was twenty-four years younger than he was, a tall, high-breasted girl with blue eyes and red-gold hair that reminded him of a sunset behind a field of ripe wheat, and full lips that were quick to smile but now had been turned sober by his tone.

She came to him, asking: "What is it, Jim?"

"It's got to be one way or the other," he said more roughly than he intended. "Seeing you for an hour once a week in Nell's kitchen isn't enough. Pussyfooting in and out so nobody will know I've seen you isn't any way for a man in love to do."

"But there isn't any other way, Jim. Not now."

"Yes, there is."

"What?"

He pulled her to him, knowing that his hands were as rough as his words, but still unable to help it. He said: "I've loved you since the day I rode into Wagon Wheel and asked Latigo for a job. You were standing under them poplars, your hat hanging back of your head, and I looked at you and knew I wasn't going anywhere else. Not unless you went along."

"I guess I loved you then, too, Jim," she breathed. "We didn't need any more hands. If I hadn't asked Granddad to hire you, he'd have sent you on."

"Then if you love me, you'll marry me," he said.

"When?"

"Today."

"Today?"

Her eyes widened as she looked at him. He felt the pressure of her breasts against him, smelled the fragrance of her hair, and he was stirred as he was always stirred by her nearness. The need of her was pressing him and adding to the violence that was in him, but he could not turn back. This was decision day. He would not be a slave to Wyatt pride and greed, even for the girl he loved.

Kitsie drew away from him and walked to the window. She stood there, staring at the zinnias Nell had planted along the base of the house. She said, without turning: "You know we can't, Jim. What's happened?"

"I just told your dad what I thought of him for trying to frame Ernie Craft for rustling," he said. "From now on it'll be me against the Wyatts. I've got to know where you stand."

She whirled to face him, suddenly and terribly angry. "Jim, are you crazy? My father wouldn't frame Ernie Craft for rustling."

"You think I'm lying?"

"I think you're mistaken."

"No." He told her what had happened between him and her father. Then he said: "When I was buckarooing for Wagon Wheel, I knew Latigo and your dad would get Bill Riley to give any-body a kick who settled within shooting distance of Wagon Wheel range, but it wasn't any of my business. Now that I'm wearing the star, it is."

Her tanned face had gone white; her mouth was pressed so tightly that it was a long-lipped line. Utterly miserable, she said: "But why would Dad want to get rid of Ernie Craft? He never bothered anybody."

Jim shrugged. "He claims the settlers eat Wagon Wheel beef."

She threw out her hands in a gesture of disbelief. "It doesn't make sense, Jim. There is only a handful of settlers, and we've got a lot of cows."

"There'd be more settlers if Latigo and Boone hadn't kept pushing," Jim reminded her.

She nodded reluctant agreement. She had, he thought, known it all the time, but she had kept her eyes closed to it, and it worried and bothered her. The things Wagon Wheel did were not governed by limits of justice and moral right. The only consideration was how far the Wyatts could go without inviting the Poverty Flat cowmen to strike back, and Jim had often thought that if Boone Wyatt ever dictated Wagon Wheel policies, even that would not be a limiting factor.

"I can't marry you today, Jim," she said finally. "You know that."

"Why?"

"A girl can't just get married any day her man says so. There's things to do."

"Like what?"

"A wedding cake to be baked," she said defiantly. "And I'd have to get Nell to make a dress."

He wiped her objections away with a sweep of his hand. "It's you and me that's important, Kitsie. Not cakes and dresses." He swallowed and forced himself to say: "And it ain't the Wyatt men and it ain't Wagon Wheel. That's what you've got to decide. It's whether our love is as important to you as a ranch that's become a god to the Wyatt men."

She stood straight and tall beside the window,

hands clenched at her sides, knuckles white with tension. "You can't say that," she cried. "It isn't true. You have no right to doubt my love, but how can I marry you after what you said to Dad?"

"How could I marry you if I got on my knees to him like the other men in the valley do?" Jim demanded. "Chris Vinton is crazy about you. He'd bow and scrape to get a chance at part of Wagon Wheel. So would Zane Biddle. Your dad would like Biddle for a son-in-law. A banker who's taken orders from Latigo ever since he opened his bank. Do you want a man like that?"

"No, but I don't want a man who calls my father a cheap thief."

"All right. Maybe I said too much, but that isn't the point now." He came to her and took her hands. "Look, Kitsie. We've both been cowards, and it's gone against the grain all the time. Sneaking in here to see each other. Afraid to tell Latigo or Boone how we felt. Trying to be satisfied with a kiss and one hour a week with you. If you love me you wouldn't ask me to wait. We've waited and waited and kept on waiting. For what?"

"For something to change," she whispered.

He laughed, a hoarse, humorless sound signaling the misery that was in him. "You think your dad will ever change? Or Latigo? The only thing that would change them would be for me to come up with a million dollars and I never will. So what'll happen? We'll put it off and off until you get tired waiting and you'll marry Zane Biddle, which same is what your dad wants."

"But not Granddad. He wants me to be happy. Oh, Jim, we've got to keep on waiting and having faith. Something will happen."

Something would happen, but it wouldn't be what they'd want. He was certain of it. He couldn't tell her why. It was a feeling that had been in him from the moment Boone Wyatt had walked along the street toward him that morning.

He put his arms around her and held her hard against his body. He felt her softness and her strength. "We can't Kitsie. It's your family or me. There's a fence between us. Which side are you going to be on?"

She stared up at him a moment, suddenly angry. "If there is a fence, you built it," she cried. "Let me go."

But he didn't let her go until he had kissed her. She stiffened and tried to break free and her fists beat against him.

Then, as she had that first time he had kissed her when he had been riding for Wagon Wheel less than a week, she went slack, her arms coming around his neck, her body molding to him. There was this moment when she could not get enough of him and she could not give him enough, a moment when the rest of the world faded into nothing and there were just the two of them. It was passion, mad and wild and crazy, but so real that there was no doubting what was in her heart.

Then Nell Craft's cough broke dimly into their consciousness. He let Kitsie go, anger stirring him. Nell had never done anything like this. She stayed out of the kitchen as long as Jim and Kitsie were together. But now when Jim looked at her, his anger melted, for he always held a pity for her. She was a hungry-faced woman whose eyes held a lingering ghost of a long-dead past.

"Excuse me," Nell said, "but I wanted to tell you something, Kitsie. Don't let your grand-father's or your father's notions make you lose the only thing in life that is worthwhile."

"I don't understand," Kitsie said.

"You will after it's too late. And don't doubt what Jim said about your father trying to frame Ernie for rustling. I was home last Sunday when Jim came out. He found the hide where your father said it would be."

# III

The doorbell gave out its metallic jangle. Some-one was pulling the cord repeatedly and angrily. Nell moved across the kitchen to the door that opened into her living room, her thin face hard-set by the worry that gripped her.

"You won't keep your secret now unless Jim wants to hide," Nell said, "and I don't think he will. Your father and your brother are outside."

For a moment Jim forgot to breathe. He looked at Kitsie. He heard Nell close the door, heard her cross the living room. He saw fear squeeze Kitsie's face, saw the beat of her throat pulse, and knew that the same thought was in her mind that was in his. If he killed her father and brother, their last chance for happiness would be gone.

"Why don't you hide?" she whispered. "Or go out through the back?"

"We'll face it," he said harshly.

Boone Wyatt's loud insistent voice came to Jim. He heard Nell arguing. Then the stomp of booted feet as the Wyatts crossed the front room, the jingle of spurs, and he opened the door before Boone reached it.

Jim said coldly: "Looking for someone, Boone?"

Wyatt stopped abruptly, surprised, and Stub, a step behind him, said: "Well, I'll be damned. Looks like Gramp gave you the right hunch."

"Get out, Hallet," Boone said thickly. "Kitsie, it's been a long time since I took a blacksnake to you."

"And you'll be dead a long time if you do now," Jim said in cold fury. "If you didn't get me straight a while ago, Boone, you'd better get it this time. You Wyatts figure you run the valley. Maybe so, but you sure as hell don't run the sheriff's office, and you don't run me."

"He talks tough," Stub breathed, his hostile intent plain to read.

He was slender like his grandfather with Latigo's fine handsome features, but he had been pampered by Boone until his sense of reality was completely distorted. Now, just a little drunk, he was bound to push until he had trouble.

Jim stepped through the door, pausing when he was a pace from Stub. He said: "Boone, since we're facing our cards, we might as well do a finish job. Kitsie and I are in love. We're asking your permission to get married."

"Married?" Stub howled. "So that's it. Well, maybe it's time."

There was no mistaking the boy's insulting meaning. Jim took one quick step, grabbed Stub's shirt with his left hand, and jerked young Wyatt toward him. "Back up, kid."

"Back up, nothing!" Stub bawled his defiance. "A two-bit sheriff don't marry no Wyatt. Kitsie knows that. She's just playing with you. She'll marry Zane Biddle."

"That's right," Boone said with biting triumph. "Just on the off chance she ain't playing with you, you'd both better know that if she marries you, all of Wagon Wheel goes to Stub. She'll starve on your wages, Hallet."

Stub laughed in Jim's face. "She ain't used to starving, tin star."

Jim released his grip on Stub and wheeled to face Kitsie. "Tell them. You're almost twenty-one."

"Old enough to have some sense," Boone flung at her. "Better know what you are, Sis. If it's the wrong thing, Hallet will be dead by night."

"That wasn't necessary, Dad." Moving around Jim, Kitsie came to stand beside Stub. "You were right. I was just playing with him."

"Oh, Kitsie," Nell cried. "You fool!"

"Shut up." Boone wheeled on Nell, triumph working through him like a drink of whiskey. "You tell your mule-headed dad to get out of the county. There's other ways of working on him if the sheriff don't want the job." Boone strode to the front door. "Come on."

Without a word or a glance at Jim, Kitsie followed her father out of the house. Stub lingered long enough to prod Jim with a grin, his flushed face alive with malice. "Wyatts take their fun where they find it, mister. Even the women." Still grinning, he followed his father and Kitsie out of the house.

Jim stood motionless, staring at the door Stub had slammed shut. It was as if a light had gone out in the room, as if there were no hope anywhere, for life had tricked him with a gaudy promise that it had never meant to keep.

He moved toward the door, stiff-legged, thinking that the smart thing would be to ride out of town and keep riding. He owed the county nothing. He had been a drifter from the time he'd been a kid until he had stopped to ride for Wagon Wheel, and the only reason he had stopped then was because Kitsie's red-lipped smile had warmed him with its promise. Yet, now that he faced this decision, he knew he would stay. His stubborn pride would hold him.

He opened the door, and then turned to look at Nell. "Thanks for trying. Tell Ernie not to budge unless he's scared."

"He's not scared. He'd rather die there than let the Wyatts run him off. He said he didn't think there was a man in the county strong enough to stand against the Wyatts like you have."

Jim grinned thinly. "My hide won't turn a bullet. When Latigo's out of the way, Boone will bring his outfit into town and fix me good."

He moved through the door, pausing when Nell said: "She loves you, Jim. Don't do anything foolish."

"She's sure got a funny way of showing it," he said, and went on into the hot sunshine.

He moved mechanically to Main Street, trying to tell himself that Kitsie had done what she had to do and what he had expected her to do, and at the same time knowing in his heart that she shouldn't have done it. He had thought she possessed strength enough to stay with him. She didn't love Chris Vinton or Zane Biddle or any of the rest who had courted her. She had reason to hate her father, and he knew she had only contempt for her brother. That left Latigo, and, like any drowning man reaching for a wild hope, Jim saw in the elder Wyatt a slim chance of turning Kitsie back to him.

Reaching the corner of the Mercantile, Jim paused, looking at the bank and wondering if Latigo was still there. He decided that the old man had had time to finish his palaver with Zane Biddle and moved on toward the Bonanza. It was then that he noticed the long string of horses racked in front of the saloon. Again, that strange monitor in the back of his mind jangled its warning bell. There were always a few Poverty Flat cowmen in town on Saturday mornings, but this was too many. Without counting the horses, he judged that every rancher on the flat was in the Bonanza.

Jim swung across the street, reaching into his mind for an explanation and finding none. He shouldered through the batwings, and stopped, for the dozen men at the bar swung away from it to stare sourly at him, their hostility a pushing force laid against him.

There was a short moment of silence. Then Chris Vinton said: "We don't want no Wyatt hands in here, Hallet. You'd better git."

This was trouble. Jim read it in their faces, in their stiff unnatural postures. To back up now under Vinton's threat would be a fatal mistake. Striding to the bar, he said: "Whiskey." Then he turned to Vinton, smoky-gray eyes locking with the other's green ones.

Vinton was close to thirty, Jim judged, a barren-faced man who courted Kitsie with grim persistence and weekly beat young Stub at poker. He had a ten-cow spread in the poorest part of the flat, was seldom home, and made his brag that he was the fastest man with a gun on the Stillwater. Jim guessed that he might be, for he wore his gun low and tied down as a professional would.

There was always a smoldering bitterness in Vinton's eyes as if he were looking for a fight. Jim, raw temper making him as proddy as Vinton, said in a flat tone: "Get this through your thick head, Chris. I'm not a Wyatt man. As long as I'm sheriff, I'll enforce the law, which same won't be Wyatt law and it won't be Poverty Flat law."

Vinton laughed. "You're a liar, Hallet, and a crook to boot."

Jim stepped away from the bar. "You want us to think you're a pretty tough hand, don't you, Chris? All right, we'll see how much of your talk is wind."

They might have set it up to go that far and no farther, hoping to break him under the weight of their bluff. Jim was never sure. In any case, that was as far as it went, for Vinton did not draw, and the rest of them moved along the bar, Buck

258

Deeter saying: "No cause for a ruckus, Jim. Chris, shut your tater-trap."

Deeter owned the Staircase, the biggest spread on the flat, and was a man Latigo considered important enough to be elected county commissioner, although he had not been in the valley long. He was tall and swarthy with strong white teeth and dark eyes that liked to laugh. A good man, Jim thought, and a level-headed one.

Not trusting Vinton, Jim said: "All right, Buck, but there is a place where a sheriff stops being a sheriff and starts looking after his own end. That time comes when a cheap-talking tinhorn calls him a liar and a crook." He watched them closely, right hand near gun butt, left hand on the bar beside his drink. "You're all proddy as hell. What's biting you?"

Even Lippy Ord, usually grinning and wanting to talk, was sourly sober. He said: "The Wyatts, Jim. You back up, you bow and kowtow to 'em, and after a while you see you've either got to quit calling yourself a man or do something about it. We're aiming to do it today."

Old Gramp Tatum lurched along the bar. "That'sh right, Lippy ole shon. Shoot 'em dead."

Somebody laughed, a high shrill laugh that was more of a release for taut nerves than an expression of humor.

Deeter said: "This ain't a question of law, Jim. You'd best stay out."

"Maybe he's aiming to look out for the Wyatts," Vinton sneered.

Too much had happened this day. Jim shoved Lippy Ord aside, the last shred of his self-control breaking, and drove a fist against Vinton's mouth. Men tumbled away. Gramp Tatum sprawled on the floor. Vinton stumbled over him, took another blow on the side of the head, and fell full out.

"Wait . . . ," Deeter began.

"Let 'em alone," Lippy Ord cut in. "Chris has been spoiling for a fight. Maybe he'll get enough."

Vinton rolled and came to his feet, cursing and spitting blood and teeth. He drove at Jim, fists swinging in round aimless blows. Jim moved in close and hit him in the stomach. Vinton snapped a fist into Jim's face; he felt the shock of it and tasted his own blood. Vinton got his arms around him, hung there, and tried to knee him. Turning, Jim took the blow on his hip, battered Vinton in the ribs, but still Vinton clung to him.

For a moment, they danced away from the bar toward the poker tables, Vinton's arms around him, chin hooked over his shoulder, squeezing and trying to bring Jim to the floor. They slammed into a poker table and overturned it, cards and chips cascading to the floor. They stumbled on to the opposite wall and fell against it, Vinton releasing his grip.

Jim's knees slid out from under him and he

went down. Vinton tried to fall on him, knees aimed at his ribs, but Jim rolled clear and came to his feet. Vinton struggled up, crazy with frustration, and lunged at Jim. It was a wild reckless attack without a thought of defense, the kind of attack that only a furious man driven by a goading sense of futility would make. Jim swung aside and chopped him down with a single sharp-cracking fist to his jaw. Vinton fell, belly down, and lay still.

# IV

Jim stepped away, rubbing his knuckles and opening and fisting his right hand, a sense of having done a foolish thing rushing through him. This was a poor time to risk a broken hand. He looked at them, Lippy Ord and Buck Deeter and the rest of them, gauging their temper and letting them feel the weight of his anger.

He said: "Let's have it. What got you boys on the prod?"

All of them stirred uneasily, eyes dropping, and he saw that they were changing their estimate of him. Deeter, turning his back to the bar, poured a drink as he said: "You're the law, Jim. Stay out of it until a crime has been committed."

Jim stooped, and jerking Vinton's gun from holster, slid it into his waistband. He straightened, gaze again running along the line of men. He said with blunt directness: "Bill Riley was a Wyatt man. We all know that. But, likewise, you know that none of you have been in trouble with the law since I took the star."

"No reason we should be!" Lippy Ord cried. "It's the Wyatts who ought to be in trouble. If our cows get on their side of the deadline, they raise hell. If their cows work up on the flat, we ain't supposed to do nothing but sit and watch 'em eat our grass, which we ain't got enough of for our own beef."

"Just what are you fixing to do?" Jim pressed.

Again he felt that sullen uneasiness grip them. He knew that someone had worked them into a killing temper, but at the same time he sensed that they wouldn't tell him who it was or what their plan was.

"All right," Jim said coldly. "If there's murder done, some of you will hang." He jerked a thumb at the motionless Vinton. "If you're loco enough to let a loud-mouth like Chris talk you into something you'll kick yourself for later, there'll be some widows on the flat afore morning."

Jim wheeled to the batwings and immediately turned back when Buck Deeter said: "What are you fixing to do, Jim?"

"I'll have a palaver with Latigo. You boys have got plenty to holler about and it's time somebody was giving it straight to the Wyatts."

Lippy Ord nodded. "Fetch Latigo over if he wants to palaver, but we'll shoot Boone if he opens his mug."

"I'll get Latigo," Jim said, and, pushing the batwings open, stepped into the street.

The bank was empty, except for the teller who stared at Jim through the grillwork of his window.

Jim asked: "Where's Latigo?"

"Mister Wyatt is in conference with Mister Biddle," the teller said with distaste as if Jim's familiarity in calling the elder Wyatt by his first name was sacrilege.

Jim pushed back the swinging gate next to the wall and stepped through. The teller called sharply: "I said they were in conference!"

"I aim to join the conference." Jim winked at the fuming teller and drummed his knuckles against the door marked PRIVATE.

"Who is it?" Zane Biddle called.

Without answering, Jim opened the door and stepped through. Biddle rose from his desk, pink-cheeked face showing the surge of anger. He was a round-bellied little man with blue eyes and a nose that twitched when emotions pressed him. He was Santa Claus without the whiskers, Jim thought, and probably a fake one, despite his protestation that his bank existed to serve all of Stillwater country fairly and impartially.

"I didn't tell you to come in," Biddle said sharply. "Get out. We're busy."

"This is official business." Jim shut the door and winked at Latigo. "Want the money-grabber to stay, Latigo?"

Latigo Wyatt had never held Biddle in high regard, and it amused him now to see Jim prodding the man who other folks held in almost as much awe as they held the Wyatts themselves.

He chuckled and nodded. "Let him stay, Jim, unless you aim to burn his ears off."

Without invitation, Jim pulled up a chair and, sitting down, began rolling a smoke. He said: "You've got trouble, Latigo."

Wyatt reached into his pocket for his stinking black briar and filled it. His cream-colored Stetson was pushed back on his head; his white hair reached almost to his shoulders. Anyone who didn't know would have guessed him far short of his seventy years, for his blue eyes were bright and sharp, his face weather-stained but less lined by age than most men of middle life.

When Latigo had his pipe going, he pinned his eyes on Jim, and said with characteristic confidence: "My troubles are all over, son. It's the other gents that have troubles now."

"I'm one of them other gents," Jim said. "I want to marry Kitsie, only Boone's got other notions."

Biddle pulled in a sharp breath, but Latigo laughed. "What does Kitsie say?"

"I thought she loved me," Jim said, his misery momentarily breaking through his mask of self-control. He told Latigo what had happened at Nell Craft's house. With sudden distaste, he jerked the cigarette from his lips and threw it into the spittoon. "Damn it, Latigo, I don't have no million dollars or a million cows, but I'd make her a better husband than some of these gents who do."

Latigo turned his gaze to Biddle and laughed. "You sure said something that time, son. You and Kitsie didn't fool me much. I seen you making calf eyes at each other ever since you started riding for us."

"That was why Boone gave you the sheriff's job," Biddle blurted, the tip of his nose working like a rabbit's. "She's young and romantic, and it'd be easy to make her lose her head, but if you really loved her, you'd want her future arranged for."

"I'll arrange for it," Jim flung at him. "She'll have a lot more fun with me than she would with a fat banker with soft hands."

Biddle had been standing behind his desk. Now he jerked a drawer open, wounded dignity whipping him into an action he would never have taken at another time.

Jim came out of his chair to face Biddle. "Zane, if you touch that gun, I'll kill you."

"Sit down, both of you," Latigo said testily. "You love Kitsie, Jim. I ain't saying she don't love you, but I do say she ain't likely to marry you. She's Boone's girl, not mine. If it was me, I'd favor you." Taking his cold pipe out of his mouth, he reached for a match. "What was this trouble you think I've got?"

"That's for you to hear and not that cottontail. Let's go somewhere."

Latigo laughed again, eyes turning to the silent, raging Biddle. "He's sure got you pegged, Zane. Cottontail. Yes, sir, cottontail with pink cheeks and a wiggly nose." He sobered, nodding at the door. "Suppose you go find something to do out front while me and the sheriff palaver. Trouble." He snorted. "Maybe some trouble would spice things up. Been damned dull lately."

Holding his shattered dignity around him like a worn garment, Biddle rose. "You are welcome to use my office, Mister Wyatt," he said, and, going out on tiptoe in his cat-like walk, he closed the door softly behind him.

I'm gonna hand it out straight, Latigo," Jim said bluntly. "A lot of folks don't like you, but they know you'll keep your word. That's a notion you never got across to Boone and Stub. They think they're little gods and they try to make everybody else think the same. That's why you've got trouble."

"Now hold on . . . ," Latigo began, quick anger sparking in him.

"Nope. I'm not holding on. I told you I was gonna hand it out straight. Nobody's supposed to talk to the Wyatts like this, but I'm doing it. I saw how it was when I rode for Wagon Wheel. I saw more of it when I started toting the star. Trouble is you're blind 'cause you're on top."

Anger and puzzlement struggled in Latigo for a moment. "What'n hell are you talking about?"

Jim leaned forward. "You bully and you shove and you kick any man in the pants who doesn't agree with what you Wyatts say. Like Gramp Tatum. Or Buck Deeter. Or any of the rest. It goes for a while. They get madder and madder and scareder and scareder, but all the time their pride's working on them."

"Pride," Latigo snorted. "They don't have none. You've got it and I've got it. So's Boone and so's Stub. So's Kitsie. It's the one thing I was damned sure they had to have, and I taught it to 'em, but Gramp Tatum . . ." He brushed the thought away with a wave of his long-fingered hand and dug for another match. "Or Zane Biddle. Hell on a fishhook! They don't know what the word means."

"They've got it," Jim said earnestly. "It just ain't our kind of pride, but after so much pushing, it gets to working on them. Then they're dangerous."

Latigo laughed. "You're spooked, Jim." He struck the match and sucked the flame into the pipe bowl. "They're weaklings. In this country, a weakling's got to stick with the strong if he

267

wants to live. Us Wyatts are strong, Jim. So are you. That's where we're likely to have trouble. When I gave you the star, I knew you'd never be a Bill Riley. At the same time, you ain't smart if you start getting bull-headed."

"Who did give me this star?" Jim asked curiously. "Biddle said Boone did to get me away from Kitsie."

"We talked it over," Latigo admitted. "I figured that you'd make a good sheriff, and Boone wanted you out from under Kitsie's nose." He rose. "If you're trying to scare me, Jim, you're barking up the wrong tree. I'm too old to scare."

"I'm not trying to scare you. I'm just trying to get you to see some sense. The Poverty Flat boys are in the Bonanza and they're sure on the prod. I dunno what got them that way, but if you don't go over and powwow with them, you've got some fighting to do before you leave town."

"What's there to powwow about?" Latigo demanded.

"They've got plenty to holler about," Jim said bluntly, "like this business of using the bank to close some of them out when they don't buckle down. Who are you after this time? Deeter?"

Surprised, Latigo scratched his nose and gave Jim a long stare. "So?" he said as if this was something he hadn't admitted even to himself.

"Damn it, Latigo," Jim exploded, "you started little once just like Lippy Ord and Buck Deeter and the rest of them. Boone and Stub can't see their side because they've always been on the top rung, but you ought to."

Latigo moved to the window and automatically began packing his pipe again. "Don't make no difference what you are, Jim. It's the same thing, human or animal. It's the strong that run things. Take a herd of wild horses. Or a wolf pack. What happens in Washington or when the state legislature meets? Same thing on a cattle range. I'm the big gun here. If Lippy Ord or Buck Deeter don't want to play my game, I'll bust 'em."

"Your hide isn't tough enough to turn a bullet," Jim murmured.

Latigo wheeled from the window. "I can still outdraw the best of 'em if they had enough guts to throw down on me."

Staring at the old man now, Jim saw all of his pride and vanity mirrored in the hard set of his face. He realized only then that Latigo Wyatt would not back up a step, would surrender nothing, and for that stubbornness he was fated to die. Jim said: "They know you four come to town every Saturday morning. They know you never bring any of your hands, but a bunch of your boys will be in tonight. That's why I'm guessing they figure on taking you and Boone and Stub today before you get a chance to leave town."

Latigo peered his disbelief in a snort of

contempt. "They'll have their hands full if they start anything, son. You tell 'em that."

"You afraid to talk to them in the Bonanza? Afraid to find out what's eating on them?"

"Afraid?" Latigo bawled the word like an enraged bull. "Hell's bells, you know better'n that. Come on. I'll talk to 'em and I'll use a language even them limp-brained sons can understand. I'll poke some hot lead down the throat of the first yahoo that opens his mug."


# V

Latigo stomped out through the bank and into the street, Jim behind him. Biddle, Jim saw, was gone, and he wondered why the banker had not stayed. He caught up with Latigo in the middle of the dust strip.

He said: "Let them get it out of their systems, Latigo. Maybe just talking will do the job. You know how it is when a bunch gets steamed up. Sometimes a palaver lets the steam down."

"I don't give a damn whether the steam's down or not," Latigo snapped, "but if they want to stop at talking, they'd better be damned careful what they say. I wouldn't let nobody else talk to me like you've done. . . ."

A gun cracked from somewhere across the street. Before the echoes of that first shot died,

Latigo Wyatt had stumbled and fallen on his face into the street dust.

For an instant Jim Hallet stood paralyzed, a dozen thoughts rushing through his brain, thoughts that were compressed into a space of a clock tick. He had expected it to happen but not this way and not this soon.

Another shot racketed into the hot stillness, the slug kicking up dust at Jim's feet. Stooping, he grabbed Latigo's shoulders and, lifting them, dragged the old man across the street to the boardwalk in front of the Bonanza. He never expected to make it. That second bullet had been aimed at him and had missed. A man who could cut Latigo down with a single shot wouldn't be likely to miss again. But the hidden killer did miss. The third bullet was wide by three feet. Jim had Latigo off the street when another gun spoke three times, fast. He was facing the Bonanza and he didn't know whether the slugs geysered the dust or not.

Jim laid Latigo on the walk. He knelt beside him, vaguely aware of the scared faces of the Poverty Flat men who had bulged out of the saloon but still held back. He heard the thump of running steps and knew that Doc Horton had grabbed his black bag, as he always did when he heard gunfire, and was on his way. He was dimly conscious of these things, for his attention was focused on Latigo. The old man was dying and he knew it, and the knowledge brought a gaunt weakness to his face. He had killed others, but like many arrogant men, he had never expected to die. Now, for the first time since Jim had known him, he was afraid.

"They done it, boy," Latigo murmured, gripping Jim's arm. "Boone ain't man enough to run the Wagon Wheel. I never thought the day'd come when I wouldn't be around. You're my kind, Jim. You've got to help him."

Jim nodded. Latigo was right about Boone, but Boone wouldn't see it.

Doc Horton was there then. He tried to nudge Jim away, asking briskly: "Hit bad?"

Jim didn't move. It was only a matter of seconds, and Latigo had something more to say. A lesser man would already have been dead. Latigo's grip on Jim's arm was vise-like; blood bubbled on his lips. Somewhere he found the strength to say: "You marry Kitsie. Don't let that damned pussyfooting Biddle get her." Then his grip went slack, and his arm fell away. Latigo Wyatt was dead, and the long shadow that he had thrust over the valley for so long passed with him.

Jim rose. "Get him off the street, Doc." He nodded at Lippy Ord and the others who stood in the doorway. "Give him a hand, boys."

They came silently and respectfully, awed by the suddenness and violence of death when only a few minutes before they had been idly threatening this man who lay before them. Jim, his eyes ranging over them, saw that not all of them were there. Chris Vinton was gone. Buck Deeter. Gramp Tatum. A braggy kid named Bud Yellowby who had squatted recently in the fringe of the timber.

"The girl," Lippy Ord muttered. "Don't let her see him, Jim."

Jim turned. Kitsie and Stub were hurrying along the walk. He moved toward them, blocking their path and gripping Kitsie's arm. He said: "It's Latigo. Get her out of town, Stub."

"He's . . . dead?" the girl breathed.

Jim nodded. "He's gone."

"Who did it?" Stub demanded, facing him angrily.

"I don't know."

"Why in hell ain't you finding out?"

"I'll find out. Right now, I'm trying to keep this from happening again. Somebody aims to rub the Wyatts out."

Kitsie was returning to the hotel. She had strength to hold back her feelings, but Jim knew how she had loved Latigo and he knew how much his death would hurt her, a hurt that would grow with time. But Stub didn't stir. He was staring at Jim, violently hating him and still realizing that Jim was his one protection. Latigo had been the keystone. Now neither Boone nor

273

Stub was strong enough to hold Wagon Wheel together, and Jim, watching Stub, sensed that the boy knew it.

"Where's Boone?" Jim asked.

"I don't know."

"I'll get your horse. Go back to the hotel and stay off the street."

The Wyatt horses were racked in front of the Mercantile. Jim strode quickly to them, fear prickling his spine. The killer might still be in one of the rooms over the Bonanza or in the hotel. Or on one of the roofs behind a false front. He had not located the dry-gulcher when the shots were fired. As he turned, leading Kitsie's and Stub's horses, he raised his gaze to rake the windows and false fronts, but there was no flash of fire, no snarling slug, nothing to indicate where the murderer had hidden or whether he was still there.

The Poverty Flat men were knotted in front of the Bonanza. As Jim swung toward them, he saw that Buck Deeter had appeared.

Deeter called: "Anything we can do?"

"You've done plenty," Jim said, and moved on.

Jim tied the horses in front of the hotel and went in. None of the Wyatts was in sight. He climbed the stairs and turned along the hall to the front corner room that Latigo had kept rented for Kitsie, but before he reached it, the door opened, and Zane Biddle stepped out. His pink-cheeked face was held very sober as he closed the door.

"I was just offering my condolences," Biddle said. "I trust you will be careful what you say. Kitsie is terribly hurt."

Anger rose in Jim. He had never liked Biddle, and the man had plenty of reason to dislike him, but Biddle's feelings for him were strictly masked behind the sympathetic soberness of his face.

"Thanks for the advice," Jim said, and started to move on toward the door, but Biddle stepped in front of him, a fat, moist hand laid on his arm. He whispered: "Do you know who fired the fatal shot?"

"No."

Biddle looked over his shoulder at the closed door and then along the hall. He brought his mouth close to Jim's ear. "Where was Boone at the time the shot was fired?"

Jim straightened, his dislike of Biddle growing. "I don't know."

Again, Biddle looked over his shoulder and brought his lips back to Jim's ear. "Don't tell them I'm suggesting this to you, but I know the situation in the Wyatt family better than anyone else. I know Boone hated his father, largely because of Latigo's attitude toward Stub's gambling losses. Boone insisted on paying them, and Latigo didn't like that. He told me

275

today that he was the only one who would draw on the Wyatt account from now on."

Jim's mind reached ahead of Biddle. What the banker had just said gave Boone Wyatt plenty of motive for murder. Wagon Wheel would go to him with Latigo out of the way, and he was the kind of passion-ruled man who might easily be touched off into doing exactly what Biddle was insinuating.

"I'll find out about Boone," Jim said.

"It was just something I thought you should know," Biddle said smugly.

Biddle had turned away when Jim asked: "Where were you when Latigo was shot?"

Biddle jumped as if he had been stung. He wheeled back to face Jim, suddenly angry. He opened his mouth to say something and then closed it. His hands fisted at his sides. When he had regained control of himself, he said with biting scorn: "I suppose it is your duty to investigate everybody, but I assure you I had no reason to kill Latigo. He was the main source of revenue for my bank."

"I asked you where you were."

Biddle jabbed a thumb at the door. "In there with Kitsie when the shot was fired. Ask her if you don't believe me." Turning, he walked down the hall, the tip of his nose working, shoulders back, an aroused and insulted man.

Jim watched him until he disappeared down the

stairs, a grim smile touching his lips. A pudgy man acting insulted had always been a comical sight to him, but he saw little humor in Zane Biddle now. He stood there a moment, letting the seed of suspicion that Biddle had planted grow in him. He wondered at the man's motives, but whatever they were, he knew he could not ignore what the banker had said.

Jim tapped on Kitsie's door. He waited, uneasiness working in him. The moments that lay ahead would be hard on Kitsie, but he saw no way to soften them. She opened the door and stood there, straight-backed and motionless. Without waiting for an invitation, he stepped into the room.

It was a sort of sitting room with expensive furniture, a thick rug, and red velour drapes on the windows. A door to the left opened into a small bedroom. The man who had built the hotel years before, when the land was new and held an unkept promise, had called it his bridal suite, but Latigo had promptly rented it permanently because, as he put it, nobody else in the valley was important enough to have it. Later, when Kitsie had grown up, it became her personal quarters whenever she came to town.

"Well?" Kitsie did not move, her tone sharp.

"Where's your dad?" Jim asked. "Does he know?"

"I have no idea," Kitsie said.

Stub, sitting beside the window, rose and crossed the room to Jim. He was still a boy, although old enough to be a man, and he could not grow up fast enough now that he faced a man's job. His voice breaking a little, he said: "Get out."

"Just a minute, sonny." Jim crossed to the door that opened into the bedroom, looked in, and swung back. "Where was Biddle when that shot was fired?"

"In here, talking to us," Kitsie said. "If it's any of your business."

She wouldn't lie. Jim was as sure of that as he could be sure of anything that depended upon the uncertainty of human behavior. He crossed the room to her, ignoring Stub.

He said: "Kitsie, I didn't love Latigo like you did, but I liked him and I respected him. I'm going to get the man that killed him."

"Go ahead."

"I need your help. Where was your dad at the time Latigo was shot?"

"I don't know. I told you that. He came up with Stub and me after we left Nell's place. We talked, and he left. He didn't say where he was going."

"How long was that before the shooting?"

"I don't know. Fifteen or twenty minutes. I don't see what it's got to do with . . ." Then she saw what was in his mind and she froze, eyes wide. "You don't think he could have killed

Granddad? Jim, why did I ever think I loved you?"

He said: "Stub, I told you to get her out of town. Your horses are in front." Turning from her, he left the room, his face hard-touched by the misery that was in him.

# VI

Again, Jim Hallet faced a decision, as brutal as any he had faced in the past. As sheriff, he must question Boone Wyatt, perhaps arrest him for Latigo's murder, perhaps shoot him if he resisted arrest. Then he remembered Kitsie's frozen, wide-eyed face, and a dull hopelessness crawled through him.

Only a few hours before she had come to town loving him, looking forward to meeting him, to going to Nell Craft's place as she had week after week. It had been a good world, bright with hope, hope that had lasted even after he had faced Boone in the street, after Kitsie had walked out of Nell's house with her father, for hope is hard to kill when a man is in love. Then Latigo had said that if Kitsie were his girl, he would favor Jim, and hope had flamed again. Now Latigo was dead, and duty laid a club against Jim's back, offering him no reward.

For half an hour Jim searched the hotel rooms

that faced the street, the alley, and roof tops behind the false fronts. For all of Boone Wyatt's top-heavy pride and loud-mouthed arrogance, Jim found it hard to believe that he had killed his father. He kept remembering that Chris Vinton had not been with the Poverty Flat men in front of the Bonanza when Latigo had been shot. Neither had Buck Deeter nor the Yellowby kid. He could count Gramp Tatum out. The old man was drunk and sleeping it off in the alley.

The half hour brought no clue. No tracks. No empty shells. No hint of where the killer had stood and no hint as to his identity. Jim had asked the Poverty Flat men to stay in town. Now he returned to the Bonanza, not liking this task and sensing that it would bring him nothing.

They were all there, idly talking, a few drinking, some trying to interest themselves in a game of poker and failing. Jim moved directly to Vinton and asked: "Where were you, Chris, when Latigo was shot?"

Vinton's battered face held no apparent resentment. He said: "In the back room with Deeter and Yellowby. We had a little poker game going." His bruised lips shaped into a crooked grin. "I was ready to pull on Latigo any day in the year, but this time I didn't have my gun. Remember?"

Jim nodded. Vinton's Colt was in his waistband where he had placed it after the fight, but there were other guns. He swung to Deeter, but before he could put the question, the Staircase man nodded. "He's giving it to you straight, Jim. We were having a game."

Without being asked, the Yellowby kid said: "That's it, Sheriff."

Jim's eyes swept the line of men along the bar, a bitter sense of frustration rushing at him. Maybe Deeter and Yellowby were lying to cover up for Vinton, but he couldn't prove it. Not yet. Yellowby was weak. He had thought Deeter was on the level, but now he was not sure. There was no sympathy on their faces, no friendliness.

"Damn it," Jim said in sudden anger. "I was bringing Latigo over to talk to you when somebody cut him down. Facing him with a gun in your hand is one thing, but drilling him like someone did is murder."

"You don't know any of us done it, Jim," Deeter said quietly. "You'd be smart to go easy on that talk till you do."

"That's right," Lippy Ord said. "I rode in today, mighty sore about the way Latigo had treated us. Wouldn't have taken much to have made me pull on him, 'specially if we found out Biddle was closing us out like he done some of our neighbors in the past just on Latigo's say-so. Now I kind of wish he was alive. We're gonna be worse off with Boone running Wagon Wheel."

"Not if our brave sheriff can see past his nose," Vinton said pointedly.

Jim swung toward the gunman. "Maybe I'm blind, Chris, but I aim to keep looking. That slug was mighty near dead center, and you claim to shoot straight."

"I do, but I didn't plug him. Keep looking, Jim. Maybe you can think of somebody else who wanted Latigo out of the way."

"Boone!" the Yellowby kid shouted. "Plenty of gents would kill their old man just to get their hands on something as big as Wagon Wheel."

"He knew we were in town," Deeter added, "and he knew we wasn't right friendly toward Latigo. It'd be natural enough to push it off on one of us."

A stomach-sinking sense of frustration crawled through Jim. What they said made sense, and they were clearing each other. It left nobody but Boone and Gramp Tatum, who was blind drunk. Jim felt as if the rush of events were washing him downstream, and he was helpless before the force of the current. Again, Kitsie's set, cold face came before his eyes. Then he thought of something else.

Boone was not much of a man alongside Latigo, but he was a man. With him out of the way, young Stub would be running Wagon Wheel, and that would mean a quick end to what was now a great ranch. Whoever had killed Latigo had planned for Boone to be taken out by the same murder. These men all had reasons to hate and fear the Wyatts, but Jim still didn't know what had finally stirred them into a violent temper and brought them to town today looking for trouble.

Jim reached for tobacco and paper, dropping his eyes as he rolled a smoke. He said softly: "How come you boys thought of Boone?"

They stirred uneasily, looking at each other, and then the Yellowby kid saw his chance to play big. He bawled: "Hell, Sheriff, Biddle told us about Latigo stopping Boone from drawing on the Wyatt bank account." Vinton jabbed Yellowby with an elbow. Yellowby squalled an oath and jumped away. "Ain't no secret. We know Boone Wyatt wants Poverty Flat for summer ranch, and the way to get it is to shove us off."

"Damn you, Bud, keep . . . ," Vinton began.

"All right, Chris." Jim slid the cigarette between his lips. "Let the kid alone. He's got the guts it takes to talk if nobody else has."

"Yeah," Deeter murmured. "He let something slip. You know why we're on the prod and you know it was Biddle that got us to thinking of Boone. Does it tell you anything else?"

The Yellowby kid had been pushed back. They formed a tight line in front of him, watchful, grim. They had united, Jim saw, and it was natural for them to consider a lawman their enemy because valley law had been Wyatt law for a generation.

They all might be guilty of murder, or just one or two, but the thing had worked so that now they were against him regardless of who was guilty.

"Don't tell me much, Buck," Jim said, "except that you boys are gunning for Boone. That might not be good."

"It's good enough to save our outfits." Deeter jabbed a forefinger at Jim, strong white teeth flashing as a vagrant ray of sunlight slanted across his swarthy face. "You're supposed to be the law, but you claim you ain't a Wyatt man like Bill Riley was. You'll prove it when you lock Boone Wyatt up."

"I'll have to find him first." Jim moved toward the batwings, cold cigarette dangling from the corner of his mouth. He turned suddenly so that he faced them, calling sharply: "Yellowby, come here!"

Yellowby hesitated, narrow face mirroring indecision, gaze swinging to Buck Deeter. Jim said again: "Come here, Yellowby."

"You've got nothing against him," Deeter said. "Stay here, Bud."

"I can see a dead man walking," Jim said. "The kid talks too easy. Yellowby, you're coming with me. I'll kill the first man who tries to stop you."

"We pegged you wrong, Jim," Deeter said. "You're a little tougher than we guessed. That makes *you* the dead man walking."

"Want to make a try, Buck?"

It was a challenge, cold and hard. Jim, standing loosely by the batwings, his beaky-nosed face signalling his intent, was not a man to be taken lightly.

Deeter shrugged. "I ain't asking for a fight, Jim. I want to see you turn Boone Wyatt up. Then we'll know what to do."

"Yellowby, climb on your horse. Get out of town. Keep riding."

The kid broke toward the batwings in an awkward, adolescent run. He went past Jim, not stopping to say, "thank you," and dived through the door. A moment later hoof thunder rolled in from the street.

"Yeah, we pegged you wrong," Deeter murmured. "You've got good eyes."

"I can see, all right." Jim's gaze probed Lippy Ord. "I've counted some of you boys as my friends, and I've figured you was square. Maybe I pegged you wrong, or maybe you're being pushed in a direction you don't want to go. I'll soon find out."

Jim backed through the door, watchful for the first hostile move, but none came. He stepped quickly away from the saloon and turned toward the hotel, pondering Boone Wyatt's disappearance and finding no logical answer, but he was sure of one thing. What the Poverty Flat boys did would be determined by Jim's action when Boone appeared.

# VII

The stage from Ontario was rolling in. Jim paused in front of the hotel to wait for it. It was a custom with him to meet the stage whenever he was in town, partly because it was the one contact between the Stillwater country and the railroad to the east, but mostly because it was a good thing for the sheriff to be familiar with the comings and goings of the people in his town.

The two Wyatt horses were at the hitch rail. Staring at them, Jim wondered uneasily why Stub and Kitsie were still in town. It was dangerous—at least, for Stub. If Jim judged the temper of the Poverty Flat men accurately, they would finish the job that had been started with the murder of Latigo.

The stage was there then, chain traces jangling, dust drifting up past the coach when it stopped in a white, suffocating cloud. There was one passenger, a young woman, close to twenty-five, Jim judged, and attractive in a round-bodied way. She stepped away from the stage to get out of the dust, saw Jim, and came toward him in a hip-swinging walk.

"You're the sheriff, Jim Hallet, aren't you?" she asked. "I'm Honey Nolan. I still go by that name, but I'm really Honey Wyatt."

He lifted his Stetson, wondering how she fitted into the Wyatt family. "Pleased to meet you, ma'am," he said.

She smiled at him, dark eyes moving appreciatively along his lean, hard-muscled body. She straightened her blue bonnet that was gray with dust, and, after unbuttoning her tan duster, she shook it. Her white silk shirtwaist and dark, tight-fitting skirt showed the curve of her hip and thigh.

"Some country you've got, Sheriff." She laid her bold gaze upon him, smiling. "Well, where's Latigo?"

"Latigo?" Jim braced himself, remembering that she'd said her name was Wyatt.

"Yes, Latigo." She stood spread-legged, hands on her hips. "Look, star-man, don't tell me I swallowed a bunch of lies when Latigo Wyatt said he was the big gun in these parts. Why, he claimed he had more cows than you could count and more land than I could ride around all day. Not that I like the land, but I took Latigo for better or for worse, and I guess I took his land with him."

"Latigo's dead. Shot this morning."

"Dead?" She stared at him blankly. "No, Latigo couldn't die. He wanted me to come out here when we got married. Trouble, I had a contract signed up and couldn't come. But he couldn't die. He's the kind of man who lives forever."

"He's dead," Jim said. "His grandson and granddaughter are upstairs. You want to see them?"

"Latigo dead. A sweet time for a bride to get home." She swung back to her valise and picked it up. "Sure, I want to see my grandchildren, but I doubt like hell that they'll want to see me."

Jim reached for her valise and took it out of her hand. "This way," he said, and turned into the lobby. He wondered what would be the end of this. Kitsie had had too much to stand already. She shouldn't have to face this, but he saw no way to avoid it.

Honey Nolan kept pace with Jim along the hall to Kitsie's door in a leggy, graceful walk. Jim knocked. The door swung open, Stub crowding out, a cocked gun in his hand, fine-featured face quivering with fear.

"Put it up," Jim said testily.

Stub's gun arm sagged. "I thought it was Vinton or Deeter or some of them." He holstered his gun and sleeved sweat from his face. "Sorry."

"Stub, this is Latigo's wife," Jim said.

"Latigo's . . . wife!" Stub stared at the woman in the dazed way of a man so shocked that his thought processes went paralyzed. "You're crazy, Hallet. He never married again."

Kitsie was standing across the room talking to Zane Biddle. She heard and came to the door. She said: "Come in."

Honey Nolan stepped boldly into the room. "So, you're the grandchildren. Latigo was mighty proud of you, and I don't blame him. Sure sorry to hear what happened. I haven't seen him since we were married a year ago in Boise, and then to get here on the day . . ." She broke off as if she felt too strongly about it to go on.

Jim shut the door. He said: "It seems a little too pat for you to get here the day Latigo gets plugged."

Honey whirled to face him. "What do you mean by that, star-man?"

"I mean a dead man ain't in no shape to deny marrying you."

"If you mean . . . ," Honey began.

"We had not heard Granddad was married," Kitsie cut in quickly. "He was an old man, over seventy. It hardly seems possible he would get married, or that he would not tell us if he did."

"He was younger than any man of seventy I ever saw," Honey said, her fists clenching at her sides. "Maybe he wasn't proud of me. Maybe that's why he didn't tell you, but I married him in good faith. He wanted me to come and live with him as soon as I could. You're not going to put me out this way."

"I don't believe it!" Stub shouted. "Got your marriage license?"

289

Honey dropped down on the bed and began to cry. "I didn't think I had to bring a marriage license to show my husband I was married. I didn't know Latigo would be dead when I got here. I never dreamed the man I loved . . ."

"Just a minute, Missus Wyatt." Biddle moved toward Kitsie, pink-cheeked face showing concern. "I'm afraid she's right. You see, Latigo did marry her."

"Why didn't he tell us?" Kitsie asked.

The tempered steel that had been in Latigo had come down to Kitsie. She had complete control of herself; her grief was hidden deep within her. Jim, watching her from the door, knew that Kitsie had become Wagon Wheel. The absent Boone didn't count. Stub, seared almost to the point of hysteria, didn't count. It was Kitsie who had the hard core of courage, the grim determination. It would be Kitsie who would hold the empire Latigo had built.

For a moment neither Biddle nor Honey Nolan spoke. The woman had stopped crying, and her gaze touched Biddle's face.

She asked then: "Who are you?"

"The banker, Zane Biddle. I'm the one who has been sending you the checks." He turned to Kitsie. "As you know, Latigo didn't like to write, so he left even the letter writing to me. Or most of it."

"Why didn't you tell us?" Kitsie asked again.

"I could not betray Latigo's confidence," Biddle said. "I have been so shocked by his death that I never gave it a thought, but I can assure you that this woman is the one he married. I have her picture. It's over in the bank. She sent it to him about three months ago when her show was in Denver. All her letters were sent to him through me because he didn't want any of you folks to see them. He was . . . well, worried over what you'd say."

Jim remembered that Latigo had gone to Boise about a year ago and he had come back feeling happier than usual. He claimed to have had a big hand in a poker game that had more than paid for the trip, but he could have married this Honey Nolan. If he had, he would probably have worked it the way Biddle said.

There was a moment of silence. Stub had gone to the window and was looking down into the street, worrying, Jim saw, more about his safety than anything else. Biddle stood beside Kitsie, his gaze on her, one hand nervously patting his bald spot. Honey, wide-eyed, stared defiantly at Kitsie.

"I won't stay where I'm not wanted," Honey said. "I suppose I'll have to go back."

"I think it would be wise," Biddle said gravely. "I assure you that you'll be taken care of financially. That is the way Latigo would have wanted it."

"No," Kitsie said flatly. "She could bleed Wagon Wheel dry, and you were just telling me that our cash was very low."

"Your herd will soon be on the trail to Winnemucca," Biddle said, "and I'll be happy to advance you all the money you need. I've done that for years, and Latigo's death will make no difference."

Kitsie shook her head. "No. If . . . if . . ."—she floundered for the right word—"if Missus Wyatt wants to be taken care of financially, she'll come home. She'll work along with the rest of us and she'll live our kind of life." She fixed her blue eyes on Honey. "I'm sure Granddad would want it that way."

"But I don't know anything about ranch life," Honey began.

"You'll learn. It will be your living the same as it's ours, and you'll have to work for it."

"Stub never worked for his living," Biddle pointed out.

Stub swung away from the window. "Shut up, Biddle."

"You shut up." Kitsie did not raise her voice, but her words slapped him into silence. "He's right, Stub. From now on, you're working. Granddad planned on that or he wouldn't have stopped the rest of us from cashing checks. And no more poker." Kitsie turned to Jim. "We're leaving now. We would have gone sooner, but

Stub was afraid of the Poverty Flat men. Are they still in the Bonanza?"

"All but Bud Yellowby. I'll see you get out of town."

"Get a horse for Missus Wyatt, will you, Jim?"

"I can't ride a horse!" Honey cried. "Latigo told me I wouldn't have to."

"Get a buggy," Kitsie said. "We'll be down in five minutes."

Jim opened the door. Kitsie had changed in the few hours since he had kissed her in Nell Craft's kitchen. He turned to look at her again, puzzled by it. Her face was as gray as the desert that ran a hundred miles to the west; she was as immovable as the Steens Mountains to the south. He thought, and it was like a slashing knife blade in him, that she didn't need him, that she was a Wyatt, and that many of the qualities that had made Latigo a success were in his granddaughter.

"I'll get a buggy for you," Jim said.

He stepped into the hall. Kitsie followed, shutting the door behind her. She said: "I understand some things I didn't when I talked to you this morning. Dad told me the same as you did, that he had framed Ernie Craft. Then he said he'd have to get rid of you because you wouldn't take orders."

He looked down at her, wanting to take her in his arms and kiss her, to tell her he loved her and would always love her. But he didn't. She didn't want it. She was looking squarely at him, holding him away with her eyes.

"I'm still looking for Boone," he said.

"You should have sense enough to know he didn't kill Granddad. Keep looking and you'll find him." She swallowed, fighting to hold her tone level. "I think you'll find him dead."

"Why?"

"They're after the Wyatts, aren't they? There would be no sense in killing one without killing the other, would there?"

"I'll get the buggy," Jim said, and turned away.

They were on the street, waiting, when he drove the buggy from the livery stable to the hotel. Kitsie stepped in and took the lines. In a cool, distant voice, she said: "Thanks, Jim." Then: "Get in, Missus Wyatt."

Biddle, standing on the walk, said: "I'll be out this evening, Kitsie, and I'll bring Missus Wyatt's picture and her letters. It should be proof enough."

That was when the Poverty Flat men, Buck Deeter and Chris Vinton in front, left the Bonanza and strode along the boardwalk, Deeter calling: "Wyatt, get away from them women."

Stub began to tremble, his face going as gray as the dust of the street. He started to reach for his gun but then let his hand drop away. He shouted: "I've got no reason to fight you, Buck!"

"We've got plenty of reason to fight the Wyatts," Deeter grated. "Make your play."

"There'll be no fighting," Jim said. "Get on your horse, Stub. Buck, if you pull, I'll drill you between the eyes."

They stopped, doubt tugging at Deeter. Vinton, still wanting to push, said: "Hell, he's just a bluff, Buck."

"I don't think so," Deeter said. "Latigo was a good judge of men. Looks like Hallet is still working for the Wyatts."

"I'm sheriff, Buck," Jim said.

Stub was on his horse and reining him into the street. He knew now he'd get clear, and a sudden rush of courage made him shout: "Us Wyatts ain't backing up none, Deeter! We started to move Ernie Craft and we'll move him. Then you'd better get off Poverty Flat." Stub cracked steel to his horse and went out of town on the run.

Honey stood beside the buggy, paralyzed by fright. Zane Biddle, backing toward the hotel, showed concern, but Kitsie's face mirrored only contempt.

"It's funny how brave you are, Deeter, now that Granddad's gone. We won't bother Ernie Craft, but Stub was right about one thing. This valley is too small for you and Wagon Wheel. Get in, Missus Wyatt."

Jim took Honey's arm and helped her into the buggy. They wheeled away, Kitsie's horse tied behind. When they were gone, Jim moved warily toward Deeter, saying: "This morning I figured you boys had a lot on your side, but I reckon I was wrong. The Wyatt's don't look like angels, but I never knew one of them to dry-gulch a man. When I find out which one of you did it, I'll get him."

Deeter swung his dark eyes to Biddle and then brought them to Jim, his bold, confident smile on his lips. "You won't last long, tin-star. With Latigo gone, Wagon Wheel will fall apart, and we'll move in. Poverty Flat, one hunk of bunchgrass for a cow. Hell," he said, and spit into the dust, "we aim to get some good graze." He swung away, saying: "Let's ride, boys."

The Poverty Flat men mounted and left town in a rolling cloud of dust. Jim, staring after them, thought how much this day had changed everything. The Wyatts had sowed their seed and reaped a harvest of lead. He turned to Biddle who was watching him thoughtfully through narrowed eyes.

"A banker's neck will stretch same as a cowman's," Jim murmured, and, stepping around him, went into the hotel.

# VIII

It was late afternoon with long shadows slanting across the dust strip, and it was cooler. This was the first moment Jim had had to relax since he had faced Boone Wyatt that morning, and he remembered he had not eaten, except for a slim breakfast shortly after sunup. He turned into the hotel dining room and ordered a steak.

"Jim." A quavering shout washed in from the street. "Jim, where the hell are you?"

The front legs of Jim's chair came down hard against the floor. It was Gramp Tatum. Jim rose and tapped on the window. Gramp saw him and lurched through the lobby into the dining room. His beard was matted with dirt and filth, and he stank of the cheap whiskey he had drunk that morning.

"Jim. My gun." He held out the old cap-and-ball revolver Jim had seen that morning. "It's been fired. Three times."

Jim took the gun, staring at Gramp and not understanding until the old man swallowed and pointed a shaking finger down the street. "Boone Wyatt. Shot three times, but I didn't do it. So help me, Jim, I didn't do it."

"Where'd you find Boone?"

"I didn't find him." Gramp gripped Jim's arm.

297

"It was Lucky. In the storeroom back of the Bonanza. Hidden behind some beer barrels. Jim, I tell you I didn't do it."

Jim slid the gun into his waistband, saying: "Come on." They left the dining room.

Gramp had to run to keep up, repeating over and over that he didn't do it. Jim said nothing more until he reached the saloon. The barman, Lucky Donovan, motioned to Jim when he came in and led the way to the storeroom. There, wedged between the walls and some beer barrels, lay Boone Wyatt with three bullet holes in his chest.

"I didn't touch him," Donovan said.

Boone's gun, Jim saw, was in his holster. There was a window opening on the alley, but there were so many tracks in the dust that none meant anything.

"I didn't hear no shooting, except when they got Latigo," Donovan offered.

Jim nodded, saying nothing, but he remembered that there had been three more shots that morning after he had dragged Latigo to the walk. Gramp Tatum stood in the doorway, trembling and chattering that he didn't do it.

"Shut up," Donovan said.

Gramp lowered his tone but kept on muttering.

"The window opens easily," Jim said thoughtfully. "Somebody could have shoved him through and then crawled in and dragged him over here."

"I don't pay much attention to that window," Donovan said. "Fact is, I don't come back here much. He could have laid there till I smelled him, but I happened to bust a lamp chimney, and the only extra one I had was in here."

Jim pushed past Gramp into the saloon. "Who bought your drinks this morning?"

"I . . . I bought 'em myself."

"You couldn't have got that drunk on the dollar I gave you," Jim said patiently.

"I couldn't shoot straight enough to kill him," Gramp quavered.

"You could at that distance," Jim said. "Boone was shot close up, judging by the powder burns. Now, who paid for your whiskey?"

Gramp began to tremble. "I . . . I disremember."

Jim glanced at Donovan, but the barman shook his head. "Nobody gave him anything that I saw after he came in. He had a fistful of silver dollars and he was showing that gun around and swearing he was gonna get Latigo and Boone."

"All right," Jim said. "You're going to jail, Gramp. You're going to stay locked up till you remember who bought your whiskey. Lucky, go tell Doc Horton he's got another carcass."

But Gramp wouldn't say anything after the cell door had closed on him, except to repeat: "I didn't do it. Don't you believe me, Jim?"

"I'll believe you when you tell me who bought your whiskey. You're a blabber, Gramp. You duck around and look in windows and listen at keyholes. Then you sell what you've learned."

"I don't neither!" Gramp howled.

"Then how come you told Boone me and Kitsie were at Nell Craft's place?"

Gramp gripped the bars with his gnarled hands, bearded face pressed against them. "Aw, Jim, I had to have a drink. I got a dollar out of Boone. Bowing and scraping just like everybody's done for years. I didn't know I was gonna get twenty dollars from . . ." He stopped and began to tremble. "I'm just a born liar. You can't believe anything I say."

"I told you they hang old men for murder."

"He won't let me hang. He's got money. I didn't plug Boone nohow." Gramp rattled the bars. "Let me out."

Jim walked away and went back to the dining room. He ate the steak he had ordered, thinking about Boone Wyatt's murder. Kitsie had called the turn when she had said they had no reason to kill Latigo without killing Boone.

It had been set up skillfully with much thought and careful planning. Jim was supposed to think that Boone had killed his father and that Gramp Tatum had shot Boone. Gramp was a safe victim for everybody. He was a washed-up whiskey bum. If Jim didn't see it that way, a dry-gulcher's slug could take care of him, and Buck Deeter, as county commissioner, could wangle the appointment of a new sheriff who would call the case settled.

It was dusk when Jim stepped out of the dining room to the hotel porch. He shaped a smoke and lighted it, the match flame throwing a quick red light across his face. Another thought had come to him, a thought that jabbed him with a sharp edge of fear. If Stub and Kitsie were dead, the Wyatts would be finished, and Jim knew there were no other heirs.

A brief crimson glory painted the western sky. Then the sun was gone and the color faded. A dry wind, strong with the smell of sage, touched Jim and rattled the hotel sign above his head. Then he heard a horse and he stepped into the street, hand on gun belt, and watched horse and rider take shape. It was, he saw with surprise, the Yellowby boy, and he was hanging to the horn as if he were wounded.

"Doc," Jim cried, "come here!"

"I'm all right," said Yellowby as he reined up. His head and chest dropped lower against the horn, and Jim, stepping to him, steadied him in the saddle. It was then that he saw the dark stain on the boy's shirt.

"Who done it, Bud?"

"Deeter. He's bad with a gun, Jim. Been acting damned pious, thinking you wouldn't catch on, and wanting to fool Latigo, but he's twice as bad as Vinton. They're gonna hit Ernie Craft's place

301

tonight and salivate him. They want you to think Wagon Wheel done it."

Yellowby fainted then, sliding off the saddle into Jim's arms. Doc Horton was there, saying: "Bring him to my office. I'll go light a lamp."

Another man who had come into the street at Jim's call gave him a hand, and they carried Yellowby to the medico's office.

"He'll be all right," Horton said after a quick look. "Slug caught him a little high to finish him. Lost a lot of blood, though."

Yellowby's eyes came open. "Jim."

"Here." Jim came close to the cot.

"I ain't plumb yellow," the boy said. "I saw you was calling it right today in the Bonanza. I blabbed, and Deeter would have got me. I got boogered and I had to make a run for it." He swallowed, fists clenched. "After I got out of town, I thought how it left you. I came back, aiming to give you a hand, but I ran into Deeter. My horse is faster'n his, or I wouldn't have got here."

"What happened when Latigo was shot?"

"I don't know for sure. We was having this poker game when suddenly Vinton jumped up and said he had business outside, but I was supposed to tell you he didn't leave the room. Deeter says he had business, too. He says to open the door into the saloon and watch for you. They pulled out, and I stayed there, watching. Then I

302

heard the shooting. Pretty soon they came back, and we started playing again."

"Where was the shooting?"

"One of the guns sounded like it was upstairs, maybe in one of them rooms facing the street. Other one was in the alley."

"Thanks, Bud."

Jim stepped into the street, knowing that he had to get to Ernie Craft's place, but at the same time realizing how long the odds were against him. Stub Wyatt was entirely unpredictable. He had shouted in what had been a mere show of bravado that Wagon Wheel would move Ernie Craft off his place. Kitsie had said they would leave him alone, but whether she could handle Stub after she got home was a question.

The bulk of the Wagon Wheel hands were in the high country with the cattle. Some would come to town to let their collective wolf loose, but there were a few older men, largely pensioners, who stayed around the ranch. Stub could use them against Craft if they'd follow him, but the real danger, as Jim saw it, came from Deeter and Vinton and the Poverty Flat boys. There was no telling what would happen if Deeter elected to move against Wagon Wheel after they had attacked Ernie Craft.

Jim saddled his horse, thinking of this and finding only one possible chance to stop Deeter. Lippy Ord and most of the Poverty Flat cowmen were good men, misled by Deeter but fundamentally sound. If he could break Ord and the rest from Deeter . . . It was only a wild hope. Deeter had fooled Latigo and he had fooled Jim. There was little chance, then, that Ord and the rest could be kept from going all the way with Deeter. Then Jim thought of Gramp Tatum. Smiling grimly, Jim saddled another horse and went back to the jail.

Gramp was sleeping when Jim came along the corridor with a lighted lamp. He stirred uneasily and sat up. "What's biting you?" he asked truculently. "I tell you and I'll keep telling you, I didn't kill Boone."

"I know." Jim unlocked the door. "I'm letting you out, a sort of parole, you might call it."

Gramp followed Jim back to the office, staring at him suspiciously. Jim picked up the old cap-and-ball pistol he had taken from Gramp, shook his head, and laid it down.

"You know, Gramp, they tell me you used to be a pretty good man. That was before I got here. Since I been in the valley, you've just been a no-good bum, a barfly mooching drinks off anybody you could. You'd crawl, belly down, like a whipped pup."

"Now you lookee here," Gramp began, "you ain't got no call . . ."

"Gramp, how'd you like to be a man again?"

Some of the truculence went out of the oldster's

face. He bowed his head, gnarled hands gripping the edge of Jim's desk. "Too late, son. I'm a crawling thing that ought to git under a rock and stay there."

Jim took down a gun belt from the wall and handed it to Gramp. "Try it on. That's a good iron in the holster. A Thirty-Eight. Be about right for you. Beat the old relic you've been toting."

Gramp extended a trembling hand. "What's this about?" He buckled the belt around him, pulled the gun and hefted it, and slid it back.

"You know Ernie Craft?"

"A damned good man," Gramp said, as if by some miracle he had suddenly become Jim's equal in toughness.

Jim turned to the door to hide his grin. He had gambled that, far inside Gramp Tatum, there was a spark of his old pride. He stepped to the saddle and said: "Let's ride, Gramp."

# IX

They rode directly south from town, following the road to Wagon Wheel until they climbed a ridge. This long finger of rock that extended nearly across the valley was, according to the law Latigo had laid down years ago, the deadline. The Poverty Flat cowmen could use the grass to the north, that to the south was Wagon Wheel's.

Actually it was as Lippy Ord had said in the Bonanza that morning. Nothing was said if Wyatt cattle drifted north, but the heavens were pulled down on the man whose stock was found south of the deadline.

Swinging west, they followed the ridge for a mile. It was fully dark now, the lights of the town lost behind a swell in the sage flat. A wafer moon showed above the eastern hills; stars freckled a black sky, beacons to troubled men filled with hungers and dreams and sorrows. The lights of Wagon Wheel glittered to the south, and Jim's mind turned to Kitsie as it did much of the time. Hers was a sorrow drowning the dreams, but because she was a Wyatt she would hug her sorrow to herself and no one could comfort her.

The ridge broke off sharply, and they angled down the steep slope to the bowl-like valley where Ernie Craft had settled beside a small spring. A light showed in the tar-paper shack, and Jim breathed a long, relieved sigh.

He said: "Ernie's all right."

"What'd you figure was wrong?" Gramp asked. "Think the Wyatts would beef him?"

"Or Buck Deeter," Jim slapped the words at him. "He wants the Wyatts wiped out, so it'd be fine to get Ernie's killing laid on them. The hell of it is, you're helping him. He got you worked up by telling you what a bunch of skunks the Wyatts are. Then he gives you a fistful of silver . . ."

"It wasn't Deeter!" Gramp cried. "It was . . ." He caught himself and swore bitterly. "You're pretty cute, Jim, but it didn't work."

"You're a damned fool," Jim flung out. "I need your say-so to bust them and you're too scared to talk."

"I know which side of my bread the butter's on," Gramp mumbled.

They had reached the bottom of Craft's valley when the thunder of hoofs from the south came to them.

"Wagon Wheel!" Jim yelled. "Damn that crazy kid Stub. Come on, Gramp." He cracked steel to his horse, heading directly toward Craft's shack. He called: "Blow out your light, Ernie!"

The light went out. Jim reined up, and, swinging down, gave the animal a slap on the rump. "It's Jim Hallet, Ernie!"

Gramp pulled up and dismounted stiffly, cursing his sore muscles. He grumbled: "What'n hell did you bring me on this joy ride for? I won't be able to sit for a month."

"It ain't a joy ride," Jim said. "Get your horse out of here. Ernie, got your cutter?"

"I've got my Thirty-Thirty," the nester said. "Who's coming?"

"You guess."

They stood in front of the shack for a moment, listening, until Gramp came back. Then Craft

307

said: "I reckon Boone's making his promise good."

"It'd be Stub," Jim said, and told him quickly what had happened. "I figured Deeter and the Poverty Flat boys would be paying you a visit, but they wouldn't come from that direction."

The horses were close now, ten or more, Jim guessed from the sound. They were racing across the valley floor in a hard run toward the shack.

"Inside," Jim said.

The thin walls of the shack gave poor shelter, but there was no time to find anything better. Jim lunged through the door and, turning to the window, smashed the glass out with his gun barrel and eared back the hammer. Craft had dropped on his belly in the doorway, and Gramp Tatum had disappeared.

The attackers were almost to the shack before the first gun sounded. Then they all cut loose at once. Lead rapped into the wall beside the window. Other bullets snapped through the open door to splinter the opposite wall. Some tore through the boards and screamed across the room. Craft's Winchester was blazing now, but Jim held his fire until they were close.

He thought they would pull up in front of the cabin and rush, for they would expect no one but Craft, and he was a notoriously poor shot, but instead they split around the shack and kept on. Jim pulled trigger twice. Then they were gone, and the sudden silence squeezed against Jim, strange and stifling after the shooting.

"They've gone," Craft breathed. "How do you figure it, Jim? Ain't like no Wyatt outfit to quit that easy."

"No," Jim agreed. "Where's Gramp?"

"Lit a shuck, I guess," Craft said sourly. "What'd you bring that old barfly along for?"

"To see if he'd whiskey-drowned all the man that was in him." Jim stepped past Craft and went outside. The beat of hoofs could be heard to the north. Then they died, and the night stillness pressed in around them again.

"Jim." It was Gramp Tatum, hiding in the sagebrush past the house. "You there?"

"I'm here," Jim growled. "Thanks for your help, Gramp."

"You don't need to be sore 'cause I was too smart to get penned up in a shack that wouldn't do no good against a kid with a bean-shooter. I figured they'd get down and fog. Then a gun outside might do some good."

"All right," Jim said testily. "Come in."

Gramp lurched toward the shack. "That wasn't no Wagon Wheel bunch, I'm thinking. The light was sure thin, but that front *hombre* rode plumb tall in the saddle. Just like Buck Deeter."

It could have been Deeter and his neighbors, circling the house and riding north to make Craft think it was a band of Wagon Wheel men. If Craft had brought the story to Jim in town, it would have set the law against Wagon Wheel. That was exactly what the Poverty Flat cowmen would want. Deeter had said: *We aim to get good graze.* This was one way to do it, and all of them, Jim and Biddle and the Poverty Flat bunch, had heard Stub, brash and rebellious and trying to hold the tag end of Wyatt glory, call out: *We started to move Ernie Craft and we will move him.*

Gramp asked: "You reckon that was Deeter, Jim?"

"Might have been," Jim grunted.

Craft had gone into the shack and lighted the lamp. He appeared in the doorway, a stooped, gentle man who showed in his weather-stained face and knob-jointed fingers the result of his long struggle against a reluctant nature. He said: "Come in, and I'll warm up the coffee." He stopped, eyes fixed on a motionless bulk in the fringe of light that washed past him from the lamp on the table. "Jim, we got one of 'em."

Jim had already seen it. He strode past Gramp and, kneeling beside the body, turned it over. Stub Wyatt! Gramp and Craft had followed him, and Craft, knowing how Jim felt toward Kitsie, said: "It was me that got him. Reckon it'd be justifiable homicide, wouldn't it?"

Jim had picked up the boy's wrist. He dropped it and, rising, faced Craft. "No, it's murder, Ernie.

310

Stub must have died several hours ago. He wasn't shot by either one of us."

"But how in hell . . . ?" Gramp began.

"We'll find out. Ernie, harness up and take the body into town. Come on, Gramp. We've got riding to do."

Kitsie was the only Wyatt left, and Zane Biddle had said he'd go out to Wagon Wheel that night. Honey Nolan was there and if she could make her claim of marriage stick, she would become the sole heir, once Kitsie was out of the way. Jim, thinking of this in one terrible moment of insight, shouted: "Damn you, Gramp, you'll give me the evidence I want or I'll cut it out of you!"

Gramp, shocked by the violence that was in Jim Hallet, laid a hand on his gun butt, and muttered in a voice too low for Jim to hear: "You'd better not try, bucko. You'd better not try."

At midnight, Jim and Gramp Tatum rode into the Wagon Wheel Ranch yard. The only light was in the long front room that, except for a small corner walled off for Latigo's office, ran the full width of the house. It was a rambling, two-story building made of pine lumber hauled from the Blue Mountains to the north. Latigo had allowed it was the finest house in the valley, and it undoubtedly was, although Zane Biddle had bragged he was going to build a stone house that would make a bigger shine than Latigo's.

Dismounting, Jim racked his horse at the pole

in front of the tall, close-growing poplars and said: "Come on." He strode across the trodden, packed earth of the yard. Gramp followed, slowly and cautiously, eyes probing the shadows.

# X

The front door was open, for the night still held evidence of the day's heat. Jim, looking in, saw Kitsie sitting on the divan, Zane Biddle beside her, leaning forward and talking in a soft, persuasive voice. Honey Nolan sat facing them, head back as if she were asleep, high breasts lifting and dropping with her breathing.

A tension that had been gathering in Jim from the time he'd left Craft's place broke in relief when he saw Kitsie. He stepped up on the porch and crossed it, spurs jingling. Kitsie jumped up and started toward the door when Jim appeared in it, a square-shouldered, lanky man, gaze sweeping the room, hand held close to gun butt.

Kitsie stopped, wide-eyed. She said: "Jim." Just the one word, and he couldn't tell by the way she said it what was in her mind.

Biddle stood beside the divan, irritated and trying not to show it. He said pointedly: "I thought your duties would keep you in town, Hallet."

"My duties take me wherever I think there's going to be trouble," Jim murmured. "Anybody else here, Kitsie?"

"No. Nobody, but Ling. The boys went to town, and Stub got angry at me and rode off."

"Stub's dead," Jim said.

Kitsie flinched as if she'd been struck, but she didn't move and she didn't cry. Honey Nolan reared up and shook her head. "What kind of a wild country is this?" she demanded.

"Wild enough," Jim said. "You'll get used to it if you live."

"I won't live long if I stay here!" she cried. "I never saw anything like it."

"Didn't your friend who brought you here tell you what you were in for?" Jim asked.

"What friend?"

Biddle coughed. "Latigo would not tell her, Hallet. You should know that."

"It's been a right peaceful country," Jim murmured. "Till today. You accept Biddle's proposal, Kitsie?"

"Did you have to come here tonight, Jim?" she asked.

"I know. You had your own ideas about how to handle her." He jabbed a finger at Honey Nolan. "It would have worked, I reckon, except you didn't count on him." He motioned to Biddle. "Everybody gone. Stub shot. You're the only Wyatt left, Kitsie. If he marries you, he wins. If you won't have him, you'll die. In that case, he still wins because he's got little Honey all trained for the job."

Kitsie kept her feet long enough to reach the divan. She dropped, her control giving way all at once. She leaned back, her face ivory white. Jim saw that she was close to fainting, but he had to keep pushing. Deeter and Vinton and their bunch might come, and this job had to be done first.

"You don't make yourself plain, Hallet," Biddle said tonelessly, "but if I understand your inference, I shall see Deeter in the morning. We will not have your kind as sheriff in this county."

Jim half turned toward the door, still watching Biddle. He said: "Gramp, get in here."

Gramp Tatum came reluctantly into the room and sidled along the wall. "He made me come, Mister Biddle, but I didn't tell him nothing. No, sir."

"Shut up, you drunken fool!" Biddle shrilled. "You don't know anything to tell him."

"He knows plenty, Biddle. Let's get our cards out where we can see them. We'll start with you. You're a soft-bellied little gent who wants to be big, but you don't know how. You had money enough to start your bank, but you needed Latigo's business. Latigo being what he was, you did your share of the kowtowing, but all the time it was festering up inside of you until you were damned near loco."

"Shut up!" Biddle cried. "Shut up and get out. You can't talk to me . . ."

"I am talking, fatty. You didn't kill Latigo or Boone, but you'll go to jail for attempted fraud. Might be, when Gramp gets done, you'll hang along with Deeter and Vinton."

"Nobody would believe a broken-down old sot like Tatum," Biddle squealed. "Not against me."

"You see what he thinks of you, Gramp?" Jim swung to face the old man. "A broken-down old sot. That's why he handed you them twenty silver dollars. He knew you had that gun. So did Deeter. They knew Latigo would come across the street from the bank. They knew mighty close to when, because I'd left the Bonanza to fetch him. They wanted Boone, too, so one of them got into the alley. Caught him in the hotel, I reckon, when he left Kitsie's room."

"Theory!" Biddle howled. "All theory. You don't hang men on theories, Hallet. You're talking big now, but it'll be different when Deeter shows up."

"You're wrong on that, too, Biddle. I'll arrest Deeter for Latigo's murder or I'll kill him. Right now, I'm after something else. That woman." He threw a hand out toward Honey Nolan. "She was your idea, wasn't she? You knew what Deeter aimed to do, didn't you? At first, you thought you'd play it safe, since Boone wanted Kitsie to marry you. Then Deeter came to you with his idea. You saw that was better, so you fetched in this floozie."

"Deeter will be along . . . ," Biddle began.

"You reckon you'll be alive to know about it?" Jim motioned to Gramp. "You never thought about it, but you did the same to Gramp that Latigo did to you, stomping on him like he was a rag to wipe your feet on. Only you didn't know Gramp had a little man left in him. Enough to fill you full of lead. That's why I gave him that iron. Look at him, Biddle. He knows why you did it. Twenty dollars to get drunk on so he'd go to sleep in the alley and Vinton could get his gun and shoot Boone. Then he'd hang. You thought he was just a broken-down old sot, but you're wrong. When he testifies in court who gave him . . ."

Jim had to keep talking, keep pressing. He had to work Gramp into admitting it was Biddle who had given him the $20. Now he got what he wanted, but not in the way he expected, for it was Biddle who broke. He grabbed for his gun, shouting: "He won't testify against me!"

Gramp tried to pull his gun, but it stuck in the holster. If Jim had not drawn and fired, shooting Biddle's gun out of his hand, Gramp Tatum would have died.

When the last echo of the shot had faded, Jim asked: "Now you see, Gramp?"

The old man stood backed against the wall,

knowledge of what Biddle had aimed to do breaking into his whiskey-fogged mind. "Sure, and damned if I know why I should save his hide when he aimed to drill me. He gave me the twenty dollars, but I didn't know . . ."

"All right, Gramp." Jim motioned with his gun at Biddle. "Now, Mister Banker, there's just one chance to save your neck."

Biddle, left hand clasping his bullet-grazed right, said in a trembling voice: "Your guesses are good, Hallet. Deeter was the one. He killed Latigo. Shot from one of the Bonanza rooms. Vinton caught Boone in the hotel lobby, told him Latigo was in the alley and wanted to see him. After he got him behind the hotel, he shoved Tatum's gun against him and held him until he heard Deeter shoot. Then he let him have it."

"What was Deeter getting at?"

"Wagon Wheel cattle. It was the biggest rustling job I ever heard of. When I married Kitsie, or got hold of Wagon Wheel through Honey, I was to pull off the Wagon Wheel riders. Deeter and Vinton aimed to push the herd south to the railroad."

"Two couldn't handle that big a job."

"Deeter knew a bunch that was hiding out over on Snake River. They were going to help him."

"Who is Deeter?"

"Wiley Coe."

Jim had heard of Wiley Coe, bank robber,

con man, and gunman who was wanted in the Colorado mining camps for a dozen crimes.

"Biddle, I can't make any promises, but I'll do what I can to keep you out of the pen. When this is over . . ."

"They're coming, Jim!" Gramp Tatum called.

Jim listened. Horses were close. Deeter and the Poverty Flat men, or Wagon Wheel buckaroos returning from town. Kitsie rose and came toward Jim. He turned his eyes to her and tried to smile. This was the test against Buck Deeter. If Jim Hallet died before the outlaw's gun, everything he had done would be lost.

"I'm all right, Jim," Kitsie said. "I'll see that neither Biddle nor the woman bother you."

She was all Wyatt now, tempered steel, but lovely in a way that only Latigo of the Wyatt men had had eyes to appreciate, and with an honest sense of justice sharing her pride that none of the men had had.

"I'll count on that," Jim said.

He stepped quickly through the door and into the shadows. There he waited, gun riding loosely in its holster, thinking he was a fool to give two killers an even break on the draw when they had murdered Latigo and Boone Wyatt. Still, it was the way he would play it because he was that kind of man.

He had heard of Wiley Coe, the same as he had heard of Soapy Smith or Butch Cassidy. Coe was a combination of the two, perhaps with a streak of Billy the Kid, for neither Smith nor Cassidy was a killer, and Coe was.

They were there then, riding boldly into the streak of light washing out through the open door, none suspecting that anything was wrong.

"Biddle?" Deeter called. "You get your answer?"

Jim stepped into the light. "Yes, he got his answer, Buck, and I got mine. I'm arresting you for the murder of Latigo Wyatt. Vinton, I'm arresting you for the murder of Boone Wyatt. Get down and put your hands up."

"What the hell, Jim?" Lippy Ord said. "You can't do that after the way the Wyatts have treated us."

"I've got nothing against you boys," Jim said flatly. "Stay out of it. You know who killed Latigo and Boone, and if I've got you pegged right, you're ashamed of it. The part I can't understand is Stub . . ."

"That was a fair fight," Ord said quickly. "He pulled first. Vinton had to shoot him. We was this side of Craft's place when we met up with him. He was on the prod. . . ."

"All right, Lippy. You can forget Stub, but you can't forget how Latigo was killed."

Neither Deeter nor Vinton had moved in his saddle. Both were staring at Jim. Vinton, pressed by the smoldering bitterness that was always

319

in him, was ready to make his try, but Deeter, smarter than Vinton, was playing for time and feeling Jim out. He was smiling, white teeth bright in the light, swarthy face masking the pressure of the emotions in him.

He said: "I thought it was understood that Boone shot Latigo."

"It was the way you wanted it understood," Jim said. "Lippy, get this straight. I'm not defending the Wyatts for what they've done. Like I said in the Bonanza, you boys had plenty of cause to holler. From now on it's a different deal. I'll guarantee that because I know Kitsie isn't like her dad and granddad. You won't get pushed around. Wagon Wheel beef will stay on this side of the deadline, and the bank won't get tough on you because Biddle won't be in the bank."

Kitsie, standing in the doorway with a gun lined on Biddle, said: "That's right, Mister Ord."

Deeter had straightened, dark eyes probing Jim. He asked: "What's that about Biddle, Sheriff?"

"He won't be in the bank. He's played your game, and it didn't work."

"Jim, I don't like it," Lippy Ord broke in. "You can't arrest Deeter until you've got more than words to use on him. He's county commissioner. His Staircase is the biggest spread on the Flat. . . ."

"I know all that," Jim cut in, "but what you don't know is that he bought Staircase so he'd have a place to hide out. Then he sent for

Vinton and began cooking up this game, taking advantage of how you boys felt about Wagon Wheel. If we don't hang him, Colorado will. His real name is Wiley Coe."

It came with suddenness that did not entirely surprise Jim, for when he showed Deeter that he knew who he was, the man had no choice. Deeter was as fast as the Yellowby boy had said, and Jim, making his choice, threw his first shot at him. The hard and bitter years that lay behind Jim had forced gun speed upon him. It had saved his life before and it saved it now. His shot came before Deeter's by an unmeasurable part of a second. The outlaw folded, dropping his gun and grabbing the horn. Then his grip gave way, and he slid out of leather, dead before he hit the ground.

Jim turned his gun to Vinton, but time had run out for him. The gunman got in one shot, the slug clubbing Jim in the chest and knocking the breath from him and taking him off his feet. He heard other shooting before he lost consciousness, tried to tilt his gun upward again, but he couldn't see. Then the guns were silent, and voices came softly from across a vast distance, and Jim Hallet was drifting out into that great unknown. The last words that came to him were Kitsie's: "Ride for the doctor, Lippy. We have so little time."

# XI

Lamp light hurting his eyes. Voices held low. The medico's cool orders: "More bandages . . . more hot water. Move that lamp a little. Get out of here, Lippy. Pull that blind, Kitsie. He'll be all right. Let him sleep. . . ."

Kitsie was sitting beside his bed when he was fully aware of things again, gaunt face dark against the pillow, stubble a rough fringe on his face. When his eyes locked with hers, she smiled, and something came alive in him that had been dead.

"You did a miracle on Gramp Tatum," she said. "He was the one who got Vinton. He's a new man. He wants a job to get the whiskey worked out of him. I've put him on."

"That's fine," he murmured, knowing it was more than that. The Wyatt men would have done nothing of the kind. It was a portent of the future.

Suddenly she reached forward and took his hand. "I was wrong in leaving you that day in Nell's place. I thought I'd save your life by breaking it up between us, but I didn't know how strong you were."

"Lucky, maybe," he said.

She shook her head. "No, it was strength and courage. It took that to tell mc what you did that day. I've thought about it so much since. You said the ranch had become a god to the Wyatt men. I had never realized it, but that was exactly what it was."

He closed his eyes, for he was thinking of what he had called the fence between them. She was rich, and he was a poorly paid lawman. Stub had called it right when he'd said: "She ain't used to starving, tin-star."

His fists clenched. Jaw muscles corded.

"I can't stay here. Loving you like I do, and you owning Wagon Wheel . . ."

"Why must a man be such a fool?" she cried. "Jim, Jim, I need your love. I need your strength and your courage if I'm to run Wagon Wheel. I need you. There is no fence between us. I've pulled it down."

"Don't pull it down," he breathed. "I'll step over it."

"Nell has made the wedding dress, Jim. She'll bake the cake whenever you say."

That was it, the last wire on the fence. He looked into her face, the blue eyes, the red lips with the smile that told him so much, the red-gold hair vibrant with life under the bright morning sun that laid its glory upon her.

He put a hand on the back of her head and pulled her down to him. "The first day I can stand on my feet," he said, and kissed her.

# ABOUT THE AUTHOR

Wayne D. Overholser won three Spur Awards from the Western Writers of America and has a long list of fine Western titles to his credit. He was born in Pomeroy, Washington, and attended the University of Montana, University of Oregon, and the University of Southern California before becoming a public schoolteacher and principal in various Oregon communities. He began writing for Western pulp magazines in 1936 and within a couple of years was a regular contributor to Street & Smith's *Western Story Magazine* and Fiction House's *Lariat Story Magazine*. *Buckaroo's Code* (1947) was his first Western novel. In the 1950s and 1960s, having retired from academic work to concentrate on writing, he would publish as many as four books a year under his own name or a pseudonym, most prominently as Joseph Wayne. *The Violent Land* (1954), *The Lone Deputy* (1957), *The Bitter Night* (1961), and *Riders of the Sundowns* (1997) are among the finest of the Overholser titles. *Bunch Grass* (1955) and *Land of Promises* (1962) are among the best Joseph Wayne titles, and *Law Man* (1953) is a most rewarding novel under the Lee Leighton pseudonym. Overholser's Western novels, whatever the byline, are based on a solid knowledge of the history and customs of the 19th-Century West, particularly when set in his two favorite Western states, Oregon and Colorado. Many of his novels are first-person narratives, a technique that tends to bring an added dimension of vividness to the frontier experiences of his narrators and frequently, as in *Cast a Long Shadow* (1957), filmed as *Cast a Long Shadow* (United Artists, 1959), the female characters one encounters are among the most memorable. He wrote his numerous novels with a consistent skill and an uncommon sensitivity to the depths of human character. Almost invariably, his stories weave a spell of their own with their scenes and images of social and economic forces often in conflict, and the diverse ways of life and personalities that made the American Western frontier so unique a time and place in human history.

Books are produced in the United States using U.S.-based materials

Books are printed using a revolutionary new process called THINKtech™ that lowers energy usage by 70% and increases overall quality

Books are durable and flexible because of smythe-sewing

Paper is sourced using environmentally responsible foresting methods and the paper is acid-free

**Center Point Large Print**
600 Brooks Road / PO Box 1
Thorndike, ME 04986-0001 USA

**(207) 568-3717**

**US & Canada:**
**1 800 929-9108**
www.centerpointlargeprint.com